Bad Girl Blvd

Erica Hilton

www.melodramapublishing.com

Library of Congress Control Number: 2012934064
ISBN-13: 978-1620780619
ISBN-10: 1620780615
Mass Market Edition: January 2016

Interior Design: Candace K. Cottrell
Cover Design: Candace K. Cottrell
Model Photo: Marion Designs

Printed in Canada

Also By

Erica Hilton

Prologue

Nate placed several pounds of weed in front of Naomi, smiled, and said to her, "It's only because I got love for you, that I'm dealing wit' this low-level stuff. If it ain't a ki or more, I don't fuck wit' it."

Naomi returned the smile. "I know you don't, Nate. You my nigga, that's why. And I'm always gonna show you the same love. Whatever you need, I got you."

"As much as I look out for you, Naomi, you better return the favor someday."

"If it wasn't for you, I wouldn't be where I'm at. Your shit really sells."

Nate nodded. "I know it do, cuz I fuck wit' nothin' but the best . . . from drugs to my women."

"Drugs, yes, but in women, I know I'm one of the best and you still ain't fuck with me yet," Naomi quipped back with a glib smile.

Nate eyed Naomi from head to toe. She was always a sexy chick but just not his speed to call wifey.

"You definitely got me on whatever? No matter what,

right?" Nate moved a little closer to her.

"No matter what, Nate. I owe you. You practically helped pay my way through school these past three years," Naomi said wholeheartedly, with her inviting gaze locked on Nate and his strapping physique.

He was tall—six-three—dark-skinned and handsome with his bald head and dark goatee—male eye candy for the ladies from top to bottom.

Nate chuckled. His attention was heavily fixed on his friend he had known for years. Every man desired to be with Naomi, with her curvy, petite physique and her balloon tits. Naomi should have been off-limits to Nate, but Nate didn't have any boundaries when it came to his dick. And with his girlfriend of three years not being around, anything was a go.

It was obvious that something sexual was trying to spark between Nate and Naomi. Their strong, lingering stares at each other were indicative that they both wanted something much more.

Naomi picked up the package of high-quality weed; it was pure Cali Kush. She couldn't wait to sell it to her college peers at NYU in Manhattan. Selling weed on the campus was Naomi's bread and butter. Her strongest clientele were mostly the privileged white students coming from affluent communities with their rich parents paying for everything. And as soon as she re-upped, shortly afterwards, she would need to link up again with Nate for more supply.

Naomi Waters was in her last semester of college and

about to graduate with a bachelor's degree in pre-law and business. She had a goal she wanted to reach in her life, and she planned on reaching it by any means necessary. School was her way to swim out of the ghetto, but hustling was keeping her afloat in the white man's world. With her tuition, books, housing, and other bills and expenses, she would have been in serious debt after her graduation if it wasn't for the Kush.

Naomi placed three pounds of Cali Kush into her school bag and handed Nate three thousand dollars for payment. It was only pocket change for Nate, something he would spend in the strip clubs later that night or splurge on one of his side chicks at the mall.

Nate was a 27-year-old major player in the drug game and on a continuing rise. His pedigree was strong throughout Brooklyn for allocating coke, weed and a special and potent heroin called "Blow Torch." It was his best seller. It was a distinctive type of heroin with a potency that had the users going crazy. It got them higher than the Empire State Building.

He lit a cigarette, took a few pulls, and said to Naomi, "Shouldn't you be leaving now? You got what you came for."

"Should I? I didn't get everything I came for." Naomi gently touched the side of his face and gazed at him with the intent to get her way.

Nate could only smile at the comment and her soft touch.

It was a bold invite coming from Naomi. The sexual innuendo that she put out there sent an exhilarating charge through Nate. Just staring at Naomi's sexiness and sassiness was making Nate highly aroused. It was obvious she was throwing her goodies out there for him to catch. And he wasn't going to miss.

He didn't have time for games or flirting. He was a busy man and wanted some quick pussy. Abruptly, he grabbed Naomi in a heat of passion and threw her against the wall of his Brownsville stash house. He hoisted her into his arms as she straddled him, pressed against the wall like wallpaper. Their tongues locked heatedly. He tore open her shirt, ripped apart her bra, and cupped and sucked on her dark, chocolate nipples.

"I want you to fuck me, Nate," Naomi bellowed with an eagerness to feel the legend thrust inside of her.

Like so many ladies in the hood, she kept hearing how big his dick was and how great a lover he was. She wanted to experience a great fuck, and see if the rumors were true.

Nate tore off her panties in a horny rage and hurriedly undid his jeans. He longed to feel her wet pussy, and she longed to feel something hard and long penetrate her. Nate was masterful at throwing his dick. He got super-hard, he had a phenomenal downstroke, and he knew how to seal the deal.

The rumors were true. Nate was definitely gifted with length and width—ten strong inches.

Naomi loved getting fucked. She adored the concept of her lover being so incredibly aroused and horny.

Nate ran his hand up the small of her back, spreading Naomi's legs more, and thrust heatedly inside of her. She jerked and gasped in his powerful grip, and then dragged her manicured nails down his muscular back as he fucked her vigorously.

"Ooooh, fuck me! Fuck me!" she cooed.

Her pussy was hypnotic. Nate filled his hands with the fullness of her ass with her legs wrapped around him firmly, giving him her wet, juicy Hello Kitty. Naomi didn't want a casual fuck, nor some maintenance sex or some sweet lovemaking. She only wanted a hard, sweaty fuck from Nate.

He continued to thrust between her soft, brown thighs, making Naomi sweat and scream and moan his name. Nate pounded repeatedly inside of her, shifting their position from up against the wall to missionary on the floor, and then curving her over into the doggy-style stance, grabbing her hips and driving his fleshy, big dick inside of her. Steady, hard and deep. She screamed with pleasure. They fucked until their bodies were glistening with sweat and their breath hitched from pleasure. He felt her pussy grabbing him pleasurably and pulling him deeper inside of her until he hit her G-spot.

"I'm coming!" Naomi hollered.

Soon, she felt the earth shattering-experience, shuddering in Nate's grasp, and creamed heavily like a spill was happening between her legs. She was extra wet. Nate grunted, as he grabbed the back of Naomi's slim neck, and repeatedly rammed his stiff, big dick inside her from the back until he was ready to create his own eruption. He didn't give a fuck about condoms; exploding inside her pussy raw was the ultimate pleasure.

Huffing and puffing, he came, releasing his seed into her tunnel, shuddering from the good nut for a quick moment, then subsiding on his back. "Damn, you got some good fuckin' pussy."

Naomi smiled. "I know." She tried to lie against him.

Nate wasn't one to cuddle and nestle after sex; he removed himself from Naomi's soft hold and started to get dressed, pulling up his jeans and busying himself around the room. Naomi watched for a moment and relished his impressive structure, the glistering six-pack and brawny chest, his body defaced with tattoos.

"Why do you fuck with her, Nate?" Naomi asked out of the blue.

"Fuck with who?"

"Luca. She ain't your type," Naomi said with distaste.

"Ain't she your best friend?"

Naomi shrugged.

"So why you dogging her out like that?" Nate asked with a raised eyebrow.

"I'm not trying to dog her—shit, sometimes she be dogging her own self out. She's my friend and everything, and I got love for Luca like a sister, but I mean, look at her, she's a high-school dropout and don't have any ambition in her life. Luca's a cute girl, but she's slow."

"Yeah, well we all can't be graduating from medical school like your man, Naomi. What, he from Africa, right?" Nate asked.

"Nigeria. And he's my fiancé, not my man," Naomi

corrected.

"Look, Luca's a good girl, Naomi. And she ain't slow, she just quiet."

"She acts like a fuckin' retard!" she blasted. "She must got something good going on between them thighs for you to keep her around as long as you did, because she looks like she can't suck dick right."

"Look, I got love for Luca, Naomi, and she got love for me," Nate weakly defended his girlfriend.

Naomi chuckled. "You sure don't act like it sometimes, because you are out there fucking everything moving. You're a whore, Nate."

"And what does that make you?!" he spat. "I just fucked you and you the one cheating on your fiancé. Luca and I don't got rings on our fingers."

"I just wanted some quick dick, because I keep hearing the rumors on the streets about how big your shit is and how good you are in bed. I know my sins. But I love my man, so don't get it twisted. He takes care of me, and I take really good care of him. We both got something big going on with our lives. You already know he's about to graduate from medical school, and I'm about to get my bachelor's degree. And I'm out here hustling to save up enough money to start up my own franchise. I got goals, Nate. I can't say the same thing about Luca," Naomi declared.

"You are a trip, Naomi. Luca's your best friend and you always belittle her. What kind of friend that make you?"

"And you are her man and you're out here fucking everything moving, including me, so what kind of boyfriend that make you?"

"Hey, I'm a man; there's a difference."

"Yeah, you a dog," Naomi replied.

"Yeah well, this dog always gets his day and loves his bone. So, we gonna do this again, 'cuz you know a nigga always gotta have seconds?" Nate asked with a sly smile.

Naomi sighed lightly and smiled. "I don't know. I'll think about it."

"So that means yes, huh?"

"I said I'll think about it," she replied faintly, reaching for one of his T-shirts to put on over her torn blouse. She stood to her feet and adjusted her clothing.

Naomi began walking toward the exit, but Nate gently grabbed her by the arm, halting her departure and gazed at Naomi for a moment. He then asked, "So, if you weren't about to get married to a doctor, would you fuck with me on that level?"

Naomi chortled with a mocking stare at him. "Nate please, you ain't even my type. I know you. I know your kind. Yeah, we've been friends for a long time, and the dick is really good, but I need a man with some stability in life, and you're not it," she frankly responded.

"Stability...I got your stability right here," Nate returned, grabbing his crotch in a sexual gesture.

Naomi shook her head at his immature act. "I gotta go."

She exited the stash house and strutted down the narrow hallway toward the elevator. She hated being in the hood even though she'd been raised in one. Her posh attitude always suggested that she was better than everyone else because she was about to marry an up-and-coming doctor and was about to graduate from NYU. Everything around her she belittled and despised, even close friends and family.

Naomi grew up with Luca in the Howard projects in Brownsville, and supposedly they were best friends, but Naomi always felt Luca was beneath her. Luca was very pretty, with a shapely figure, but she was insecure, weak, stupid, and naïve, allowing people to always take advantage of her. Luca put Naomi on a pedestal because she looked up to her, respecting her style and mannerisms.

Naomi stepped into the elevator, being careful not to touch anything or step into something disgusting, as the floor was littered with debris. She nimbly pushed the button for the lobby. The elevator reeked of urine. As the lift descended, she couldn't help but think about Nate and how good the sex was. Yeah, she was ready to give him seconds, but she couldn't have him think that.

While Naomi left the building, Nate went back to his business in the stash house. He had to pick up another shipment from his Harlem connect soon. The demand was high and product was low—but his attention was briefly on Naomi. Her pussy had his mind drifting somewhat.

As he was putting his affairs in order in the apartment and opening his secured safe for some cash for his re-up, his girlfriend of three years watched the entire affair take place from her smart phone while she sat in her GED class thirty miles away. Everything that had transpired in the apartment in the past twenty-four hours was being watched and recorded via Luca and her home security video recording system she'd personally set up. Nate had no idea it was there and it only streamed video to Luca.

Chapter 1

Nate placed sixty thousand dollars from his safe in a brown paper bag, removed his pistol from the table, checked the clip—which was fully loaded, and stuffed it into his waistband. The gun was only a precaution, like always. He had to drive into Harlem to re-up with his connect, Squirrel.

The new heroin he was selling on the streets of Brooklyn was moving like hotcakes at a lumberjacks' breakfast. His specially stamped Blow Torch was so potent and becoming so infamous in the streets that users traveled as far from Queens and Long Island into the treacherous streets of Brooklyn to cop the drug. He was sitting on a gold mine and was the only one in Brooklyn pushing the special brand of heroin that was almost ninety percent pure.

Nate wanted to become the Nino Brown and Frank Lucas of Brooklyn and control the game. He always idolized notorious mobsters and gangsters of the underworld and wanted to wear the crown like the king he saw himself as. And with Blow Torch making a strong name for itself, he saw power and riches raining down on him like never before. He couldn't wait to get his hands on four kilos of heroin at fifteen thousand a ki; the turnaround alone would profit him two hundred thousand or more.

Dusk was settling over the city, and it was a balmy evening. The projects were alive with numerous kids playing outside enjoying the summer weather. The older young men with their sagging jeans and urban attitudes loitered in front of the corner bodegas, gambling and drinking malt liquor. Aging residents lingering in front of their buildings, playing cards or dominoes, and gossiping about all the other folks' business except their own. Everyone tried to keep cool under the blazing sun that was gradually setting. Brownsville was always an area bustling with the good and the bad.

Nate walked toward the living room window and glanced outside. He stared at his gleaming E-Class Benz coupe parked across the street from his building. It was the prettiest car on the block with tinted windows, a ground kit, and blinding chrome rims. The car was a status symbol that he came up and was making major moves.

However, a sure sign of his rise in the game was where he rested his head. His true residence wasn't in Brownsville, but a few miles away in Canarsie—a middle-class residential and commercial neighborhood in the southeastern portion of Brooklyn. There, Nate rented a well-furnished three-bedroom flat that he shared with Luca.

Nate learned a long time ago to never shit where you

eat. And where he now ate was ten times better than where he had grown up and now sold drugs. His poverty-stricken lifestyle was a distant memory to him. There was no more picking roaches out of the cereal boxes every morning, or wearing hand-me-downs that were either too big or too small, or watching the only one or two stations that worked on the television. Now his lifestyle was pushing fly rides, sporting heavy jewelry, dating diva-style women, and being able to afford to buy anything he wanted. Hustling was the way and his only way.

Nate picked up his cell phone and dialed Cheez, one of his die-hard soldiers in his crew. As he listened to his phone ring, he lit a cigarette and continued to gaze out the window, admiring how his car shimmered on the block like a diamond. With the top down on a nice summer day, it made him want to stunt even harder.

"Yo!" Cheez answered.

"Where you at?" Nate asked.

"Comin' from the store. Had to get some smokes. What's good?"

"I need you to come take a ride wit' me," Nate said.

"Uptown?"

"You already know."

"A'ight."

"Two hours, and we out," said Nate.

He hung up and took a few pulls from the burning Newport between his lips. He lounged on the couch and listened to some R&B music. It was a good night and yesterday's sexual rendezvous with Naomi was a good feeling. Good friend of his or not, Nate had been wanting to fuck his girlfriend's best friend for the longest, and he should have felt content, but he was greedy.

The pussy was good, really good, but he'd had better. Luca might be somewhat docile and square, but his girlfriend of three years knew how to treat her man, and sex with her was mind-blowing. She always wanted to please him, from sex, to strongly being by his side. She made Nate her world—her primary. He always came first in her life, but the reverse couldn't be said. Sometimes Nate would wonder himself why he always cheated on Luca. She was good to him. She truly loved him and would do anything for him. She was a good woman, but sometimes he felt she was too green and too soft.

Nate thought about Luca with Jagged Edge playing in the background. A mellow feeling swept over him. He wanted to roll up a blunt and get high, but he knew he needed to be focused when going into Harlem. In his line of work, you always had to be alert and on point. The wolves were always lurking and hungry in the streets, sniffing out weakness and ready to sink their teeth into any vulnerable prey.

As minutes passed, with Nate's mind on business, his ringing cell phone on the glass coffee table broke him from his relaxed mood. He leaned forward and looked to see who was calling. It was Luca. Her phone calls were always routine to him. He answered, "Hey."

"Hey baby, what you doing?" Luca asked. Her voice was soft and almost childlike. She was twenty-three years old, and it seemed that everything on her had matured except her high-pitched tone. At first, it was cute to listen to, but then most times it would become annoying for Nate. Sometimes it felt like he was talking to a young teenager via the phone. And it was hard for Luca to be taken seriously when she opened her mouth and her high-pitched voice resembled that of a cartoon character. It was one of her insecurities.

Nate dryly responded, "I'm kinda busy, Luca. I'm about to make a run into Harlem,"

"Can I come?" she asked.

"That ain't happening, Luca. You know I got business to take care of, and besides, I don't need you around that life."

"But baby, I missed you and I haven't seen you in three days," she whined.

Luca knew his business and she understood he was only going into Harlem to get his work from Squirrel. She had never met Squirrel, but she'd heard Nate speak about him a handful of times. She wanted to spend some quality time with her man, even if it was riding along to pick up drugs and come right back to Brooklyn.

But Nate was against it, feeling Luca was too soft to be around that type of life. She was a good girl, and although she grew up in the hood and poverty, with her moms smoking crack since she was pregnant with her, Luca wasn't built for that lifestyle. He always felt his girl was just too classy. And also, though he loved her, he felt she was too fragile and could easily be broken.

Nate felt like he had to protect his girl. He always took

care of her needs and wants. Luca didn't have to want for anything as long as Nate was hustling and clocking major figures.

But Luca was adamant to see her man tonight. She wanted to ride along.

"I missed you, baby, and I wanna see you. What did you do yesterday? Naomi said she came by to see you. What was that about?" Luca mentioned.

A slight lump developed in Nate's throat and he wondered why Naomi had brought up yesterday to his girl. What kind of game was she playing?

"She did, huh? What she talkin' about?"

"Nothing new. She wanted to do something tonight, to go chill and talk, but I told her that I wanted to see my baby tonight."

A wave of guilt engulfed Nate like he was drowning in regret. The hard fuck inside that wet piece of pussy yesterday was fun, but he didn't want to lose his girl over some bullshit.

"You know how Naomi is, she just came by to be in a nigga's business," Nate dryly explained.

"But why yours? I mean, I'm feeling some kind of way, Nate. My best friend can come see you, but I can't? Why? I just wanna see you, baby, and spend some quality time with you. But you always seem to be too busy for me lately. I'm supposed to be your woman, not Naomi," Luca complained and pouted.

The guilt trip made Nate give in. He sighed and halfheartedly replied with, "Okay, but just this once."

Luca smiled through the phone.

"You at the house?" Nate asked.

"No, I'm at my mother's place."

"I'll be there in forty minutes. Don't have me waiting," he said.

"I'm already dressed, baby."

Nate hung up feeling like he was going to have to babysit her all night. He sighed heavily and shook his head. "Fuckin' melodrama fo' real," he uttered with contrition.

Luca walked out of her mother's building on Rockaway Avenue looking stunning in her skinny jeans, revealing her long, thick legs, along with a pair of white Nikes and a fitted T-shirt that accentuated her petite breasts. Her Asian-cut hair complemented her Chinese-shaped eyes and smooth light skin, and the smile from her full lips aimed toward Nate as she approached his car was contagious, causing him to smile, too.

Gazing at Luca's beauty reminded him why he fell in love with her three years ago. He had always noticed her around the way, roaming with Naomi all the time—they were like night and day. Naomi was the pretentious and showy friend, while Luca was always in her shadow. She would talk, but never had much to say.

Nate had always been attracted to Luca; she was the mystery behind door number one. Unbeknownst to everyone else, Luca was extremely smart, and her forte was technology. She had a knack for computers and other gadgets. And even though he was a cheating dog, Luca and her personality captured his heart. She could be shy and docile, but she was so patient and understanding with him. She'd had a hard life growing up, and had a reason to be angry at the world, but she wasn't.

Luca noticed Cheez in a gray Chevy Impala parked behind Nate's Benz coupe as she climbed into the car and gave Nate a kiss on the lips. Her perfume lit up his nostrils. He was reclined in his seat pulling on a cigar, trying to emulate a don. It reeked in the car and caused Luca to cough.

"Hey baby," she still greeted him warmly. "I don't know why you keep smoking those."

"'Cuz they relax me, and all the great kingpins smoke cigars. But you look and smell good, Luca," he complimented.

"Thank you."

Nate was about to put the car in drive when Luca asked him, "Why is Cheez parked behind you? I thought it was only going to be us?"

Nate chuckled slightly and shook his head. She was truly green to his world. He looked at her like he was about to explain a simple math problem to a child and said, "You don't drive into Harlem to re-up on some of the purest heroin in the city without some muscle to have your back and a pistol on you. Cheez is my insurance. And it's a bait car, to transport what I need back to BK."

"Oh," Luca said.

Nate had nothing more to say. He slowly drove off the block and headed toward the highway. The ride was a quiet one for a moment. Jay-Z and Kanye West were playing from the radio, and with it being dusk out, the traffic going into the city was light.

Luca stared at Nate with yesterday's events still eating away at her. She kept her cool, though, but was tired of being the pacifist in her troubled relationship. They were crossing the Tri-Boro Bridge with the New York City skyline lit up in the background. With them about to enter into Harlem, she needed to ask him and see what his response would be. Nate spent most of his time on his cell phone talking to various people during the duration and repeatedly glancing in his rear view mirror to see if Cheez was still following behind them. But he ignored his girl. Everything else seemed more relevant in his life than she was.

When Nate finally ended his last call, in her highest pitch, sounding like a young Rosie Perez, she exclaimed, "Nate, do you really love me?"

Nate swiveled his head at her and uttered, "What? You know I do."

"I don't feel it, Nate. It seems like everything else in your life has been more important than me. You're never around. And I hardly get to see you," she griped.

"You're seeing me now," he quipped. "And besides, you know I'm a busy man. I'm tryin' to get this paper for us."

For us? She frowned at the phrase.

She couldn't hold it in anymore. As Nate steered his Benz down 125th Street, Luca blatantly asked him, "Are you cheating on me, Nate?"

She already knew the truth and had captured his infidelity on camera, but she was waiting to see if he was man enough to be honest with her.

Nate looked dumbfounded by the question. "Hell no, I'm not cheating on you, Luca."

It was a slap in her face. He was too nonchalant with his response. Like daddy cool, he had the audacity to say, "You're the only woman in my life and the only woman I choose to be with, Luca. I don't care for any of these bitches."

Luca's blood boiled, but she still remained pacifist. She strongly felt that now wasn't the time for an argument, or a confrontation with him.

Luca decided to change the subject since she wasn't getting an honest answer from him. Coolly, she said, "After I get my GED, I'm going to enroll in school and get my degree. I'm going to better myself."

"That's good, baby. You should, and you should take up communication and technology, cuz you definitely have a way with computers and gadgets," he chimed.

Luca smiled. "You believe in me?"

"You know I do . . . always." It was a halfhearted reply from him. She didn't feel the encouragement was genuine.

"I'm not gonna end up like my mother, Nate. I refuse to. I know what people think and say about me. That I'm a nobody, that I'm soft and need to stand up for myself. They think I'm weak," she proclaimed.

"You're not weak, Luca. You're just different from everybody else," he replied.

"Different?"

"Yes, different. And I love you, baby."

"How am I different?"

"You just are. But it's good to be different. And like I said, it's the main reason why I love you."

Nate smiled at her. He actually did love her in his own special way.

But Luca wasn't a fool. She'd seen the video and heard everything that was said about her. She disliked how her boyfriend barely stood up for her when her best friend was kicking her back in.

"Love . . . shit is so overrated," she spat.

"Where is all this coming from, Luca?" he exclaimed.

It was all coming from her being so sick and tired of being used and mistreated by everyone else, especially from those she loved and trusted. And being lied to.

But she didn't feel bold enough to come at Nate the way she wanted to. She didn't want to get into a full-blown argument with him while they were in Harlem. Once again, the passive side of Luca took over, and she meekly replied, "It's coming from nowhere, Nate. I was just talking, that's all."

She frowned.

Nate noticed her sudden sadness. When he turned onto the block of his drug connect, he smiled at Luca and said, "Listen baby, when you finally get your GED and start doin' ya thang, then I'm gonna buy you the biggest engagement ring. Let's get married, right? What the fuck we waitin' on? I love you and you love me. How's that sound?"

It sounded promising to her, but knowing his history and cheating ways, it would probably be more hell than matrimony. She faintly replied with, "It sounds nice."

"Nice? It's gonna be you and me baby. Watch. I love you and I'm gonna give you the world," Nate said with conviction.

He parked in front of the towering and sprawling project known as the Wagner Houses, also known as the Tri-borough houses. Its twenty-two buildings occupied a vast stretch of land on the four blocks below East 124th Street, from Second Avenue to East River. The place was home to two notorious gangs who called themselves 20 BLOCC and Flow Boyz. They were violent, but loosely organized and had no hierarchy. Squirrel ran everything with an iron fist and was a legend to the locals.

Nate parked on the bustling city block with Cheez parking directly behind him. He locked eyes with Luca. She remained quiet. He had been the only man she ever loved. There was a loving confidence about Nate that made Luca want to forgive him and move on. Yes, he was a nasty dog with the gift of gab, but her reasoning was that he never disrespected her in person and they'd had three years together—he was the evil she did know.

Nate opened the door and had one foot on the ground and the other still in the car. His attention was still on Luca. She was ready to say something to him, maybe let bygones be bygones, but something out of the blue caught her immediate attention. A masked gunman came from out of nowhere with his arm extended and a .9mm at the end of it. Nate had his back turned toward the approaching gunman, unaware of the threat. Her eyes widened and she tried to warn him, but her voice became mute, and before her man could turn around, the frightful sound of gunfire cracked opened the air.

Bak! Bak! Bak!

The back of Nate's head exploded, his blood and brains spraying all over the leather seats and dashboard. His head dropped into Luca's lap with his eyes wide open, dead. She screamed, "Ohmygod!"

Chaos followed with people fleeing the danger.

Luca locked eyes with the masked gunman, seeing the whites of his pupils. She quickly ejected herself from the passenger seat and threw herself on the ground, scraping her knees, her hands covered with her boyfriend's blood. She closed her eyes and panicked.

"Muthafucka!" she heard Cheez yell out. He rushed out of the Impala with fury, the gun cocked back and ready.

His shouting was followed by erratic gunfire that lit up the cool, spring air. Luca hugged the hard, concrete ground, as a shootout ensued between the men. Cheez erupted on the masked assailant with heavy gunfire from a Glock 17 shattering car windows and lighting up the night with shells. He wasn't intimidated by gunplay.

Boom! Boom! Boom! Boom!

The cannon came alive like fireworks in Cheez's hand, forcing the assailant to take cover behind a parked car. Cheez observed Nate's body sprawled out in the front seat of his Benz Coupe and Luca taking cover on the ground. He scowled heavily and charged like a madman to take revenge for his fallen friend.

"I'ma kill you, muthafucka! You fuck wit' me!" he screamed. "You fuck wit' me! That's my nigga!"

Boom! Boom!

Luca continued to scream, trapped in a hail of bullets from both directions. Cheez wildly rushed forward, adamant to kill someone. What he didn't see was that there were two masked gunmen in the mist. The second gunman came from behind him like a thief in the night and opened fire. The hot slugs tore into Cheez's back, and he went crashing face-down into the street, taking four shots in the back, his gun spilling from his hand. It was a setup. The lanky gunman stood over Cheez and pumped four more rounds into his body. He was heartless killer.

Luca saw her chance. She picked herself up from the ground and went running away from the chaos. She dared not to look back. The terror displayed in her eyes and the fear in her heart made her run like she was the Flash. She ran on air, determined to survive. She hadn't seen their faces, but hers was as clear as day. The screams she heard came from her own lungs.

The police sirens wailing in the distance made Luca run faster. She rounded the city corner, nearly toppling over an old woman carrying groceries. She had no time for apologies. In the distance was the train station, the sign illuminated for the A and C lines. It was her escape from the nightmare.

She ran for it, jumping the turnstile with the token booth clerk paying her no nevermind, her boyfriend's blood still coating her hands and sprinkled across her face. She descended the stairway rapidly. It was empty, the weekend—no rush hour, no crowd, so there weren't any judgmental stares at her, no speculations as to why the blood was all over her. Only the drunks and homeless occupied the littered platform with the rats scurrying in different directions.

Still in shock, she dropped onto a bench with her face etched in suffering from what she'd witnessed. She was tired and drained. Scared, she picked up a discarded brown bag and wiped away the blood away from her hands and face, doing a half-assed job. Soon after, the A train came roaring into the station and Luca leaped into the last car. Thank God it was empty. She sobbed and collapsed into a seat, thinking, *What now?*

Chapter 2

Instead of going back to Brownsville, to either her mother's or grandmother's place, Canarsie was Luca's destination. It was an hour train ride from Harlem to Brooklyn. She mostly lay in the fetal position on the long seat, trying to black out the horror from her memory—but the bloodshed was rooted deep inside her like a terminal cancer. She was a nervous wreck. She had never witnessed a murder, let alone seen someone she loved snuffed before her eyes.

When the A train came to a stop in the Brooklyn station, almost two miles from her home and Nate's private stash house, under the cover of night and thanking God for empty streets, she jumped into a idling gypsy cab parked on the corner. The driver was somewhat startled by her abrupt entry, but then relaxed when he noticed the pretty, young girl in the backseat. Luca hid herself from the driver's view, throwing him a twenty, saying, "Please, just drive off," and giving her address. Ten minutes later he came to a stop in front of her home.

Luca immediately jumped out of the cab, rushed up the stairway, and barged into her home like she was being chased. It was a miracle that she'd made it back to Brooklyn in her condition—blood staining her clothes and flesh, a nervous wreck, haunted by the shootout.

She ran around the house closing the blinds and making sure the doors were locked. She turned on a few lights and went into her bathroom to wash away the remnants of blood and shed her soiled clothing. Then she went into the bedroom. She took a seat at the edge of the queen size bed and said to herself, "Think Luca, think!" Nate was dead and she was afraid and alone.

Luca dried her tears and looked around her bedroom. She would no longer share it with the man she loved. Everything seemed different without him. Her life had changed within the blink of an eye.

She felt herself drowning. Then with a sense of urgency, she jumped up and went scurrying around the bedroom looking for something. She swung open the door to her walk-in closet and wildly began tossing clothes out. She saw the safe embedded into the wall. She had no idea what was inside, but she knew where the safe was, because every night when Nate came home late, he would go into the closet and spend a moment inside either depositing or withdrawing something from it assuming that Luca was asleep. But she never was.

Luca stared at the safe. It was a medium-sized combination safe and she didn't know the combination. Knowing Nate had all kinds of valuable things inside from cash to jewelry, she started to guess the combination, starting from his birthday, then her birthday, but to no avail. She started to brainstorm, trying to come up with the right numbers to crack it open. For twenty straight minutes, she entered numbers after numbers, but still nothing.

Frustration started to grow; it had been three hours since Nate was murdered. Luca wanted to get everything she needed from the house and then get ghost.

Luca stared at the safe and said, "Think, Luca...you're smart, you can crack this safe. It's only numbers from zero to ninety-nine."

She started to brainstorm, thinking of random things to identify with Nate and the safe's combination. And then like lightening, it suddenly struck her: What was the one thing Nate loved the most and always talked about? Cars. His favorite car was the Benz CLK. Nate was smart, but Luca considered herself smarter. Each letter in the alphabet had a number. C was 3, L was 12, and K was 11.

Slowly, Luca turned toward the chosen numbers, taking a deep breath with each one. When she spun the dial onto 11, she pushed the lock and the door came open. It was the advantage of knowing her man. She pulled the door back to see inside, and *wham!* Luca hit the jackpot. Inside stood revealed three kilos of pure heroin, some cash, guns, jewelry, and some paperwork. She stared at the contents for a moment. It was all amazing to her eyes. It was a goldmine.

Luca had never really dealt with guns or drugs before, but she knew enough to know everything was valuable.

She grabbed a large garbage bag and dumped everything in the safe into it. She would sort everything out later. The guns she handled extra carefully. Remembering what Nate once taught her about pistols and how to put the safety on, she did so and placed four pistols into a book bag. She then grabbed a few clothes and shoes. There was too much to take all at once, so if it wasn't important, then it was left behind.

Luca stood in the center of her home and carefully looked around. She had everything gripped in her hands or slung over her shoulders.

She called a cab and waited until it pulled up outside before leaving the place she'd called home.

Luca climbed into the backseat of the cherry-scented gypsy cab with the female driver behind the wheel and placed her things beside her: two lumpy trash bags and a black book bag with deadly firearms. She looked more like a bag lady than anything else.

"Where to?" the dark-skinned woman with long dreads and a nice smile asked.

"Brownsville," she replied, and then gave the address.

The woman nodded and drove off with Luca brooding in the backseat. She placed her head against the window and started to shed some tears, exposing her sorrows. It had been a long and terrible night. And with dawn approaching soon, the only thing on her mind was sleep, knowing tomorrow would be a new and frightful day.

The driver noticed the tears while glancing at her passenger's anguished face from the rearview mirror, and out of her mouth came, "Girl, you know he ain't worth it. You're leaving for a reason."

Luca opened her eyes and looked at the driver, befuddled by her statement. What was she talking about?

The driver continued with, "Sometimes men take a good woman for granted. What was it; did he beat on you, cheat on you? Whatever it is, I can tell that you're a strong black woman and you'll get back on your feet."

It suddenly came clear to Luca, the woman driver saw the bags, and then the tears and hurt along with her leaving in the middle of night, and it appeared she was running away from a failed relationship. It was too far from the truth.

Luca felt she should have told the woman to stay out of her business and just drive. Naomi wouldn't hesitate to scream on the driver, but she wasn't Naomi. She wasn't as straightforward and harsh like her friend and others. Luca just dried her tears and kept quiet. If the driver wanted to believe she was running from a relationship, then so be it. She would never see this woman again. And she was running, but from the storm she knew was coming.

"I'll safely take you wherever you need to go, chile, because us black woman need to stick together. You just have faith and never look back, keep moving forward. People are out of your life for a reason," the cab driver said.

Never look back, keep on going, people are out of your life for a reason. It was solid advice coming from a complete stranger. Luca didn't respond, and her aloofness didn't bother the driver. She was a talkative, spirited person.

The streets were empty and quiet going toward Brownsville. It was after 1 a.m. when the cab came to a complete stop in front of one of the buildings in the Howard project. The area was still somewhat rough— it was the hood, violent with drugs and gangs, but tonight things were quiet like the suburbs with no late-night hustlers, gamblers or fiends wandering about. The dilapidated twenty-four-hour corner bodega was still open for business, feeding its late-night customers through a revolving slot for security reasons.

Lingering in the backseat of the cab, Luca gazed at her grandmother's building and sighed. From Canarsie back to the troubling Brownsville once again; she felt like she was in a pinball machine with all the bouncing around.

The first time she'd left was at sixteen years old, when she had gotten pregnant and had gone to stay with her boyfriend's family. She ended up having a miscarriage because of the STD she caught, Chlamydia. Her boyfriend blamed her for it and threw her out like trash. Luca knew better; *he'd* given it to *her*. She'd never cheated on him, and she had lost her baby because of the STD—and because of his infidelity.

The second time she left Brownsville and came back was when she was nineteen years old; it was a job program in Long Island for high-school dropouts with high IQs. The program didn't pan out too well for her because of Naomi. When her friend came to visit, she had gotten into a fight with some girls, and it was against regulations. The incident caused Luca to be removed from the program. Naomi had cost Luca in finally attaining her degree and getting a proper education—and yet, Luca didn't fuss or get angry about it. She took everything in stride, believing that things happened for a reason. Naomi had halfheartedly apologized and had said, "That school was bootleg anyway, Luca."

Luca handed the driver her twenty-dollar fare and opened the back door. But before she could place one foot on the ground, the driver turned around and gave Luca a supportive look. "Chile, let me tell you something. Things will only get better for you. You just gotta have faith and believe in yourself. You are quiet, I see, but I see strength in your eyes. I don't know you, but I feel you will have a special outcome after all of this."

Luca softly replied, "Thank you."

"You're welcome."

Luca finally stepped out of the cab with her belongings in her hands and her tears finally dried. She proceeded toward her grandmother's building with the cabbie still parked on the street and idling by the curb. It was odd to run into a stranger who cared. Luca shrugged it off and walked into the lobby.

She took the elevator to the seventh floor and stepped into the narrow project hallway with heavy-duty graffiti and gang signs scrawled across the walls. It also reeked of weed permeating into the hallway from someone's apartment. Luca walked down the corridor, tugging her bags along. Her grandmother's apartment was the last door down the hall.

With it being one in the morning, Luca wasn't apprehensive when it came knocking at her door and waking up the elderly woman.

"Grandma, it's me, Luca," she hollered, banging her fist against the door.

Luca knocked repeatedly knowing it always took her grandmother time when it came to answering her door. She was in her late seventies—a wise and also nosy woman who had seen and been through a lot.

"Who?" Luca heard her grandmother answer.

"It's me, Grandma. Luca," she reiterated.

The apartment door opened up. A woman who stood five-foot-five with a waifish figure, twiggy arms, aging skin, and luxuriant, long gray hair stood in front of Luca with a frown.

"Luca, do you know what time it is?" her grandmother barked.

Luca meekly nodded. "I need a place to stay for a moment, Grandma."

She looked lost and disheartened. Hours of crying had turned her eyes red and puffy, and her face was stained with grief. Her grandmother noticed the bags and the desperation in Luca's face.

"Did that boy put you out?"

Luca nodded. The truth was just too devastating for her to speak. With a thoughtful gaze, the old woman moved to the side, allowing her granddaughter into her apartment.

"You can stay as long as you want, Luca," her grandmother said warmly.

Luca managed to smile. "Thank you, Grandma."

Luca walked into the living room, which was sparsely decorated with antique furniture, couches with torn plastic covering, wobbly dilapidated chairs, pictures old and new of family and friends framing the walls, some going back to the Civil Rights Movement, and a retro television set with the rabbit ears that came straight out of the eighties. The place smelled of Bengay and was seriously outdated. Her grandmother, Lucinda, was a simple and God-fearing woman.

The apartment had three bedrooms. Luca would stay in her mother's old room. The second bedroom was cluttered with laundry and books. Luca went into the bedroom and closed the door. Her grandmother gave her some privacy. She dropped her things on the floor and sat on the bed, looking and feeling defeated. She looked around the bland room and groaned. She didn't even bother to unpack anything. She curled into the fetal position on the bed, closed her eyes, and wished that the next time she opened them the night she'd experienced was nothing more than a nightmare.

Chapter 3

Luca woke up in a cold sweat to the sound her cell phone ringing and ringing. She jumped up from her sleep and became a little frantic, the shooting playing out in her head like a bad movie. It was morning with the sun percolating through the window. For a moment she forgot where she was, and then it quickly came to her: Grandma's second bedroom. She looked around, not knowing what to do. She picked up her cell phone, seeing all the missed calls. She already knew why everyone was calling her. By now the whole neighborhood had to have heard about Nate and Cheez's violent murders.

Luca stared at the missed calls and the five voicemails she had. The first to call was Naomi. But Luca wasn't in any rush to call her back, or anybody else. She went to the window and looked outside, expecting to see hell on earth; she only saw a bright and sunny spring day.

Making sure the bedroom door was locked; she carefully dumped all of the contents of the bags onto her bed. She gazed at the drugs, guns, money, and jewelry for a moment. *What to do with everything?* she asked herself.

She counted the money; it was only thirty-five thousand. She went through the jewelry: two Breitling watches worth five thousand apiece, two rose-gold chains, diamond rings, and bracelets. The most expensive watch and chain Nate had was on him when he was murdered.

Luca started at her jewelry also: diamond tennis bracelets, diamond earrings, and a Rolex watch. Everything was a small fortune in her eyes. With her things secured underneath the bed, she walked out, hearing her cell phone ringing again. It was an unknown number, probably someone trying to reach her after they'd heard the news about Nate. She chose to ignore it.

Luca walked into the kitchen. She didn't have an appetite. Her grandmother was seated at the table near the window in a blue housecoat with rollers in her hair. She nursed a hot cup of coffee while gazing out the window like she did every day and every night, watching the activities and people around her building.

"Good morning, Grandma," Luca greeted with a faint smile.

"Good morning, Luca. Did you sleep well last night?"

"I did," she lied. The small bags under her eyes showed otherwise.

"That phone of yours has been ringing all morning. Is it that boy calling you?" she asked, always referring to Nate as "that boy."

"I don't know. I didn't answer."

"Well, I never liked him, Luca. I always felt he was

nothing but trouble in your life. What did he do to you this time to make you leave? Or did he kick you out? Did he beat you?"

"No, Grandma, he didn't," Luca weakly replied. She tried not to get choked up while speaking with her grandmother about Nate. The pain was still lingering, and the experience still had her shaky.

"That boy you're dating reminds me too much of your deadbeat daddy. I told your mother about him like I'm telling you about that boy. He's no good. They will bring you down no matter how much or how hard you try to love them. Your no-good daddy brought your mama down. I warned her. And the sad thing Luca, your daddy was really smart . . . very intelligent. He was good with math and numbers. But he chose to worship the streets and do drugs." Lucinda shot a stern look at her granddaughter.

Her grandmother was never afraid to speak her mind and give her opinion. Luca was the opposite. She always felt afraid to speak up for herself, even when people would slander her character and defile her name. She hated drama and thought if you didn't acknowledge the problem and left it alone then it would go away. She was afraid to add more fuel to a burning fire. Sometimes she was afraid to be noticed, afraid of conflict—an introvert in so many ways.

Lucinda wasn't finished preaching. She knew her granddaughter was smart like her father, but somewhat saw the threat of her father's downfall in her—a high school dropout and being with a loser.

"I heard you're trying to get your GED. That's good,

Luca. I'm gonna be so proud of you when it happens. It's about time. You always been a smart girl," she stated with an encouraging smile. "Just keep that boy out of your life and everything will be okay for you."

Luca heard her grandmother talking, but she was far from listening. Her mind transitioned to the shooting again. She could hear her phone ringing again from the bedroom. She felt another breakdown coming, but she didn't want it to happen in front of her nosy and preachy grandmother. Her hand trembled and she felt the tears welling up again. Her grandmother was still talking, but Luca had to excuse herself quickly and retreat to the bedroom.

When she got to the bedroom, the caller ID on the phone read *Naomi*. This time she decided to answer it, knowing that the trifling backstabber was going to keep on calling.

"Hello," Luca answered with a distorted tone.

"Ohmygod . . . Ohmygod, is it true? Luca, are you okay? Where are you? I heard about Nate," Naomi cried out, her voice distraught.

Luca started to choke up.

"What?"

Hearing Naomi's voice like she was such a concerned friend felt disturbing to her on so many levels. It had only been yesterday when she'd caught Naomi on camera fucking her man.

"Luca, you haven't heard?" Naomi asked.

"What happened, Naomi? Tell me what happened,"

Luca asked hysterically.

"Nate was killed last night. He was shot to death in Harlem. Him and Cheez," Naomi informed her, sorrowfully.

"No! No! What?" Luca shouted out.

"Nate's dead, Luca."

Luca pretended to be shocked and grief-stricken by the news. She had to pretend it was news to her because she didn't want anyone to know that she was there when Nate was killed. Luca wanted to separate herself from the entire night. She wished she had never gotten into the car with Nate. She wished she had stayed home.

"I'm coming to see you, Luca. Where are you now?" Naomi asked.

Luca was silent, feigning being too traumatized by the information to even speak. She sat on the floor, the phone loosely to her ear, tears falling once more.

"Luca, speak to me, where are you?" Naomi hollered.

Luca slowly responded, "I'll be at my mother's place."

"I'm there," Naomi assured her and hung up.

Luca sat still for a long moment. Her grandmother was knocking at her door asking, "Luca, are you okay?"

The door opened and her grandmother walked in, seeing Luca on the floor with tears streaming from her eyes. Right away, Lucinda knew something was wrong with her granddaughter. Luca stared up at grandmother and uttered, "Nate was killed last night, grandma."

Lucinda placed her hand against her chest and cried out, "Oh sweet Jesus!"

Chapter 4

Lucia Linn was a thirty-nine-year-old black woman living a mediocre life in the projects after going through years of hell battling a serious addiction to crack and heroin, prostitution, and prison. She'd been in numerous abusive relationships since she was fifteen years old Lucia had seen it all and been through it all. Despite her hard life, she still managed to hold on to her good looks with her long, raven-black hair, light skin, and curvy figure. But she carried scars, both physically and mentally—and the years of stress were beginning to show. Her eyes were dark and told a story of struggle and survival.

Lucia sat by the window in her living room like her mother Lucinda always did, watching things going on in the courtyard below in the early morning. She took a few drags from her cigarette and listened to some Michael Jackson songs. Lucia's life was calm now but still shaky; it hadn't been so long ago since she maxed out from her parole and was neck-deep in trouble. And not only had she risked her own life but her daughter's too when she smoked crack while pregnant with Luca. It was a blessing and miracle that Luca wasn't born deformed or with any birth defects. Luca was a healthy baby girl but caught hell from her mother.

Lucinda, Lucia, and Luca were three generations of woman born and raised in the projects with difficulties in life and their own personal struggles to deal with. Luca inherited the struggle and hardship, but she didn't inherit the backbone and fight that her grandmother and mother both had in them.

Lucia smoked her Newport and stared at her daughter trotting across the courtyard in a hurry. She knew Luca was coming to see her and it was always a pleasure having her come by. She stubbed out her cigarette in the ashtray, removed herself from the window, and quickly straightened up her untidy place a little. A few minutes later, there was a knock at her door.

"I'm comin', Luca," Lucia hollered.

Her two-bedroom apartment was a palace to her after doing five years in a rough women's prison upstate for drugs and robbery, and living on the streets for a lifetime. Now with things somewhat easier in her life she noticed her daughter had picked up the torch of hardship, having a drug-dealing boyfriend and no high school diploma or GED.

Lucia opened her door and Luca immediately fell into her mother's arms with grief.

"Luca, what happened to you? What's going on?"

Lucia asked.

"They killed him, Mama! Nate was murdered!" Luca exclaimed.

"Ohmygod," Lucia cried out.

She pulled Luca into the apartment, held her tightly, and tried her best to console her. The tears fell against her and the anguish she saw was something far too familiar from her own past. Lucia knew the feeling of losing someone close. She'd lost men she loved over the years. Nate's death wasn't much of a shock to her, because men like him never lasted too long in society. Luca needed to go through her own trials and tribulations for her to learn.

"He's gone, Mama . . . he's gone," she cried.

"I'm here, baby. I'm here," Lucia softly said to Luca with her arms still wrapped around her.

It was time for Lucia to be a mother to her distraught daughter. Drugs, prison, and the streets had made her an absentee parent for too long, and now with her life back on track, it was a warm and humble feeling to help Luca out during these trying times.

Lucia decided to make her daughter a cup of tea, and they settled into the kitchen where Lucia comforted her daughter with stories from her own past.

"It hurts, baby girl, and it will continue to hurt for a long time. I went through the violent loss of three boyfriends, including your father, but sometimes the men we choose to be with can leave us one way or another," Lucia said.

Luca didn't know much about her father except that

he was a smart man with many gifts who chose to waste his life. Now he was doing life in prison for murder. She'd never met the man. Nor did she care to meet him.

"But you don't let this shit fuckin' break you, Luca!" her mother continued harshly. "It hurts, but you're a got-damn Linn, and Linn women aren't weak. You understand me?"

Luca nodded.

But Luca knew she wasn't like her mother or grandmother. She was so far from being a strong and opinionated woman—a fighter. What happened to her? She wanted to know. Did the aggressive gene skip her?

"You gotta let all these muthafuckas know that my daughter ain't no punk!"

"I'm just tired, Mama."

"Tired of what?" Lucia snapped.

"Everybody. And now with Nate gone . . ."

"Luca, he's gone and you can't bring him back!" Lucia intervened. "But you cry for him, then dry your damn tears and keep it moving. Don't shed tears for any man for too long."

Luca listened. She sipped her tea, stopped crying, and received the encouraging words from her mother.

"I know I haven't been around to raise you up like a mother should, but please don't make the same mistakes I've made growing up. I was stupid, Luca. I was lost and chasing behind men and a high. I wasted so many years of my life being in the dark that when I finally saw the light, it almost killed me to see. Be better than me, Luca. Yes, Nate is gone, but let his death strengthen you, not destroy you. You understand, baby girl?"

Luca nodded.

Lucia went over to her daughter and gave her a loving hug. Luca hadn't been hugged by her mother since she was in her early teens. It was a warm feeling. It was a great feeling. Though Lucia wasn't around while she was growing up, Luca always understood that her mother cared greatly for her and loved her a lot.

The tender moment was interrupted by knocking at the door. Lucia went to see who it was. She looked through the peephole and saw a young woman standing in the hallway. Lucia turned to her daughter and asked, "You expecting anybody at my place? There's a young woman out here."

"It's Naomi, Mama."

"Naomi?" Lucia replied with an incredulous tone.

She opened the door. She hadn't seen Naomi in years, not since she was thirteen years old. Naomi looked at Lucia and asked, "Hey, Ms. Linn, is Luca here?"

"She is."

"I need to see her, it's important," said Naomi, who looked like she was ready to break down in tears.

Lucia stepped to the side, allowing Naomi into her home.

Naomi spotted Luca in the kitchen and rushed straight toward her with open arms. She pulled Luca into a concerned hug, saying, "I'm so sorry, Luca. I can only imagine what you're going through right now. I don't know what I would do if I ever lost my man like you did yours. But I'm here now."

The condolences felt forced, but Luca went along with the act, hiding her sudden contempt for Naomi.

She remained silent while Naomi went on to say, "I'm here for you, Luca. Whatever you need, I got you. I'm by your side through this tragedy. I loved Nate, too."

I bet you fuckin' did, Luca thought. As her best friend continued to hug and console her, Luca had the urge to put her hands around her neck and squeeze. She wanted to strike Naomi so hard that her grandkids would still feel the pain. But it wasn't in her. She remained passive and humble.

Lucia walked into the kitchen and stared at Naomi. There was something about her daughter's friend that she didn't like. The vibe in the room didn't feel genuine to her. And even though she'd known Naomi since she was a little girl, Lucia out of the blue didn't like the little, smug bitch.

Naomi cried with Luca, but the pain Naomi truly felt was losing her drug connection. With Nate gone she didn't know anyone else to run to for her re-up. And it also hurt that she wouldn't get to fuck him again.

Naomi looked at Luca with a sudden after thought and asked, "Do Gloria and Tanya know?"

Luca dreaded to hear those two names. Gloria and Tanya were both hell on earth, and she didn't want any dealings with them. The further away Luca stayed from them, the better.

Bad Girl Blvd

***

The Howard projects along with all of Brownsville were shocked when they heard about Nate being murdered in Harlem. His goons were ready to take up arms and start a war with an entire neighborhood. "Fuck Harlem!" many niggas heatedly shouted out. But Nate's foes and competitors were singing a different tune. They praised his death, and it was open market on the streets of Brooklyn.

Twenty-four hours after his murder, Nate's family charged into his Brownsville stash house expecting to receive a huge payoff. Nate wasn't taking it with him, so the drugs, cash, and other valuables could be put to better use somewhere else. In other terms, they wanted it all. But everyone got the surprise of their lives when they found the stash house empty—everything was gone—cash and drugs.

Gloria, Nate's ghetto mother, and his older sister, Tanya, were the ones leading the charge. Yeah, they were both devastated about the death of a son and a brother, but at the same time they needed to eat, too. Nate always took care of them, and with him gone, panic started to set in. They had both always hated Luca. She was cute, but that was it. They felt Nate was giving her way too much.

Gloria and Tanya turned over furniture, knocked holes in walls, and uplifted everything that wasn't bolted down, and if it was bolted down, they unbolted it and tore it open. But the Brownsville stash house didn't produce a damn thing valuable.

"There's nuthin' here, Ma!" Tanya shouted.

"I see that, Tanya!"

"That bitch took it! She took everything! She got here first and fucked us! I knew Nate shoulda never trusted that bitch. She probably the one that set him up!" Tanya exclaimed.

"You got that bitch's number?" Gloria asked.

"Yeah."

"Call that fuckin' dumb bitch and tell her I want to see her right now. My son is dead, so she better have the balls to come see me and explain what the fuck is goin' on," Gloria barked.

Tanya smiled. She had no problem calling Luca to start some type of dispute with her. First, they wanted everything that was stolen from the stash house back, and second, Tanya wanted to finally beat the shit out of Luca. When Nate was alive he'd prevented his sister from putting any hands on his girl. Now there wasn't anyone to stop her.

They had nothing right now—penniless. They couldn't go to the police because Nate was a drug dealer and everything of his was ill-gotten. In their hearts Luca was the main culprit behind it all.

It was midnight when Tanya made the phone call. Both of them were seething. They felt betrayed and cheated. But unbeknownst to them, the Brownsville stash house never held anything valuable for too long. Drugs and cash came and went like the wind blowing through it. Nate wasn't stupid enough to keep tons of cash and drugs around. The place was a front and a drop-off point for cash

55

coming in from the streets. Mostly guns were in the place. Nate kept anything of real value at his Canarsie home, and only a handful of people knew the address. Not even his mother and sister knew of the place. They were family, but he didn't trust them at all.

Luca knew his operation but never got involved. He didn't allow it. But being around Nate for three years, she had learned a few things from him and picked up on how his world moved.

Luca wasn't asleep when she heard her cell phone ringing after midnight. She was back at her grandmother's place after spending the day with her mother. Naomi lingered around for a moment but left her side the minute her Nigerian fiancé called her phone. Luca didn't care; she had bigger concerns.

Luca was seated at the foot of the bed inspecting the kilo of heroin in her hand. What was she going to do with three kilos of heroin and four guns? She wasn't about that life. She didn't like violence. She had never sold drugs, and the only drug she'd ever tried was weed.

Luca looked at her cell phone and didn't recognize the number on her screen. She hesitantly answered. "Hello?"

"You dumb, fuckin' bitch! Where the fuck is everything?" Tanya screamed through the phone.

Luca was taken aback by the abrupt screaming from Tanya. She was the last person Luca wanted to speak to.

Tanya continued to shout, "My fuckin' little brother is dead and you have the fuckin' audacity to take all of his shit out of the apartment!"

"Tanya, what are you talking about?" Luca responded meekly.

"Bitch, don't fuckin' play games wit' me, I ain't fuckin' stupid! Me and my moms is over here at Nate's place right now and ain't shit in here."

Luca knew what they meant. Of course it was empty. Nate always kept the golden egg away from the nest.

"What do you want from me, Tanya?"

"You better come meet wit' us right now or I swear to God, next time I see you Luca I'm gonna beat the shit out of you until I break all your fuckin' bones," Tanya exclaimed through clenched teeth.

Luca knew her threat was real. Tanya was a bully and a badass in the streets. She had an extensive arrest record, from drug dealing to violence, and she seemed to always be angry. Maybe it was because she wasn't a pretty girl and was overweight and bald headed. No one liked her. She was ugly. She was rude.

Gloria snatched the phone away from her daughter's hand and immediately screamed, "Listen to me, Luca, if you ain't at my son's apartment in fifteen fuckin' minutes then I'm raising hell at your fuckin' door. I don't give a fuck if it's your mother or grandmother's door. My son is dead. All of his got-damn shit is missing and someone better have a got-damn answer for me, cuz right now I don't give a fuck about anything. I'm pissed off and people are gonna pay. So no playing fuckin' games!"

Luca swallowed hard. She didn't want any problems with Nate's family.

She timidly replied, "I'll be there soon, Ms. Gloria. I'm sorry."

"I fuckin' thought so. Don't fuck wit' me bitch!" Gloria snarled. "You know I'm fuckin' crazy."

The phone call ended. Luca's heart was banging against her chest. They wanted what she had in the bedroom, but she wasn't giving it up. They didn't deserve to have any of his things because they didn't love him like she did, and they didn't have his back and put up with his ways like she did.

Luca didn't want to meet with these two women, especially not alone. Reluctantly, she called Naomi. Despite how she felt about her, Naomi was the only person she could count on to have her back, especially this late.

***

The moment Luca and Naomi stepped into the apartment, they felt the intensity of anger and frustration coming from Nate's mother and sister. Nate's Brownsville stash house was ransacked from top to bottom. Everything was turned over and broken apart. The place looked like a post police raid. Looking like two fiends, Gloria and Tanya glared at Luca and her friend.

Tanya rushed toward Luca and shouted, "Where is everything? Huh, bitch?"

Naomi got in between the two, shielding her friend from any harm and matching Tanya's scowl. As long as she was there, they weren't going to put a hand on Luca. Luca appreciated the support.

"I don't know what you're talking about," Luca replied.

"Bitch, don't fuckin' play stupid wit' me. We know you took all of his shit!" Tanya retorted.

"Bitch, don't fuck wit' us!" Gloria spat.

They both looked like they were ready to tear Luca apart. Naomi shook her head in disgust and spat, "Nate ain't even been dead twenty-four hours yet and the two of y'all are only worried about money and drugs. Seriously? Y'all should be more concerned about who killed him, and second, his funeral."

"Bitch, don't tell me shit about my son!" Gloria shouted.

Naomi sucked her teeth and locked eyes with a coldhearted mother. Luca stood timidly behind her friend. They always intimidated her. And they weren't leaving the apartment until they'd gotten what they came for.

Tanya stepped closer toward Luca, ready to push through Naomi and sink her teeth into her victim. With her ugly face scowling heavily and acting unruly, she tried to reach for Luca, shouting, "I'm gonna fuck that bitch up if she don't start talkin'."

Naomi pushed Tanya back, ready to fight. It was sad enough that she had to fight Luca's battle, but once they tried to put hands on her, Naomi wasn't going to stand for it. She turned and stared sadly at her friend. Luca seemed to be shaking in her boots. Acting scared and quiet like a mouse was only going to get her disrespected even more.

"Bitch, you better start talkin'," Gloria shouted.

"I don't know where everything is at. Nate always kept me in the dark," replied Luca with aggravation.

"Bitch, you fuckin' lying!" Tanya exclaimed.

"For all we know, you probably was the one that got my son killed in the first fuckin' place!" Gloria chimed.

"What?" Luca was shocked at the absurd accusations.

"You heard me, bitch!"

Luca wanted to run out of the room, but she remained close to Naomi. Though she disliked her friend, if she hadn't been there, they would have jumped on Luca long ago and made things a lot harder. But the mother and daughter gave Naomi some respect, knowing how she got down.

"It wasn't me. I had nothing to do with it. He was probably set up by one of his friends, someone he trusted. The last time I spoke to him, he said he was going to Harlem to re-up. He never takes me with him," Luca proclaimed uneasily.

"And I can vouch for that, because she was with me last night," Naomi lied.

Gloria and Tanya weren't buying it. They weren't leaving Nate's apartment without some type of payday.

"Y'all bitches is lying. You her friend, of course you gonna cover for her, but you can get beat down too, Naomi. I don't give a fuck!" Tanya exclaimed through clenched teeth.

"Bitch, what?" Naomi spat back with her fists tightened.

"You heard what the fuck my daughter said, you conceited, fuckin' dumb bitch!" Gloria intervened harshly.

Gloria was an OG—a hardcore gangsta bitch that done

shot niggas and bitches, moved weight in the nineties, did prison time, and gained her respect in the streets. Her son followed in her footsteps and excelled where she didn't. She was proud of her baby boy; he was a man in Brooklyn, and word on the street was he went out like a man.

Gloria was forty-five years old, stood five-nine with dark skin, and styled a long blond weave because her own hair couldn't grow. She was thick in weight from hips to booty with tits like balloons. She was an intimidating woman, from her ghetto attitude to her sketchy history. Her life in the streets was over. She'd lived off her son, who always took care of his mama even when he didn't trust her—but now that he was gone, things looked scary and the future looked bleak—for Tanya too. She was too lazy to work, with no GED, four kids, and three baby daddies. She was the epitome of loud, ghetto trash.

Naomi refused to back down, knowing she was outnumbered. She had Luca's back, but Luca was just too much of a coward to have hers. It was sickening to think about, but Naomi, feeling somewhat guilty about her recent affair with Nate, needed to make it up to her friend somehow, and this was the way to do it.

"It's whatever, Gloria," Naomi hissed.

"Yeah, it's whatever, bitch. But I tell you this, if we don't get what we fuckin' came for, I guarantee you, Luca, I'm gonna personally fuck you up in this apartment and then have my peoples beat you down every time they see you in these streets. You and your friend ain't never gonna walk these streets in peace again," Gloria warned sternly.

Luca swallowed hard. Gloria was known to always make good on her threats.

"Tell her, Mama!" Tanya uttered with a smirk on her face.

Naomi felt things were escalating to a full-blown war, but they were the only ones without any soldiers to fight for them. She looked at her friend, her eyes saying to Luca, *If you know something just tell it. It ain't worth all of this.*

But Luca wasn't about to give up her own personal payday. She had enough cash and drugs to move out of the hood. She coyly responded, "I never disrespected you, Gloria. I don't know anything and I didn't take anything from out of here. Nate kept that away from me."

"Bitch, stop fuckin' lying!" Tanya screamed frantically. She charged for Luca, ready to attack, but Naomi quickly pushed her back.

"You need to chill, Tanya!" Naomi boldly responded.

"Bitch, what? You gonna get fucked up, too! For this weak-ass bitch?" Tanya screamed out, smacking her hands together heatedly.

Gloria marched up to Luca and Naomi like a general with five stars on her shoulders. She frowned heavily. With an afterthought, she said to them, "You know what, if it ain't here, then I know where my son's shit is at."

Tanya was ready to hear where at.

Luca remained silent.

Naomi was sick and tired and was ready to go.

"At y'all place. The house my son stayed at wit' you, and if you deny it, Luca, I swear to God, I'll fuckin' murder you right here," Gloria added. "I'm the bitch that can make problems happen."

Luca nodded. "I'll take you to the house."

Tanya smiled like a child getting away with snatching a cookie out of the cookie jar before dinner.

"What's the fuckin' address?" said Gloria.

Chapter 5

Like lions tearing apart prey in the jungle, Gloria, Tanya and two hoodlums tore apart the home Luca used to share with Nate. Couches and chairs were flipped over; they knocked holes in the walls and shredded furniture with a blade to check for drugs or money inside. Pictures were thrown off the walls, the kitchen ransacked. They tore the house apart going over the place inch by inch, looking everywhere for drugs, money, or jewelry.

Luca watched helplessly as they tore her home apart. She didn't care, because she wasn't coming back to the place. It wasn't her home anymore. Without Nate, it was meaningless to her.

Naomi stood beside her. It was a shameful thing to see. She felt sorry for Luca, and didn't want to be in her predicament at all.

Gloria was growing frustrated. It was the next day and getting late or early, depending on how you looked at things.

Tanya glanced at her mother and growled, "There's nothing here, Ma."

"I can see that," Gloria snapped back.

Gloria pivoted toward Luca with a dark grimace and asked, "His jewelry? Where is my son's jewelry? I know he had plenty of it, and he bought you plenty of shit, too. Where is everything?"

"Nate always wore his jewelry. And I don't have any," Luca lied. "He knew I would never wear that gaudy stuff."

Gloria didn't believe her. She stepped toward Luca with the intention of causing her some bodily harm, but when she heard one of her goons yell out, "I found a safe. In the closet," Gloria went rushing toward it.

The mother and daughter smiled, feeling this was the moment. But the only flaw was that it was locked. Tanya looked at Luca and asked, "What's the fuckin' combination?"

"I don't know," Luca quickly replied. "You think Nate would give it to me?"

"Shit."

"We just gonna have to take it wit' us and crack it open later," said Gloria in a civil tone.

Everyone nodded, agreeing with her. Luca remained calm. She was the only one that knew the safe was empty. They were going to look like fools after all their hard work in trying to get it open to find out it didn't bear any fruit. The safe wasn't the only thing they planned on taking out of the house. In the pettiest of moments, they began taking flat-screens off the walls, going through Luca's closet and throwing her clothing in trash bags, and even taking a Cuisinart coffeemaker. These were the only few things they were able to load into the SUV parked outside, until they could come back for the rest.

Naomi didn't say a word to her friend at first. She just truly felt sorry for Luca, who seemed so weak. Everyone was taking advantage of her. When the vultures finally left, to return later for more, Naomi said to Luca, "Why you let them run all over you like that? You need to stand up for yourself someday, Luca, for real. It's pathetic. All I know is that couldn't be me. It couldn't. I wouldn't have stood for that kind of disrespect, especially after your boyfriend's murder you gonna let them take his shit. Shit, he probably would have wanted you to have. I just wish you had a backbone, Luca."

Luca blankly stared at Naomi. Just like the house, she felt empty. Though Naomi had her back, she was just as bad as Gloria and Tanya, maybe worse. She could respect them two—at least they told her they didn't like her up front, didn't perpetrate some fraud on who they really were. Naomi was the type to smile in your face but stab you in the back at the same time.

Luca could only walk away. The tears would come later.

Like looters, the next day Gloria and Tanya came back to the house with a U-Haul truck. They were ready to take everything out of the house. Gloria felt that what used to be her son's now belonged to her. Luca had no say so at all. And with cousins and other family members, they started removing expensive furniture and piling it into the truck—a $5,000 living-room set, $6,500 bedroom set, rugs, dressers and other amenities. It all was going. They were picking apart the flesh until nothing was left but the bone.

Luca didn't have any more concern for those things. She had a plan. She was still attending her GED classes and planned on getting her diploma in a few weeks. She was lying low at her grandmother's place, but visiting her mother's apartment regularly. But her gut was telling her that she needed to leave Brownsville all together—disappear for a while. She had the cash to lay her head anywhere in the city. She understood it would be best to leave, because once Nate's family finally got the safe open and they saw it was empty, it was inevitable that they would come after her.

They could have the house, the clothes, the furniture, and everything their greedy hands touched. She had what really mattered: cash, drugs, guns, and jewelry. Now, she needed somewhere safe to stay and stash everything. Her grandmother's place was cool, but Grandma could get kind of nosy with her snooping around and questions. Luca was running out of hiding places in the bedroom. And her mother's place wasn't the best place either. Lucia used to be an addict, and Luca felt it wasn't wise to keep three kilos of that kind of heroin in her mother's apartment. She didn't want her mother to relapse, and when they came looking for her, she didn't want to involve her loved ones. She'd already had enough hell growing up; Luca didn't want to add more to Lucia's shaky life.

Bad Girl Blvd

✳✳✳

The Comfort Inn in downtown Brooklyn was home enough for Luca. It was in a subtle location, out of the hood, and she didn't have to worry about any nosy neighbors or people that knew her. She paid cash for the room and only needed two weeks. The room had free wireless Internet, a nice-sized bed, and cable, and Luca loved that the subway was down the street and that she had access to a cab stand. She didn't drive, so these two places were definitely going to come in handy for her.

She hid away her stash in the closet and refused any room services to her room. The last thing she needed was housekeepers finding everything and alerting the police or treating themselves to something nice.

Luca went to the window and gazed outside. She was staying on the fifth floor. Downtown Brooklyn bustled with people and activity. It was the place to be in the spring with summer approaching—mixing in with the lunch crowd and going shopping on Fulton Street. Gradually, the weather was getting warmer and warmer, and Luca didn't have any real spring or summer clothing. Gloria and her ghetto family had taken everything.

Luca had the urge to go outside and see the town—she had money to spend—but it didn't feel right. Her boyfriend was dead and she was in trouble. Sighing heavily, Luca took a seat on the bed and continued staring out the window. The room was still, but her mind was spinning like a theme-park ride. She needed a plan. She had her

GED class tomorrow morning and needed her rest. She was yearning to finish up the program and move on to better things, maybe college. Also, she didn't want to keep carrying around three kilos of heroin and guns, or sit on them for too long. It made her edgy. Nate always got rid of his work the minute he received it. His brand of heroin moved promptly, like a flowing creek. But she was naive to the game. She didn't have any clientele and was in fact clueless where to start.

Luca wished she could go to the library and pick up a book on how to hustle, learn the fundamentals of the game without getting her head blown off or getting locked up. Just thinking about the consequences made her cringe.

As the day faded into the night, Luca was still clueless on what to do. She needed her rest, and most important, she had to get her GED. She was smart when it came to technology, and math, but when it came to the streets and knowing the game, Luca's intelligence was subpar or less.

***

The algebra problem written on the blackboard was too easy for Luca. Like adding 2+2=4. It was her forte, but majority of her classmates in the room looked at the problem like it was rocket science. Their faces were frustrated and flabbergasted. The men and women taking the course were a mixture of young and old, from as young as seventeen to as old as sixty-four. They were black, white, Latino, Asian, Indian, Russian, and so on. It didn't matter what creed or ethnicity they were. They were all in the same predicament—trying to get a proper education and better themselves in life.

Luca knew she was going to pass her GED exam with flying colors. The only reason she hadn't graduated high school with honors, and probably the valedictorian of her senior class, was that she had gotten pregnant at sixteen and dropped out. Now she had a chance to redeem herself.

While the students tried to decipher the three algebra problems on the blackboard, Luca just sat there motionless and in a daze. She thought about Nate. Since his murder three days ago, he was all she could think about. And then the trouble brewing in her hood. As she'd predicted, once Gloria and Tanya got the safe open and saw it was empty, they were furious. Word went around the projects that they were looking for Luca, and it wasn't going to be pretty. They had also warned that she had better not show up to Nate's funeral; if so, she was going to truly regret it. Luca was so saddened by the information. She had been with Nate for three years, and not being able to attend his funeral and say her proper goodbyes was about to make her cry. She was hurting a great deal, but she kept strong and kept it moving.

When lunchtime came around, Luca needed to use the restroom. She had an hour break and wanted to use it to sob for a minute. She was ready to implode with emotions. With everyone piling out of the classroom talking about lunch and other things, Luca headed toward the bathroom.

She walked into the bathroom to find she wasn't going to be alone. There was a young girl leaning by the window getting high. She put a blunt to her lips and took in a deep pull. The weed permeated throughout the bathroom and Luca began to cough violently.

"Sorry 'bout that, I just needed a smoke. This is my lunch right here," said the young, butch-looking teenager with long cornrows and a hardcore look. It took balls to smoke weed inside a college bathroom.

"It's cool. I won't tell," Luca replied with slight humor. The teen nodded and smiled.

Luca went toward the sink to splash water on her face. *Get right, Luca, get right,* she told herself. She felt the teen's eyes watching her while she continued splashing her face with cold water and then fixed her eyes on her reflection in the cloudy mirror.

"You a'ight?" the teen asked.

Luca nodded.

"Ya name Luca, right?"

"Yeah," she replied.

"Yeah, I be seeing you in class. You really smart," the young teen complimented. "You be kickin' the shit out that math, fo' real."

"Thanks," Luca returned nonchalantly.

"I'm Phaedra," she introduced with a genuine greeting.

"Hey, Phaedra."

"How you get so smart, yo? I mean, you be doin' ya thang in the class. Why you tryin' to get ya GED anyway? Shit, wit' ya mind, you should be in Harvard or sumthin'."

"It's a long story," Luca coolly replied.

"I feel you. It's a long story for me, too. Well, it ain't that long. Judge and my probation officer both told me, you can either get ya GED and advance yourself, or go to jail. Shit, a bitch ain't tryin' to be locked up over the summertime. You feel me?"

Luca nodded. "I feel you."

"You smoke?" Phaedra asked, getting ready to hand the blunt over to Luca.

"Nah, I'm good."

"You sure? Cuz this that Ooh Wee type of weed, gonna have ya ass lifted and higher than heaven," Phaedra joked.

Luca laughed. She needed the smile and laugh.

"I'm okay. But do you think it's wise to smoke in the bathroom?"

"Man, that class be kickin' my ass. I need to relax some way. Shit, I ain't asked to be here, a bitch was forced to join this program. Ya feel me? I ain't no Einstein and shit, Luca. I just come, act like I'm payin' attention, and leave. All they told me to do was show up, they ain't say shit 'bout passin' this muthafucka," Phaedra said.

"Well, at least you should try. You never know, Phaedra," Luca replied.

"I do try. I just don't get this shit. It's fuckin' hard."

"You should get a tutor then."

"What I look like to you, the Fresh Prince of Bel-Air? Fuck I'm gonna do wit' a tutor? I can't afford one and I ain't tryin' to have some nerdy-ass geek think they better than me. Fuck that, I do what I do, and that's get by.

Either the easy way or the hard way, but I get by," Phaedra proclaimed brusquely.

"I didn't mean to offend you," Luca said with a sheepish gaze.

"Nah, we good. You ain't offend me." Phaedra took another pull from the burning blunt.

"If you don't mind me asking Phaedra, how old are you?" Luca asked.

"I'm seventeen. And if ya wondering, yeah, I dropped out of high school at fifteen. I just got bored of school and started makin' money on the streets."

"I got pregnant at sixteen but had a miscarriage," Luca blurted out.

"Sorry to hear about that."

"It's cool. You can't miss what you never had, and besides, the baby's father was an asshole anyway. The miscarriage probably did me a favor."

Phaedra laughed.

From there, the two ladies had a striking conversation with each other. Luca liked her newfound friend's vibe. She was easy to talk to and rough and hood, but she seemed fun to be around. Talking to Phaedra actually made Luca feel good. She no longer felt like crying.

Phaedra was a little rough around the edges and hardcore, but deep inside, she only wanted to belong to a family. She was cool peoples. She had grown up moving around from foster home to foster home since the age of five. Her parents were hardly in her life. When she was born, her mother would disappear for months on end, not wanting to be a parent. Phaedra was left with neighbors, friends, and an alcoholic grandmother, until finally the Administration for Children's Services was contacted and she was taken away. ACS tried contacting her father, but he was killed when she was two years old.

Phaedra grew up in the mean streets of Bed-Stuy, and since she was eight years old, she had learned how to take care of herself. The streets taught her about survival. Hustling, stealing, guns, drugs—anything illegal— Phaedra knew how to do it well. She moved around in group homes, and then transitioned from one foster home to another. Some were okay, and some were pure hell.

Luca and Phaedra spent their entire lunch break talking in the bathroom. After the break, the two went back to class with a firm understanding and respect for each other. Luca had volunteered to tutor Phaedra so that she could get her GED. It was the most that anyone had ever done for Phaedra, and she seemed appreciative.

Luca's GED classes were three times a week, and during every lunch break, Luca and Phaedra went into the bathroom to talk and be alone. Phaedra even convinced Luca to smoke with her. Luca was nervous at first, fearing they were going to get caught. But once the weed started to flow through her system, Luca felt more relaxed.

"You smoked before," Phaedra said.

"I never said I didn't smoke, I just don't smoke often," Luca replied.

"Shit, if it wasn't for weed, I don't know how I would get through my days. This shit calms me," Phaedra stated.

***

Today was the day that Luca definitely needed to get high. It was Nate's funeral, and she wanted to go, but she felt too threatened. It pained Luca that she couldn't give her final farewells to her slain boyfriend. But his family was after her, and it was too risky to go back to Brownsville. She had gotten news from her mother that someone had broken into her apartment while she wasn't there. The place was a wreck, and everything had been destroyed. It was obvious that whoever broke in was desperately looking for something. It didn't take a genius to figure out that Gloria and Tanya were behind it.

Luca told Phaedra about her murdered boyfriend. Phaedra could relate. She had lost her boyfriend when she was fourteen. He was gunned down in a parked car on Fulton Street. That afternoon, the two created something between them, a bond of understanding and somewhat trust. It seemed like they could tell each other anything and wouldn't be judged for it and it would stay between them. Unlike Naomi, Phaedra was real and never judged her. Unlike Naomi, Phaedra was becoming a true friend to her.

Chapter 6

Ponce Funeral Home on Atlantic Avenue was packed with mourners, family, and a lot of Nate's friends and associates. The area was teeming with Brownsville residents and hustlers. Cops were watching the area heavily, knowing that there could be some sort of retaliation for Nate's murder and trying to keep peace. Nate had enemies everywhere, and his death had created a vacuum for violence in the hood. Everyone in the drug game wanted to step into his place and flood their drugs in territories where Nate once had control.

Nate's murder and funeral were what everyone was talking about. But the real gossip in the area was how Gloria wasn't going to tolerate Luca being at Nate's funeral. She put it out in the streets that Luca was a snake and had something to do with his murder. If Luca showed up, it would be war at her son's homegoing service.

Gloria was a greedy bitch, and she went reaching out to Nate's drug-dealing friends crying about how she was broke and didn't have any cash or insurance money to bury her son. She practically begged Nate's old associates for burial money, using the argument that funerals were expensive and Nate had always looked out for them.

She collected nearly thirty thousand dollars from over a dozen hustlers in the area, but only spent a very small portion of the cash on his funeral. It took a special kind of person to profit from her son's funeral, and Gloria was that special kind of person. She was always about money.

Nate was sharply dressed in a three-piece black-and-white Tom Ford suit with his gold Rolex around his wrist, diamond-encrusted earrings in his ears, and a diamond ring. He lay still in an 18 Gauge Presidential casket that was inundated with flowers and cards, and a large picture of Nate in his early years with his golden smile was posted near the casket. Gloria was counting down the seconds until the service was over so she could promptly remove the jewels that adorned her son's body. Hell would freeze over before she put him into the ground with that amount of bling on his person. Not when she was starving.

Family and friends seated in the front row were sobbing; grieving heavily over his murder. Tanya sat with her kids, dressed all in black and her heart heavy with grief. Gloria was seated next to her, and she was deadpan during the service. Her face was like stone as she fixed her eyes on her son lying perfectly still in the casket. The mortician had done an exceptional job with the body. He looked more asleep than dead.

Behind the family, there were dozens of attractive females pouring their eyes out with tears and agony. Nate was definitely a ladies' man, and he was truly going to be missed. When it came time to view the body, ladies, some scantily clad, were falling over his casket, screaming and hollering how they loved him so much and how they were going to miss him greatly. But the shock came when two females went to speak at the podium and mentioned that Nate was the father of their children. There was even one eye-catching female that had Nate's name tattooed across her chest with falling hearts around it. It was too much.

Gloria was ready to curse these bitches out and snatch out their weaves. But she didn't want to cause any drama at her son's service. The only female she truly loathed was Luca. And if that bitch came walking through them doors, then she was ready to create a scene.

Naomi didn't bother to walk toward the front to view the body. She decided to pay her respects from the back of the funeral home. She wasn't on good terms with the family, and the last thing she needed was a confrontation. She felt she looked too good in her classic Chanel dress and her six-inch heels to get into a fight with any bitch. Also, she wanted to remember Nate the last time they were together—him deep inside her, throwing her up against the wall and then thrusting between her thighs and punishing her pussy.

Naomi smirked as she watched Nate's alleged baby mamas grieve and pour out their hearts in front of dozens of people. Fake-ass bitches, she thought. She would glance around to check for Luca, but there wasn't any sign of her. She hoped Luca didn't have the nerve to show up, because she didn't want to have to her back with Nate's people. They would be outnumbered, and it could get ugly. But Naomi knew Luca was going to be too much of a pussy to show up. She told herself that if her man was killed, nothing on earth would keep her away from his funeral—nothing.

It was a long and teary-eyed service. Naomi didn't stay for the whole thing. She was out the door the minute the preacher got behind the podium to give the eulogy. It was dark out, and warm. Naomi strutted toward her Lexus and called Luca to give her the 411 like Luca had asked her to do.

Luca was taking a long time to answer. Naomi couldn't wait to tell her friend everything that had gone on at the funeral. She started the ignition and drove out of her parking spot, still waiting for Luca to answer her damn phone. Naomi hadn't seen her around the hood lately and figured she was hiding out and staying low somewhere.

"Hello," Luca finally answered.

"Girl, you ain't gonna believe this shit," Naomi replied.

"I assume you just came from the funeral?" asked Luca.

"Yes, I did, and it was a fuckin' zoo. First of all, there were so many bitches at his funeral confessing their love for him, and then two bitches got up there talking about how Nate fathered their kids," Naomi said.

The news was traumatizing to Luca. "What?"

"Yeah, girl, your man was a straight-up dog. These bitches was falling out over the casket, crying and hollering like he was Jesus Christ himself. And then Gloria and

Tanya were looking ghetto as ever. I swear to you, Luca, that bitch Gloria didn't shed one tear while I was there. She just sat there like a statue staring at her son's casket. There's something wrong with that bitch."

Luca couldn't believe it. Even with his death, Nate still managed to hurt her deeply. Luca listened to Naomi halfheartedly, feeling explosive. Her friend was rambling on about Nate's infidelity and his supposed baby mamas like it was cute. It seemed she was indifferent to Luca's feelings.

"Yeah, Luca, talk about a zoo and drama, girl, you're better off without him," Naomi added.

Luca remained quiet. How could she say such a thing? Luca loved Nate, and for Naomi to say that she was better off without him was straight-up blasphemy.

"Luca, hello? You still there?"

"Yes, I'm still here," Luca replied dryly.

"Anyway, it was best that you didn't come. Gloria and Tanya really have it out for you. They were constantly looking around the place to see if you would show up. I mean, at least you get to remember Nate your own special way—and you got his drugs and money, right?" said Naomi flippantly and then snickered.

Luca didn't find it funny.

"So you believe I took everything, too? Huh, Naomi?"

"Girl, you know I was just joking with you. Shit, I wouldn't blame you, though. As much shit you put up with, with Nate's cheating and having to deal with his ghetto-ass and disrespectful family for three years? Shit, you need some kind of compensation for the hell you put up with. Fuck his family, just do you, girl."

Yes, do me, thought Luca.

"Oh, and you know what the streets are saying, Luca," Naomi continued on like she was some machine. Her mouth was like a river, always running. "They saying that his connect, Squirrel, had him set up. He was going uptown to re-up when he was killed. Shit out here is getting heavy. I don't know how y'all are doing it, dating these gangsters and hustlers, having sex with these niggas and putting y'all's lives at risk like it's in fashion. At least you didn't have any kids by him. Could you imagine the horror you would have to deal with? Having that bitch as your child's grandmother."

It was a blow below the belt for Luca. Naomi was inconsiderate with her words and easily could become disrespectful in a cunning kind of way.

Luca was ready to hang up on her. She had heard enough and was becoming too emotional. She didn't want to cry, but when her friend was expected to make things better, she was only making things worse for her.

"How are things with you, Luca? Are you okay?" asked Naomi.

Now the bitch was concerned.

"I'm good."

"Where are you? I haven't seen you in a few days."

"I'm where I need to be. That's all you need to know."

It was a first from Luca; something of a backbone coming from her. Naomi was shocked.

"Excuse me?" Naomi replied.

"I'm just somewhere safe at the moment. But I have to go, Naomi. Thanks for the update," Luca said hurriedly.

"Yeah, of course. We're friends, right?" Naomi asked, reaching for Luca's endorsement.

"Yes, friends, that we are," Luca replied matter-of-factly.

She hung up.

Naomi stopped at the red light, thinking about Luca. Her friend had seemed aloof from the conversation. Naomi figured Luca was going through a lot right now and was about to break down. She definitely had a lot on her plate. Naomi wanted to be there for her, but she had her own life to live, and she planned on living it well. With her college graduation coming up, and her fiancé in her life, she wouldn't trade shoes with anyone in the world, especially Luca.

Chapter 7

Phaedra arrived home way after her 10 p.m. curfew with her foster parents. It was twenty minutes after 11 p.m. and the house looked dark. But she had known better. Someone was up; they were always up. A house with eight people, three bedrooms and two bathrooms—yeah, there was no such thing as privacy. Curfew? Phaedra laughed at having such restrictions. She was seventeen, already grown, been through hell and back since she was a kid and the streets taught her everything she knew. The foster home the agency placed her with this time was temporary, but the folks that took her in, they were creepy, especially the dad. He was overweight, underpaid at his janitorial job, and looked like he could play the serial killer in a horror movie. The Simpsons had three other foster kids to take care of and two biological children of their own.

Besides the mother, Phaedra was the only female in the house. And why her social worker decided to place her in a home with mostly males was mind-boggling to Phaedra.

She didn't fear anyone, but it was getting tiresome to fight with niggas every time she was home, especially the dad. He was the biggest pervert. Since she was placed in their custody three months ago, Mr. Simpson's eyes were always transfixed on his foster daughter. Phaedra was a dyke and dressed like one too, with her sagging and baggy jeans, oversized T-shirts, cornrows, and the dark shades she liked to wear. She liked pussy. A balding, middle-aged blue-collar worker was of no interest to her.

Phaedra decided to come through the back window of the kitchen that she had purposely left open. She didn't have her own key to the house, and ringing the doorbell after her curfew was a no-no. She used a milk crate nearby to help her reach the window, and she carefully made her way through it and inside like some cat burglar. She climbed inside the dark kitchen—so far so good. The downstairs area was quiet. She slept on a couch in the basement. It was comfortable enough for her and she didn't mind. Compared to other places she had spent the night, the basement was made up nicely for her. But she had to creep through the house first to get to her makeshift room.

With her sneakers in her hand, Phaedra slowly crept through the living room toward the basement door. Easily, she opened it, turned on the lights, and made her way downstairs. But she didn't get to settle in peacefully and quietly like she hoped too. When she made it inside the room, Phaedra saw that her night wasn't going to be so peaceful after all. Her smooth attempt to come home without any notice was shaken up by seeing her foster father seated on the couch where she slept, smoking a cigarette and clad only in a wifebeater and shorts.

"Where you been at?" he spoke coolly.

Phaedra stood there frozen with a scowl.

He stood up, towering over Phaedra by almost a foot. Phaedra looked down and saw the leather belt in his hand. She refused to answer him.

"I asked you a question, you little delinquent tramp. Where you been? Don't you know it's past your damn curfew?" he spat with his own matching scowl at his foster daughter.

"I was out!" Phaedra barked.

"Out? You ain't grown. And when you're staying under this roof, you will abide by my rules or get dealt with accordingly. You understand me?"

She remained silent.

He stepped closer to her, gripping the belt tightly in his hand. His scowl turned into a lecherous grin.

"You have two choices—either you come this way and allow me to give you a proper ass whooping for breaking your curfew, or you do something else for me in return."

Phaedra continued to stare at him contemptuously. She didn't want to understand him. She didn't plan on staying there for too long. And she knew this day was coming. The way he always looked at her since the day she arrived, it was inevitable. He was a man that couldn't control his sexual urges for the young, pretty teen. He didn't care if she liked dick or not; in his household, he was the boss.

His wife and the other kids were upstairs asleep. He had all the privacy he needed.

The man slowly unzipped his shorts and pulled out his stubby, fat dick. With his free hand, he slowly began stroking himself and said to Phaedra, "All I want right now is a blow job, and then we can work our way up to other pleasing things later on. And I'll forget all about this incident of you coming home late. You comprehend?"

She didn't. It wasn't going to happen.

With a strong conviction in her voice, Phaedra harshly replied, "Go fuck yourself!" She had her fists balled and was ready to fight him off.

"Bitch, what did you say to me?"

"I said, go fuck yourself!"

He gripped the belt with both hands and snapped it loudly, indicating he was going to fuck her up with it.

He violently grabbed Phaedra by her shirt and yanked her in his direction. She yelped and swung at him with all her might, but he was a monstrous sized man with tremendous strength. He tossed Phaedra on the bed like a tornado had lifted her off her feet and pressed all of his weight against her. He began roughly grabbing at her breasts with his massive hands, and then swiftly, he stuck his finger into her panties and penetrated her vagina. Pinned to the bed, she screamed, "Get off me! Get the fuck off me!"

Phaedra continued to struggle and wiggle free. His hand was removed from her panties. He struck her with the belt, and then again, and again. She tried to fight, but was overpowered. He breathed heavily against her and then punched her in the stomach. Phaedra folded over from the blow and coughed aggressively. The blow hurt. He knocked the air out of her and shouted, "Bitch, this my house!"

"Your house? The state pays me for me to live here!" she screamed back, challenging his authority. "You *need* my money."

He scratched his stubby beard drinking in her words. "Is that so?"

"You ain't shit without them checks. You're old, and fat and a fifty-year-old janitor." Phaedra was on a roll. It felt good to say what had been on her chest for months. "Your wife don't want your sorry ass that's why she's fucking your foster son Mark whenever you ain't around. She wants that good dick. A young stud who knows how to put his back in to it."

The news nearly knocked Mr. Simpson off his feet. His mouth fell open in shock. He took a couple steps backward and leaned on the wall for support.

"That's why you down here pulling out your little sausage dick trying to fuck a lesbian. How sad and pathetic are you?" Phaedra snickered, mockingly. "If my real father was alive he would put his foot in ya ass! He was a gangsta and woulda fucked you up something good. He murdered perverts like you."

The first slap silenced her. It was quick and powerful. The second blow came with a closed hand, but it purposely landed in her gut. The litany of blows were hard and fast—

mostly back and kidney shots so as not to leave any visible marks.

For the next hour Phaedra's foster father whipped her ass. He pounded on her flesh until his hands were raw. He no longer wanted to fuck her; he only wanted to fuck her up. He beat on her until his manhood felt restored.

"Stop! Please . . . stop!" Phaedra screamed loudly. And when he didn't stop she began screaming for help. Everyone upstairs heard her pleas but no one came to her rescue. His wife cut on the stereo to drown out her cries and her foster brothers clicked on their televisions and began playing video games. No one in the house liked Phaedra and what they felt were dykish ways.

Phaedra's cries became moans of agony as she endured the worst beating of her life. Every inch of her was sore.

After he couldn't lift his arm to strike her with another blow, Mr. Simpson began to mock her. It was his turn.

"I might be a janitor, I might even take handouts from the state. My wife might even be getting dicked down by a boy living under my roof—" he paused to wipe the sweat from his brow, "but even with all of that said I got two parents who love the shit out of me and would never have given me up to live like a dog, begging for love and attention from strangers. I got family who would lay down their lives for me. What you got? No one loves you, kid. No one. I can live with my shortcomings. Can you live with yours?"

And just like that, he left the room, leaving Phaedra frozen to the couch looking lifeless and in pain. She cried her heart out, feeling humiliated, desperate, and filled with rage. She curled into the fetal position against the couch and wished he was dead.

***

Luca walked into the ladies' bathroom expecting to see the same lively and exciting Phaedra she befriended last week. But to her surprise, Phaedra wasn't smoking weed this time by the window, but she was curled up in the corner of one of the bathroom stalls, crying.

"Ohmygod, Phaedra. Are you okay? What happened?" Luca asked with grave concern.

Phaedra looked up at her friend. She felt weak and hurt. Her foster father pulled something to the forefront of her mind that she thought she had tucked far away. She did feel unworthy and unloved. How could no one in her family come for her? How could they just toss her away like they did?

"Just leave me alone, Luca. I'm okay," Phaedra replied faintly.

Luca knew that was a lie.

It had to be serious, Luca thought, because Phaedra was a tough girl. She was hardcore to the bone, had many war stories she told Luca and some scars to prove it. She had a reputation out there and had survived this far.

"No, I know you're not okay. What is it? We're friends, remember? I'm gonna always be there for you and you the same for me. You can talk to me. Somebody hurt you?"

Phaedra had her head lowered and mumbled with contempt, "I'm gonna kill that muthafucka!"

"Who?"

"My foster father."

Luca was ready to be her crutch. She sat next to Phaedra in the bathroom stall with open ears; quick to listen and last to judge. Luca took Phaedra hand in hers and tried to comfort her. During the entire lunch break, Phaedra told her everything that had happened the other night with her foster father.

Luca was furious when she heard what had happened to her friend. Anybody that beat on a child the way he beat on Phaedra should be locked up. And then the fondling and mental abuse—saying all those ugly words to her was just wrong. Her friend was hurting and Luca wanted to fix it.

Two days later, Luca walked into the bathroom to see Phaedra like her usual self. She was by the window smoking weed. Her mood was lighter, but the humiliation of being touched sexually and then beat down was still rooted inside her. Luca carried her black bag into the bathroom.

"Luca…what's in the book bag?" Phaedra asked.

Luca motioned for Phaedra to follow her inside the stall, she took a deep breath and removed a pistol from the book bag. It was black .9mm Beretta and it was fully loaded. She held it like she didn't have any clue how to handle a gun.

"Oh shit, where you get that from?" Phaedra was shocked to see a woman like Luca carrying such a deadly firearm.

"I got it from a friend."

"A friend?" Phaedra asked with a raised eyebrow.

"It was my boyfriend's."

Phaedra took the .9mm out of Luca's hand and held it. She felt more comfortable with the gun than Luca did. She knew how to remove the clip and check the safety and the ammunition.

"Damn, this is nice," she said.

"It's yours," said Luca.

"What?"

"The gun, take it. It's to make sure your foster father won't ever bother you again."

Phaedra smiled. She had fired a gun a few times and loved the power she felt. Luca was unaware of Phaedra's infatuation with guns. It was like putting crack into a recovering addict's hands. Phaedra continued to smile and inspect the gun inside the bathroom. She got comfortable with the .9mm really fast.

Phaedra locked eyes with Luca and nodded with assurance. "If he ever comes near me again, whether to hit me or try to fuck me, I'm gonna blow his fuckin' face off. I swear."

"Yes, you can do that, but I have another option for you, Phaedra," Luca mentioned. "But only if you want it."

"And what's that?"

"Just leave."

"And go where?" asked Phaedra.

"I have a place. You can come stay with me. It isn't much. I stay in a room at the Comfort Inn not too far from here. We can be roommates, just you and I. And you can still keep the gun," Luca said.

It sounded promising to Phaedra. She hated where she was at now and had been tempted to run away numerous times, but then she would violate her probation. The judge and her probation officer had given her a stern warning: If she messed up this time, it would be jail for several months.

"But I have a social worker that always comes by to check on things. What am I supposed to tell her, or my foster parents?" Phaedra asked.

Luca thought for a moment, and then she said, "Let me take care of that."

"How?"

"I'll figure something out, but until the meantime, you have a place to stay and you can feel safe. I got your back and you have mine. Right?" Luca asked tentatively.

Phaedra nodded. "I got your back, Luca. I swear I do. Thanks for this."

"No problem. Oh, and give me his name."

"Who?"

"Your foster father."

Phaedra nodded and smiled furtively.

Phaedra concealed the gun on her person and walked out the bathroom feeling like a new bitch.

Luca went to the computer lab and immediately went to help Phaedra out of her unpromising situation.

Mr. Simpson exited his janitorial job at the Manhattan Housing Authority feeling exhausted. It was late in the evening and it had been a long day for him. It seemed like every tenant in two buildings needed something fixed or handled, and called for his services. He had been working for Housing for nearly twenty years, and he was good at his job. He was a handyman with adept skills, but behind the mask, the feigned smile the family man manifested in front of his coworkers and supervisors, was something much more sinister and corrupt.

Mr. Simpson approached his car under the fading sun. He got behind the steering wheel and was ready to start the ignition, but a folder and a cell phone in the passenger seat caught his immediate attention. It was something that he hadn't put there himself, and he was bewildered by its sudden appearance. Curious, he picked up the folder and removed the contents. It was paperwork, signed, notarized affidavits from numerous girls—underage girls—who used to be under his roof when he was their foster parent. These girls, now young women, were easy enough to find. Luca trotted them all down to her attorney's office where each one wrote out a sworn statement detailing how they were molested, raped, or sodomized by Mr. Simpson. He was a scumbag who'd taken advantage of kids in need for the past five years.

Now this information didn't come free. Luca had to pay each girl two large for their troubles and promise that they wouldn't have to testify in open court. She didn't plan on taking this information to authorities, she just wanted Phaedra free from him. And the strong letter, from a fake attorney stating that his clients are entertaining a class action lawsuit and criminal charges was the coup de grâce.

Mr. Simpson was shocked at what he saw. He was wide-eyed and looked around frantically to see if anyone was watching him, but he seemed to be alone. Suddenly, the cell phone rang. Cautiously, he picked it up and the voice on the other end was Luca's.

"You've been a naughty boy, Mr. Simpson. Probing into your personal life was easier than I thought."

"What is this? What do you want?" he asked desperately.

"What do I want? I want Phaedra completely out of your life. But unfortunately, that just can't happen because she has a social worker who frequently comes by to check on her. Now, she's coming to live with me, but what I need from you is to pretend like she's still living there when this social workers calls or comes by. Do you understand?"

Mr. Simpson remained silent. He was being blackmailed. He didn't recognize the voice. He took a deep breath. Reluctantly, he replied, "Yes, I understand."

"You hurt her the other night, and the only thing stopping me from sending everything to your home, your job, and the authorities is that you are of great use right now. But you make sure your wife gets with the program. If not, then with one phone call and a drop into the mailbox, your little foul life will be ruined," Luca threatened.

"Please, don't. I understand. I'll get her on board and you won't have any problems with us. I'm sorry," he pleaded.

"Yes, you are sorry. Phaedra is to be left alone."

"She will be."

Luca hated his voice and what he was—a nasty, foul pervert. She so badly wanted to destroy his life right now for what he'd done to Phaedra and the other girls, but she couldn't let her emotions overcome her. She was smarter than that.

Luca had a love for computers and had learned programming and computer science at an early age from a teacher. It was amazing how easy it was to hack into his world by getting from Phaedra a copy of his paystub, which had his social security number, the name of the foster care agency, and his home address. It took her several hours, but being the elite "black hat" hacker that she was, she was able to violate any computer security system with the stroke of her keys and break into ACS' secure network to attain the complete history of all the children that went in and out of his care. Mr. Simpson had a lot to hide, and it was a wonder he had kept his vile life hidden from everyone for this long.

Luca hung up. It felt good to have control over someone like that, even though it was indirect. She felt the power she had over him and it was exhilarating. She used her wits instead of brawn—though she didn't have any brawn—and it was empowering to see him crumble like paper, to see how he was too willing to do whatever she told him to do. She never had anyone succumb to her like Mr. Simpson had.

She smiled. She'd gotten something done for a friend, and it was for a good cause. *This is what power feels like,* she said to herself.

Power—Nate had power in the streets, and he had power over her in the home. Naomi had power over her, too, being the dominating friend. Gloria and Tanya had power over her through fear and intimidation. So for once, it felt good for Luca to have someone fearing her and under her power.

She'd once read that power was the ability to get results. Power was an addiction, and Luca wanted to get high off of it and never come down.

Chapter 8

Phaedra walked into the Comfort Inn hotel behind Luca with two trash bags in her hands. It was everything she owned and took from the Simpson's residence. She walked into the neat but lived-in hotel room feeling like she was at the Trump Plaza. It was home for now. Luca stopped in the middle of the room and joked, "I would like to show you around, but as you can see, we're under renovations."

Phaedra laughed. "You silly."

"But this is it, until I can find something better. I've been looking around."

Phaedra dropped her bags on the floor and looked around the room. She noticed a lot of books on the table. Luca was a reader. The books ranged in areas from computers, technology, and surveillance to history, some urban fiction novels, and self-help books. Phaedra picked up a paperback book entitled *Python for Data Analysis*.

"What?" she uttered.

She opened the book and looked through it. It was written in English, but it might as well been written in a different language, because Phaedra didn't understand any of the content inside. It was four hundred and seventy pages, and too long and difficult for her attention.

"Damn, you're really smart," said Phaedra with admiration.

"I just like to read and know about things. But don't get it twisted. I'm not sitting around reading all day like some geek. Just in my down time instead of watching mindless cable and reality TV shows, I pick up a book as a hobby."

"Well, my hobby of course is smoking, and doin' me," Phaedra said. "In fact, I think it's about time to start up wit' my hobby again."

She pulled out a dime bag and two Dutch Masters cigars. "You smoking?"

Luca nodded.

Phaedra smiled.

As Phaedra began rolling up the blunt, she looked at her friend and said, "Yo, that shit you pulled wit' my foster pops, it was smooth. I mean, I was ready to murder that muthafucka, but the minute I got home to get all of my shit, it was like he was a different person and shit. You spooked that nigga somehow. How did you do it?"

"I have my ways," Luca replied with a grin.

"Thanks, once again," Phaedra said with much gratitude.

The girls settled in as roommates. They talked, watched TV, and laughed.

A sisterly love was forming. Luca continued to tutor Phaedra for her GED, and in return, Phaedra taught her how to use a gun. Phaedra wanted Luca to learn how to protect herself with the weapon, not just how to flip the safety on and off.

"This is how you hold it and cock it back," said Phaedra, positioning herself like a gangster with the .9mm in her hand. She slid the chamber back. The gun wasn't loaded and it was safe to practice with.

Luca nodded. She was eager to learn.

Luca tried emulating everything about Phaedra, from her talk to her style. She had respect for the seventeen-year-old. There was something about her that was intoxicating. Luca wanted to know her world. She wanted to grab a hold of it and absorb herself into something or someone she never was. She wanted to be feared and respected like Nate once was.

"Have you ever shot someone?" Luca asked Phaedra out of the blue.

Phaedra looked at her with difficulty and replied, "Yes."

The night moved on. It was getting late, after 2 a.m. The two had been talking and teaching each other, sharing talents and knowledge for hours. But they were far from tired. It was intriguing for them both to learn and know new things from each other.

Luca had gotten high, and the weed that flowed through her system made her feel more relaxed. Her eyes became heavy and she suddenly had the munchies. But she was still focused and aware. She trusted Phaedra. She wanted to let her in on her secret. She stood up from the bed, gazed at Phaedra seriously, and asked, "Can you keep a secret?"

Phaedra nodded. "Of course."

Luca went over and opened the small closet in the room, revealing two trash bags buried underneath some clothes. Luca removed the bags from the closet, and then began removing their contents and placing everything—money, kilos of heroin, guns and jewelry—on the bed.

Phaedra was wide-eyed. "Oh shit!" she uttered in disbelief. "What are you, a queenpin?"

"I might need your help with this," said Luca.

"Wow! Fuck a GED," Phaedra said with reverence. "We about to get paid."

And then, there were two—book smarts and street smarts.

***

Luca walked around the three-bedroom brick home on Seaview Avenue clad in an all-black, belted Tahari pantsuit, looking like an attractive businesswoman. She wore wire-framed glasses, and her posture and attitude spoke honesty to the middle-aged realtor with the receding hairline. He showed Luca around the home he wanted to rent out with a welcoming smile.

The property in Canarsie, Brooklyn was really nice. It was immaculate, and across the street were a baseball field and park. The neighborhood was very quiet. Inside the home were hardwood floors, high ceilings, and a finished basement, which could either be Luca's home office or a recreation room. There was a large living room and an eat-in kitchen with walnut-stained cabinets and granite countertops. And entering the front door of the home invited you into the picture window and great sunlight.

Luca turned to the realtor and asked, "How much do they want a month for it, again?"

"Twenty-five hundred," he said.

Twenty-five hundred a month for one year was thirty thousand. The price wasn't a problem for Luca; it was getting the realtor to rent to her when she didn't have any credentials or a legitimate job, but did have a shabby credit score. She had cash to give him though. She was still sitting on close to fifty grand. She and Phaedra fenced all of the jewelry and received fifteen thousand for everything. The jewelry was worth a little more, but Luca needed the cash. And besides, they still had three kis of heroin to profit from.

"How many people are looking?" Luca asked.

"Oh, I have plenty. There's a school not too far from here, it's right near the park. It's a quiet area. The subways and buses are down the road. Oh, this is a resident's dream place," he mentioned with a smile.

"I'll take it."

"Well, you'll have to wait; I already have a few people ahead of you that showed interest, including a couple that's expecting their first child. They seemed very nice."

Luca didn't have time to wait or keep looking for a place. She loved this one.

"And besides, I need to do a background check and run your credit history. You can't rent to just anyone nowadays," he added.

"I understand. But listen, I'll double your fee plus give you first months' rent and the security deposit," Luca assured him.

Money talks and bullshit walks. It was ten thousand dollars cash, up front.

Luca looked at him seriously. She went into her bag and pulled out a wad of cash. The realtor's eyes bulged.

"Double my commission, huh?" he uttered.

"Yes."

"And what is it that you do again?" he asked with a raised eyebrow.

"It's not what I do, exactly; it's who my father is. Have you ever heard of a company called Quest-Zion?"

Of course he hadn't, Luca knew that. She'd made it up. Luca sized the man up with his protruding belly and subpar intelligence. He seemed like a *Sports Illustrated*, *Playboy* type of guy who never picked up a business magazine or turned to CNN or MSNBC a day in his life. She tried to steer the conversation in that direction.

"Who?" he replied in a low voice.

"Well my father is one of the partners and I'm the graphic designer. It was created in 2009 and doing really well. The headquarters is based out of Manhattan, but we're from California. I just moved here several weeks ago—I need a decent place to stay and I always dreamed of living in Brooklyn.

"To put it simply, Mr . . ."

"Anderson."

"Mr. Anderson, I want this location and I'm willing to pay whatever. My father is a wealthy man so the owner will always get their rent. I guarantee, you won't regret renting to me," Luca said with conviction and an aristocratic tone.

He thought for a moment. He didn't know a lot of things in life but he knew not to believe one word that had just come out of her mouth. However, he could remember times in life when he needed someone to just cut him a break. He didn't know what the young woman was in to and didn't want to know. He would be making an extra $2500.00 under the table that the IRS wouldn't have to know about, and that was enough to bypass any red tape.

"I guess it's yours, then," he said.

Luca smiled. "Thank you."

The transaction was made and a one-year lease was signed. She'd actually pulled it off. She was sweating like an addict in rehab, but she and Phaedra needed a place to stay, somewhere quiet and away from the hood, and renting the hotel room was eating up all her cash.

When Luca was blocks away from the property, she met up with Phaedra, who stood on the corner, patiently waiting to hear the news.

"Well?" Phaedra asked with anticipation.

"We got it!"

"Oh shit, fo' real?"

Luca nodded and assured her that everything was taken care of. They hugged each other and felt life was changing for them. They had big dreams of living life like superstars, with sprawling yachts and stretch limousines, moving coast to coast through the sky in private jets like tycoons.

Chapter 9

Before she started to sell the heroin, Luca wanted to know the history and chemistry of it. She felt that you should always know and understand your product or commodity like you knew yourself. She always saw Nate moving his brand, titled "Blow Torch," in the streets like it was water to thirsty people, and it made him rich. Luca was always curious how such a small, light brown, powder-looking product could create such a euphoric feeling that made people addicted to it and destroyed and even took lives.

She went online and researched everything there was to know about heroin.

For hours and hours, Luca read about it all—about its medical use, recreational use, prescription for addicts, the detection in biological fluids, its adverse effects along with withdrawal, the etymology of it, and the different ways users of the potent drug got high—by either smoking it, snorting it, or shooting into the arms or some other extremity of the body.

What she had in her possession was an intriguing drug that, over the years, netted drug kingpins, hustlers, and many other players, millions or even billions of dollars.

Luca had a plan, though. She was on a different mission. It was nerve-racking having three kilos of it around, so she needed to get rid of it; to make money, but at the same time stay undetected by the local authorities and rival drug dealers in Brooklyn. She had Phaedra on her team, who was streetwise and her muscle for now.

The girls quickly set up shop in their Brooklyn home. Luca decided to stay out of her old hood, or any other troubling and violent neighborhoods, and move the drug in Canarsie, a more suburban and residential area. Staying in a residential area meant less risk of competition or of bumping heads with an already established dealer or crew. She feared that her neighborhood and others were too hot to move the distinctive drug in. She was ready to run everything like a business—first, giving her drug a name, making it a brand—like Pepsi or Nike. It had to be something catchy, appealing to its users, but at the same time get word of mouth going around.

Nate once called it "Blow Torch." They had to separate themselves from that. Luca and Phaedra came up with the name "Bad Girl." They both loved it. Bad Girl—it was something Luca wanted and needed to be, that bad girl in the streets no one messed with, talked about or picked on. *Bad Girl*, her metaphor for something strong out there.

Phaedra immediately went to work with the kilos. Her boyfriend, Smurf, used to teach her how to cook up crack and process heroin on the scale. She knew what to cut it with and what not to cut it with. Having Phaedra around was a blessing for Luca. What Luca lacked, Phaedra made up for, and what Phaedra lacked was compensated through Luca. They were the perfect chemical compound.

There was the black tar heroin, a gooey, sticky and generally quite nasty substance in both appearance and texture. And there was the white powder heroin, which was like the day. Phaedra sat in the ventilated basement with a surgeon's mask covering her face and gloves on, and began grinding the substance into a powder form. It was one of the more popular ways of consuming black tar heroin for those who didn't like to use needles. Luca figured that the customers she was trying to attract weren't too fond of using syringes to get high, so selling a smokable or snortable form of heroin would be more appropriate. The heroin was put into some sort of blender and mixed with lactose. It then created a fine powder that could easily be snorted.

Slowly, but surely, Phaedra began transforming the ki for street distribution, creating packages for their clientele that they soon were about to establish. She would cut the drug with diluents such as lactose or maybe caffeine, and then ready the drug package for retail. Using this method, one kilogram of nearly 100 percent pure heroin was about to be cut and divided into approximately thirty thousand individual glassine envelopes. A small portion of the drug was measured out in the appropriate increments and was laid on the end of a regular party-type balloon. The balloon was then turned wrong side out around the small wad of heroin and the ball then tied into a knot. This was done for a reason. The rubber material kept the drug from bleeding out or wasting away. It also made the portion of heroin look a bit larger than it really was.

For the white powder heroin, Phaedra used glassine envelopes, which was a very effective method for packaging heroin since the waxy material is moisture and grease resistant.

Phaedra was very meticulous when it came to her work. Most dose-size glassine bags were about the size of a postage stamp. She measured out about one-twentieth to one-tenth of a gram of the drug on a digital scale and scooped the drug directly from the weighing device into the glassine container using a razor or matchbook cover. And then came the branding/stamping of their product— Bad Girl, so their consumers could readily identify its indirect source. This would assure return of business for the sellers.

The white packages had a new label which was now stamped pink with the white powder, and the balloons the same. Phaedra wanted it to be spelled "Bad Gal," but Luca absolutely didn't want that. She wanted to appeal to a higher-end clientele. She wanted women who were classy, who wore red-bottom shoes and did functions, went to brunches, and donated to charities, but would use the drug maybe on weekends, recreationally. And the men, who held board meetings, belonged to clubs, and drove high-end cars. These people had long money and tried to be more discreet about their drug use, having a lot to lose, unlike an addict or fiend relying on public-assistance checks twice a month.

Luca saw the bigger picture and had big dreams. She wanted to become bigger than Nate. She had so much to prove to everyone. She wanted to be known and to have power and respect. She set out to accomplish something. Everyone said she was a loser; now it was her time to prove them all wrong. There was a yearning for revenge in her heart, and Naomi's name was written all over it.

First, she started off small in Canarsie, realizing that in the middle-class neighborhood where the senators, proprietors, lawyers, a few blue-collar workers, and many well-to-do blacks, among other races, lived, there were a lot of functioning addicts out there. Addicts who held great jobs and went to work every day, but they all had habits. Some liked to sniff, some liked to smoke it, and maybe in the middle-class neighborhood, there was a small, very small percentage that even wanted to shoot it directly into their bloodstream.

Luca just wanted their business.

And with her trademark package, she was about to step out of her comfort zone and into a whole new world. It was a stimulating feeling for her—already, she was feeling like a whole new person.

Immediately, Luca upped the price on her product. Instead of the usual ten dollars addicts paid for a hit, it was now fifty dollars a pop for her distinctive merchandise. Luca's heroin was 80 to 90 percent pure, so 50 milligrams sold for fifty dollars and was marked for snorting. Thinking like a CEO of a Fortune 500 company, Luca came to the conclusion that when something came for cheap, it was inferior and weedy, but when something was pricey, then people assumed the quality of it must be very good, and knowing not everyone could afford it made those that could want it even more. Also, functioning addicts were under the impression that they weren't addicts, so the packaging and new price points would appeal to them. It would be like buying caviar in their minds. They would be willing to pay more for the potent drug, and they wouldn't have to venture out of the comfort of their cushy neighborhood to make a purchase.

While Phaedra handled her end of things with cutting and packaging the product, Luca fortified their place with state-of-the-art surveillance equipment, including front and back steel doors. She had five dome cameras placed outside the house, along with a few indoor cameras and night-vision cameras, motion sensors, an alarm contract that allowed Luca to receive alerts, and a live video relay system sent to her smart phone if any unusual activity happened around or inside her home.

Luca had a thing for toys and loved her gadgets.

***

Her name was Tiffany and she was Phaedra's first cousin. She was young, nineteen years old and a beautiful woman with angelic features and high cheekbones, and her face was surrounded by straight, shiny black tresses.

Her hair flowed freely and framed her face and head perfectly. She was dressed in a turquoise halter-tie summer dress and had legs that stretched out like a marathon. She talked with elegance, and it was hard to believe that she was Phaedra's first cousin, on her father's side. It seemed like they'd been born and raised on different sides of the tracks, but Tiffany was from Bed-Stuy.

"I can get you your clientele," Tiffany said with conviction.

"How?" Luca asked.

"Phaedra didn't tell you? Since I was sixteen years old, I've taken advantage of the co-op program in high school and worked office jobs at some big corporations, and I've done banking jobs for two weeks out of each month since I graduated last year. And I had the privilege of knowing and mingling with some of New York's elite. These men and women, they know me, they love me, and they trust me. I know the users. I personally know the ones that are looking to have a good time with some pure drug, whether it's cocaine, weed, or heroin. The white people I know, they like to get high . . . really high. And if I introduce it, they'll definitely try it," Tiffany declared.

Luca liked her already. She was firm, attractive, smart, and about her business—and she knew potential clientele to bring Luca's way.

"I told you, Luca, my cuz is about her business. She don't play," Phaedra chimed, smiling.

"So, what is it you're pushing? Coke, pills, weed?"

"It's heroin," Luca answered.

"Heroin. Okay, well, I can tell you now, a lot of people I deal with don't deal with syringes—"

"They don't have to. It can be sniffed like coke, smoked, or taken orally," Luca said.

"I see you already thought ahead."

"I had to," replied Luca.

"And what's my cut?" Tiffany asked.

"Ten cents on the dollar," Luca said.

"I want fifteen," Tiffany replied seriously.

Luca looked at Phaedra. Phaedra could only shrug and say, "Hey, she graduated high school with honors. She knows her shit."

Luca smiled, but wasn't too keen on Tiffany.

"Fifteen it is, then."

It was agreed on.

Luca was putting a team together—young girls who were driven with ambition but could also be trusted, and who didn't stand out. With Phaedra's help, girls as young as sixteen who needed work, who wanted to be a part of something big and rousing, a family, flocked her way. They were all coming to Luca for a job. A few came straight from the GED class she was taking, and they all looked up to Luca. She started to feel like a queen, a mother to them. They were ready to work, and she was ready to grow.

Chapter 10

Bad Girl, Bad Girl, it was the name ringing out in Canarsie, Brooklyn. Over the next two weeks, the potent drug infiltrated the streets with a sonic bang. With hordes of clientele rolling in, from lonely housewives to lawyers and teachers, there was an abundance of cash that came in. Selling the portions at fifty dollars a pop, Luca was drowning in sudden wealth. She remained discreet, setting up a tight system and a number of rules for her and her crew. No talking on phones. Everything done or said was face to face. No outside associates coming to her home. Of course, no cops. No excessive anything, from clothing to attitude. Luca wanted her girls to be low-key and on-point. Also, the girls had to continue with their GED classes and try to maintain regular jobs. But her young soldier-workers were proving to be thorough employees and were moving Bad Girl on the daily like McDonald's moved burgers.

Luca and Phaedra had one problem: The supply was running out, and they needed a connect. Luca only had one choice—to meet with the man that had supplied Nate in the first place, Squirrel. But how could she get a man she had never met to trust her and resupply her with the good stuff? She just had to risk it, and ride uptown, and speak to Squirrel in his language—money.

***

Luca and Phaedra jumped on the A train going toward Harlem to meet with Squirrel in the late evening. It was risky for them both. Squirrel had no idea that they were coming, and there was no guarantee that he would meet with them and then get into business with a chick he didn't even know. But, as in *The Godfather*, Luca was about to make him an offer that he couldn't refuse. She was desperate to do business with him, but she couldn't show it. Somehow, she had to act like she was the one in control when she really wasn't. Getting rich in life was about taking risks, and she had come too far to be shut down.

From the three kilos they netted almost two hundred thousand dollars after the crew was paid and supplies were purchased. It was something unprecedented for a newbie in the game. It was a high profit in just two and half short weeks. Bad Girl was becoming a notorious brand in Canarsie, but it was spreading out quickly like a virus throughout Brooklyn. Bad Girl, Bad Girl, it was what the users were craving. Tiffany had provided them with 60 percent of their clientele. The Wall Street players, the bankers, executives and investors, along with the ladies with the red-bottom shoes and those who worked the evenings, and et cetera—they all liked to dabble in some nose candy from Luca. Tiffany was definitely worth her 15 percent cut. She knew everyone. She was their sales rep. She was their lifeline.

She felt herself changing every day she was in the game. Luca understood that if she was to survive in a dog-kill-dog world, then she couldn't be feeble. She was tired of looking and feeling frail. Out of the blue, she had cut her hair really short and dyed it blonde. The transformation made her feel different. It felt like she was someone—else. And making lots of money also helped.

On the night of her dramatic transformation, she gazed at herself in the mirror and thought about the things she hated about herself—allowing people to take advantage of her—no more. People thought she was stupid; it was far from the truth. The hood confused timidity with stupidity. She was a people pleaser and put everybody else's needs before her own; Nate, Naomi. It had to be about Luca. She yearned to suddenly shine brighter than everybody else.

After the cut and hair color, Luca truly looked at herself for the first time—she looked amazing. She smiled heavily and couldn't believe it was her.

"Ohmygod . . . look at you," Phaedra replied in awe.

"You like it?"

"I love it."

Luca rubbed her shaved blonde head. She loved it too. She nodded. It was a whole new her. She couldn't wait for her family and Naomi to see her now.

But in order for Luca to be different, become someone else, she created an alter ego for herself, someone who was the exact opposite of her; a second-half self, distinct from her normal, original personality; someone leading a double life. That someone was Vesta. Why the name Vesta? Luca didn't know. It sounded intriguing and she liked the name Vesta; she liked being the bad girl. Her alter ego Vesta had accomplished something in a short period of time that Luca hadn't done at all: getting respect and being a leader. And making her own damn money. She was no longer anyone's puppet.

Tonight, everything would change, for good or bad. Phaedra carried the book bag filled with cash, a hundred thousand dollars of hardcore cash, for them to do business with the kingpin Harlemite. Also in the bag was a loaded .45 with some hollow tips; an extra precaution for the wolves lurking out there.

Luca couldn't help being nervous, but she remained stoic, completely absorbed by her alter ego as the A train roared through the dark tunnel. She sat quietly next to Phaedra in the nearly empty car thinking about everything that could go right or wrong. They were three stops away from their destination. It was now or never.

"What's he like?" Phaedra asked.

"Who, Squirrel?"

Phaedra nodded.

"We never met."

"What? You never met him before."

"He's my boyfriend's old connect."

"Shit. We need this to happen. I mean, we're, like, rich right now, Luca, with no supply. This thing we started, it gotta continue on," Phaedra said. "I never had this much money on me in my life."

"It will," Luca replied. "It will."

Phaedra stared at Luca. Luca seemed so sure of herself. If she was nervous, she didn't show it.

The train came pouring into their station. The two ladies stepped out and made their way toward the surface. The balmy night brought Harlem alive with police sirens wailing, evening traffic swelling from block to block, and the residents, out in full force, enjoying the comforts of spring.

Phaedra followed behind Luca. They remained cool, trying to look like they belonged. They were only blocks away from the Wagner Houses, and also from the spot where Nate and Cheez were gunned down. Luca felt a lump in her stomach and felt her body tense up as she approached the crime scene. But she couldn't get emotional. Now wasn't the time to freeze up.

She quickly moved by the area, blocking out the nightmare. It was about business, not the past. Phaedra was her right hand, and Luca felt ten times safer with her around.

They entered the towering Wagner houses where it seemed like all the thugs were lingering outside gambling, drinking, and taking up every space in the walkway and courtyard. It felt like they were Daniel in the lion's den. Instantly, the locals knew Luca and Phaedra didn't belong.

There were five men huddled around a dice game with cash and bets rapidly growing. They shared a burning blunt and looked like the ones running the block with their gleaming bling and hardcore attitudes.

One individual goon with his sagging jeans and wifebeater took a pull from a Newport in his hand with the dice in the other. He was ready to roll, raising his arm over his shoulder and shaking the dice in his fist, exclaiming, "I'm 'bout to break ya niggas tonight! Have all of y'all come out the fuckin' pocket, fo' real."

"Nigga, whatever. Just roll, nigga!" another goon chimed.

The dice went flying out of his hands and rolled onto the concrete with everyone anticipating the outcome. Five hundred dollars was in the pot and up for grabs. When they stopped, the man who tossed the dice screamed out, "Muthafuck! A nigga can never get a fuckin' break!"

His cohorts laughed and some scooped up the scattered bills in the circle.

"I told you nigga, this is what I do, get fuckin' money from gambling or hustling! Yeah, fuckin' pay me," a tall and slender black male hollered, clutching a fist full of dollars.

Money was being collected and insults were tossed at each other. And then the loud chatter amongst them stopped and everyone stared at Luca and Phaedra approaching.

"Y'all bitches lost or sumthin'?" the tall, slender male asked roughly.

"What? Who you callin' a bitch?" Phaedra retorted.

She wasn't going to let anyone disrespect her no matter where she was.

"Fuckin' Thelma and Louise over here," he joked. "Nah, Amber Rose for the blonde-hair bitch."

There was slight laughter coming from the group. They found the young girls quite amusing, and the eyes fixed on them proved that they were eye candy, too.

Luca didn't come to Harlem to be disrespected. She stepped up and said frankly, "We're looking for Squirrel. Where that nigga at?"

More laughter erupted from the group. The alpha male, the tall and slender one, who also seemed to be in charge, moved closer to the girls and said, "What the fuck Squirrel gon' want to meet wit' y'all two hood rats for? Who the fuck is y'all, police or sumthin?"

"Nigga, do we look like fuckin' police to you?" Phaedra shouted with the heart of a lion around the thugs.

This was going to be harder than she thought. Luca quickly sized up the man talking. Six-one, looking sloppy with his attire, and with his hair unkempt, he was doing the talking, but she quickly read that he wasn't the important one. Nothing but a loudmouth; a fool.

She needed to tell them something that they needed to hear. She needed to catch their attention, and fast.

"We're here to talk business with him," Luca said coolly.

"Business?" There was more laughter. The man doing all of the talking continued with, "Yo, look here, unless y'all bitches are tryin' to get on ya knees and suck dick, it ain't no business wit' y'all," he replied harshly.

Phaedra scowled, looking like she was ready to fight him. But Luca kept her cool, not trying to give up. Several weeks ago, she couldn't imagine herself doing what she was doing—taking charge of something. But her alter ego forced her to push forward and not worry about the consequences with these thugs. She had started a business—illicit, but it was still a distribution business, and Squirrel was her wholesaler. There was no going back to Brooklyn without some kind of understanding and product.

What came out of her mouth next was both bold and defiant. "Listen, y'all niggas do what y'all gotta do. But we came up here for a purpose and we're not leaving until we fulfill that purpose. And that's to meet with Squirrel."

Phaedra stood by her friend and felt the same way.

"Oh, y'all some bold-ass bitches. Shit, it's like that, ya might just end up not leaving the scene talkin' that shit," the tall man rebuked, while lifting his T-shirt to reveal the .9mm tucked smugly in his waistband.

He stepped forward, with his eyes brimming with anger for having his dice game interrupted by foolishness. But quickly a voice boomed out, "Tater, chill the fuck out and fall back!"

It was spoken with authority. His tone was commanding. Luca's and Phaedra's eyes shot toward the man it came from.

Tater did what he was told, compliantly. The man who'd given the command stood nestled in the back of the crowd, looking introverted to all outward appearances, but it was obvious that he was respected. He was well fit, and tall. He was also extremely handsome with his dark goatee, smooth black skin, and gleaming bald head. His defined, muscular arms were tatted up and his demeanor suggested a man in power. He wore a black tank top that highlighted his physique and showed off his arms. His jeans didn't sag, but were creased in the middle—old school style, his Timberlands were laced and brand new, and he was well groomed. He wasn't showy with heavy jewelry or loud clothing like the thugs huddled and gambling near him with their monstrous pendants, over exaggerated bling, and sagging pants.

Luca locked eyes with him. She figured he had to be Squirrel, or at least his right-hand man. He didn't budge from where he stood. He smoked a cigarette, and the way everyone suddenly became quiet after he spoke—spoke volumes.

Luca wasn't intimidated. "You Squirrel?" she asked.

It was silent for a moment. He took a few pulls from the Newport between his lips and sized up the young girl. She was pretty and shapely, her short, blonde hair unique in his part of town.

"You don't need to worry about that name around here," he replied in his raspy, deep tone.

"And why not?"

More silence. Luca could be patient.

"Listen, y'all don't belong here, so just turn around and leave. It ain't no need lookin' for Squirrel. You don't ask for the devil unless you're ready for hell," he said coolly but with a firm stare at them both.

"You think I give a fuck about the devil when I give niggas hell?" Luca spat back sharply. "I'm Nate's girlfriend."

Hearing Nate's name brought an uneasy silence throughout everyone. Everyone knew his fate; no one wanted to speak up on it.

"And you think that changes things right now?" the mystery man replied stoically.

Luca shrugged. "I took over his operation, made a profit, and now I need to, you know, get those things," Luca mentioned with a smug stare, careful not to say "heroin" out loud.

"This bitch lying. She probably police," Tater argued.

The man in charge stood in silence. His stone-cold look was fixed on Luca. In his eyes, she looked far from being a player. She was cute, but his first impression was that she wasn't built for this shit. She wasn't cut from the same cloth as he, or Nate, even if she was his wifey.

Luca already knew what he was thinking. It was what everyone who saw her always thought of her: This wasn't her world.

Luca was ready to take the risk. Her alter ego had to fully take over. She removed the book bag from around Phaedra's shoulders, unzipped it, and removed a bundle of money. She tossed it at the man and said, "Do that prove I know what the fuck I'm doing?!"

Eyes got wide and greed could be seen behind the sly smiles. She passed the bag back to Phaedra who slyly slipped her hand into the bag and gripped the pistol on the low. She wasn't taking any chances; anyone moved wrong and she was going to start blasting.

The man leafed through twenties and fifties, remaining deadpan. It was a large wad. He gazed at Phaedra and said to her in a cool way, "You can take ya hand off the gun inside the bag, Ma. We don't even get down like that. I'm a businessman, not some common thug or stick-up kid."

Phaedra scowled. She refused to relax. She didn't trust anyone. She knew the game, the streets and the code. When it came to large sums of cash like a hundred thousand, it could make your own mother set you up.

"I don't take orders from you!" Phaedra spat.

"Ma, you need to calm your dog," replied the man.

"Dog?" barked Phaedra.

"Phaedra, chill," Luca chimed in.

She did that, having respect and trust in Luca. If her friend felt everything was okay, then it was okay.

The man focused his attention back on Luca and said, "So ya tryin' to be a businesswoman. Then let's talk. Upstairs, apartment 6B. Ten minutes."

Luca nodded.

He then tossed Luca back her wad of cash and said, "Don't be stupid. You never know who's watching out here."

The man pivoted on his feet and disappeared into the building. The wolves remained outside, snarling and showing their fangs. But out of respect and under their boss's command, Luca and Phaedra were hands-off.

Luca and Phaedra walked into the lobby on high alert. They didn't know what to expect upstairs. They'd already let the cat out of the bag about the hundred thousand in the book bag, and about Luca being Nate's girlfriend. And there was no guarantee that the man talking to them outside was Squirrel.

Luca knocked on the apartment's black, reinforced-steel door with the hope she'd made the right choice. The hallway was quiet. Phaedra removed the pistol and placed it on her person. Anything could go wrong.

After Luca knocked, there was a moment of waiting, and then the door opened. They walked in. Inside was a drug haven with product and guns displayed in the living room, the threat of danger in the air. Weed could be smelled burning. Two goons were in the room glaring at their sudden guests. The third goon was the one who opened the door, and he stood closely to the girls like he was ready to snatch one in his arms as his own personal prize. He took a pull from the cigarette between his lips and eyed both ladies heavily.

"So, you Nate's old lady, huh?" he asked.

Luca nodded.

"My condolences to you."

"Thanks."

Nas' "One Mic" could be heard playing from a radio in the room. The girls lingered in the foyer, remaining on high alert.

Luca looked around for Squirrel. The knot in her stomach started to twist even harder. Everything smelled and looked bad—like a setup. Anyone with sense would have left, but she didn't have a choice.

She stepped forward like a bitch that didn't give a fuck, her eyes fixed on the two goons in wifebeaters and sagging jeans, the hood cliché, and she barked, "We came here to do business with Squirrel, not to be gawked at like we about to get fucked."

The men laughed. One returned with, "Relax, ma. We ain't thirsty like that, just cautious 'bout who come through this bitch. Female or not, we don't give a fuck."

It was understandable. The girls were searched and the pistol was removed from Phaedra's possession. She expressed her disapproval, but wasn't in the position to win her argument.

The girls moved deeper into the living room. The windows were blacked out and the place was sparsely furnished with some leather couches, a table with work on it, and a sixty-inch flat-screen with the NBA game on mute.

Luca and Phaedra refused to have a seat. They felt better standing. Phaedra clutched the book bag containing a hundred thousand tightly.

Soon the man who spoke to them outside exited from one of the bedrooms. He smoked a Newport and took a seat on the couch in front of them, looking like a thorough G and a cold-blooded killer. Luca couldn't help but stare and admire how fine he was from head to toe. His powerful stature was intriguing.

He exhaled smoke from his lips, focused his attention on Luca, and said, "First off, I ain't had shit to do wit' ya nigga's murder. I know the streets are talkin', putting me into it. And yeah, I put that murder game down, but this one wasn't me. Nate was good peoples; he was about his business and I had respect for him."

Luca nodded. "I believe you."

"And second, I'm kinda curious—nah, more like fuckin' skeptical of why his chick just out of the blue comes up to Harlem to see me talkin' 'bout she wanna do business."

Squirrel took another pull from his cigarette, blew out the smoke, and leaned back into the sofa with his hard, black eyes cutting into Luca.

"What's ya angle, ma? I mean, yeah, ya Nate's lady, but who the fuck is you? I don't know you," he asked harshly.

Luca removed the book bag from around Phaedra's shoulders and tossed the cash in front of Squirrel. She matched his hard look. "That's who I am. A bitch about her business. My man is dead and I'm trying to carry on with his legacy."

Squirrel pulled the bag closer, unzipped it, and looked inside. It was a beautiful thing to see, money. He chuckled and then took another drag from his cigarette. He then coolly returned with, "It ain't just about the money wit' me, ma. It's about that trust and loyalty, and you ain't got 'em. I got money, and I got loyalty and respect out there. Trust, shit, that's the hardest thing to get from me. I know niggas for over twenty years, and we still don't have trust. But you come into my domain with neither one, and already I'm supposed to trust you?"

He chuckled.

Luca remained silent.

Squirrel continued. "How do I know ya not tryin' to set me up? I got enemies tryin' to come at me every which way. You can be an angel tryin' to plot my downfall. You wired up?"

"We ain't fuckin' police!" Phaedra shouted.

"I'm talkin' to ya home girl, not you," Squirrel relied sternly.

Phaedra wanted to lash back, but Luca gave her a stern look. Luca locked eyes with Squirrel and heard him continue with, "Like I said, I'm 'bout trust, loyalty and respect. What you choose to start wit', it's ya choice, ma. Are you wired up?"

Squirrel's goons started to smile like clowns. Squirrel remained deadpan. His cold look was transfixed on Luca. Trust. Luca knew what he was insinuating. She didn't need any more hints. The buttons on her shirt began to open, along with the button and zipper on her. She shimmied out of her jeans, stripping down to her underwear. Phaedra looked on in shock and uttered, "Luca, what are you doing?"

Luca didn't respond. She knew what she was doing. Trust. This was her way of getting him to trust her, to show that she wasn't wired and also to show she didn't give a fuck. The goons stood speechless at her curvy, smooth figure. One muttered, "Oh shit!" feeling himself becoming aroused by the sight of her.

Luca did a little turn for him to show off her backside— her booty plump and body looking enticing. Squirrel was unemotional. Smoking his Newport, he definitely liked what he saw. He simply said to her, "You musta made Nate a very happy man wit' all that on you, I see."

Luca smiled.

"You good," Squirrel said.

"What about her friend?" one of his goons asked.

"Ain't no need for that, they good," Squirrel replied, not interested at all in seeing Phaedra's goodies. "Get dressed, ma."

Luca did, quickly. And then she said, "I have established some high-end clientele with your product. And look at us. You doubt us because we're young, like schoolgirls. But it's an advantage for us. We don't catch attention, and we can go on selling undetected with no suspicion our way. The people we mess with—let's just say it's good to fuck with people with a higher pay grade."

"Nate always said you were smart. He said you like to fuck wit' gadgets and shit. That you into technology," said Squirrel.

"I do."

Squirrel finally stood up and walked over to Luca. He towered over her by almost a foot. "Well, I might need a favor from you."

"What kind of favor?"

"I don't like bugs. I don't like surprises, you feel me?"

Luca nodded.

"I need something to keep my shit private. I need to be ahead of the curve. Too many niggas talking and I wanna shut a few muthafuckas up."

"Then let's work something out," Luca replied.

Squirrel nodded, and he started to see that there was more than meets the eye with the young Brooklyn beauty. When she spoke, he saw that she was much smarter than the average nigga trying to come up in the hustle.

Half an hour later, Luca and Phaedra left the apartment with five bricks of heroin for eighteen thousand a ki and a new connect to further their rise in the game. Squirrel wanted to sell them coke and weed too. But she only needed heroin, the good stuff like before. She was smart enough to know you had to crawl first, and then walk, before you could run.

"Let's just take the stairs," Luca suggested.

Phaedra followed behind Luca, and when they came to the third floor, Luca suddenly curved over, leaned into the wall, and threw up. "You okay?" asked Phaedra.

Wiping her mouth, she replied, "Yeah, just give me a minute."

It had been a very tense time for them both. Luca couldn't believe that she'd actually pulled it off, but she had. She went in there with the mind-set of being a powerhouse player, and she was willing to win by any means necessary. It was Vesta that pulled her through everything. She had to black herself out and allow Vesta to take over. In the stairway, a little bit of the old Luca came out. She had to purge herself.

When Luca was done throwing up, she looked at Phaedra and smiled. "We did it!" she hollered.

"I know."

They hugged each other. They had just accomplished something really huge—getting a lifeline. Now they didn't feel like they were sinking.

"This is it. We on our way into doing this," said Luca.

"We sisters for life, Luca. I love you," Phaedra proclaimed with a huge smile.

"I love you, too."

The girls hurried out of the Harlem projects and jumped back on the train to Brooklyn.

Chapter 11

The red Corvette did 85mph on the Belt Parkway in Brooklyn. The sleek sports car was a crimson flash on the highway, moving like lightning on the winding road. And with the weather being perfect— a blue sky and a warm day—it was the right time for Abioye to throw the top back on his prized ride.

Abioye: It was a Western African name, and it meant "born to royalty." And Abioye was definitely from royalty in his homeland, Nigeria, where he was born and raised. He was from a proud and wealthy family of doctors, and he was about to become a third-generation doctor. He had come to the States when he was thirteen and graduated from high school when he was only sixteen years old. He was third in his senior class and steadily on the honor roll.

He had started doing his internship at Beth Israel hospital in the city and was well on his way to becoming a very successful surgeon. A brilliant and ambitious man— and also handsome, standing six-two with a chiseled physique and smooth skin—he had the ladies surrounding him. But his heart was with Naomi and hers with him. They were in school and soon to graduate and loved each other deeply.

Naomi's fiancé was straitlaced, and he was her type all the way—handsome, rich, smart, and blessed with a big dick. Abioye was the epitome of the man of her dreams. She couldn't wait to become a doctor's wife. The posh and classy lifestyle was what she had yearned for since she was ten. Maybe she would give her man two or three kids, and they could get a dog—a small one. She'd always wanted a Yorkshire Terrier. The small dog fitted her too well.

Naomi loved to brag about her man to anyone who would listen, and if they didn't, then she would still brag about him, even harder. If she wasn't bragging about her fiancé, then she was boasting about the franchise she planned on starting, or her being about to finish school and attain her bachelor's degree. She was about to have the perfect life with a fine, rich, and established husband, and her own career. Who didn't want to be her?

She thought that she was better than everyone in her hood. She was getting out. She wasn't a statistic. She wasn't a ghetto baby mama with multiple kids and her baby fathers locked up or being deadbeats to their children. She didn't work a dead-end job. She wasn't on any public assistance. She wasn't a slut or talked about. Naomi always bragged about how she was smart enough to date someone with a future, not a hustler. She especially expressed this to Luca a few times over the months. Fucking a nigga was one thing, but to get into a relationship and have babies by a drug dealer or a no-good thug— it was blasphemy in her book.

Abioye gripped the steering wheel with one hand; the other was tangled in Naomi's long hair. Her face was in his lap, his nine-and-a-half-inch dick shoved down her throat. She enveloped him with her mouth. She sucked and licked on his mushroom tip while jerking off his big dick in her manicured fist. She heard a sharp intake of breath come from him as she swallowed him whole. Naomi aimed to please her king by any means necessary. She sucked his dick like a porn star, gave him anal, and would always transform into a little freak for him.

It turned her on, sucking his dick in the convertible Corvette while he sped on the highway. He felt the warmth of her mouth and the softness of her lips slide sensually up and down his hard erection. His knees began to buckle. He wanted to close his eyes and lean on something or pull her closer, but he couldn't; he had to remain focused on the road and keep from crashing his pricey Corvette while she painted indescribable pleasure with her mouth.

Naomi licked every inch of his hard cock as his breathing got louder and louder with the wind blowing in his face. She was ready to feel his release and have it slide down her throat like a smooth drink. She was on a mission and there was only one goal—making her man cum.

Her lips clamped around his swelled dick like vise grips, and the muscles in her mouth went to work, causing her man to moan and groan, hollering out, "Oh shit! I'm gonna cum!" in his thick Nigerian accent.

He fought to keep from swerving on the road. He wanted to recline back and enjoy every single bit of her. But now wasn't the time to fully indulge in all her glory. He had to be at work in a half hour.

Naomi's head rapidly bobbed up and down in his lap, sucking his hard dick, feeling him pulsating between her lips. She could feel the speed of the Corvette flying like it was on air. She could feel him about to cum. He cradled the back of her head and felt the warm sensation coming. Naomi looked up at him with lust in her eyes and said, "Cum for me, daddy."

"I'm gonna cum for you, baby."

She was ready to taste him. He began moaning uncontrollably, in a different time and space. She continued to lick and suck and jerk him off at the same time. Abioye shifted gears bringing the car down to a lower speed. And Naomi had her own gear shift to work with.

"Aaaah…aaaah," he cried out.

The Corvette took a curve at 65 mph and he had complete control over the car, but his family jewels being polished wasn't his to control.

"You okay, baby?" Naomi asked, pausing her blowjob for a brief second.

"Don't stop! Don't stop!" he exclaimed.

She smiled and with that, she made one more descent with her mouth and wrapped her full lips around his dick again. She swallowed him completely, and he reached the point of no return. The orgasm hit him hard as he released the evidence of his arousal into her mouth. He jerked for a moment, becoming spent. The blowjob was so good that he had to pull over to the side of the road and collect himself.

Naomi lifted her head out of his lap and wiped her mouth. Job well done. Her man was satisfied and was ready to have a good day at work. She looked at him and asked, "So, I'm still getting the car today right?"

Abioye could only nod.

***

Naomi felt untouchable behind the wheel of her fiancé's red Corvette. She dropped him off at work at Beth Israel in the city and made her way back to Brooklyn to meet up with Luca for lunch. It had been several weeks since they'd last seen each other and hung out. Since Nate's murder, Luca had made herself scarce from the hood. Not even her own family saw her. Everyone thought she was in hiding from Gloria and Tanya, or maybe depressed from losing her man. The neighborhood was talking and coming up with assumptions about why Luca wasn't around anymore.

Naomi came to a stop in front of the college where Luca was studying for her GED. It was a busy area with many people around and many things going on. Downtown Brooklyn was like a miniature replica of Manhattan.

Naomi sat double-parked in the street. She received much attention. A sexy woman in a hot car with R&B playing—everyone who passed her had to turn and look her way. Naomi grinned slightly at the attention. It felt good to be a bad chick riding around in an eighty-thousand-dollar car.

She opened the sun visor to check her hair and makeup. Perfect. She then got on her cell phone to call Luca.

Luca answered. "Hello?"

"Yeah, it's me. I'm outside the school waiting for you. How long are you going to be?"

"I'll be down in ten minutes," replied Luca.

"Okay, hurry up, because I'm double-parked."

She hung up and sighed. Naomi felt she could be doing something better on such a lovely day. It was bright, it was hot, and summer was right around the corner. But Naomi was worried about her friend and decided to treat her to lunch. Everything was on her. It was the least she could do after everything Luca had been through lately.

Naomi waited, becoming impatient. She lit a cigarette and decided to step out of the car to stretch her long legs in her new Jimmy Choos and show off the red, silk, Gucci summer dress she wore.

She stared at the front entrance of the school, keeping a keen eye out for Luca. Students of different ages and ethnicities started to pour out of the building in hordes. It was hard to spot Luca in the crowd. It was making Naomi upset. She wanted to be nice, but suddenly everything was becoming inconvenient for her. She had to find Luca and at the same time keep an eye out for cops and traffic police.

Finally, she saw her friend and couldn't believe what she was seeing. Luca was walking her way, flanked by some young girl with cornrows, and they were smiling and laughing. Naomi instantly thought the girl was a hood rat—and why was Luca with her? But what caught Naomi off-guard was her friend's bold new look.

They spotted each other. Luca went toward Naomi, and Phaedra followed.

Naomi feigned a smile and hollered, "Luca! Ohmygod, what did you do to your hair?"

"You like it?" Luca asked, touching her head.

"It's different. I mean, wow . . . look at you," Naomi replied halfheartedly. "It was better long, though. Why did you cut it?"

Phaedra cut her eyes over at Naomi. Right away she disliked her, picking up on her pretentious attitude.

"I just wanted to try something different."

"Well, it is different. Looking like Eve and a ghetto Amber Rose," Naomi joked.

But Phaedra didn't find it funny.

"Well, I love it," Phaedra interjected.

"Of course," Naomi hissed with sarcasm.

"Oh, I'm being rude," Luca uttered. "Naomi, this is Phaedra, and Phaedra, this is my friend from around the way."

Immediately, Naomi became standoffish and dryly replied with, "It's nice to meet you." She couldn't even look the girl in the eyes and didn't want to shake her hand.

Phaedra knew the greeting wasn't genuine. *Fake bitch,* she wanted to shout out. But since she was a friend of Luca's, she held her tongue and remained polite.

"You ready? Because I'm double-parked," Naomi said with a slight attitude in her tone.

Luca looked at Phaedra and asked, "You hungry?"

But before Phaedra could answer, Naomi quickly chimed, "It's a Corvette I'm in, Luca, and I only have room for you. See?" She pointed to the car.

Phaedra glared at the uppity bitch and was ready to beat her down in public. But in return, she simply replied, "Nah, I'm good, Luca. I see you got ya hands full and shit. I'll see you around."

"Okay."

They hugged each other, and before Phaedra walked away, she glared at Naomi and smirked, knowing that she could destroy this bitch in so many ways. Luca's friend wasn't on her level at all.

The two of them began walking to the car.

"She's interesting. Where did you find her?" Naomi asked.

"We're in the same class."

"I'm surprised she's in any class at all," Naomi said.

Luca let the comment slide. She climbed into the red Corvette and admired how sleek the car was with its cream interior and polished grain dashboard.

"Nice car," she uttered.

"I know. It's Abioye's. He let me borrow it for the day, right after I finished doing him a pleasurable favor in the front seat," Naomi proclaimed with a proud smile. "And you can't believe how much attention I've been getting."

It was too much information for Luca to hear. She didn't need to know her friend just got finished sucking dick in the same car. Luca didn't even know why she agreed to have lunch with Naomi. It was clear to her that Naomi was a fake bitch. And besides, she had found a new best friend with Phaedra. She was young, but she was real and very caring. Despite knowing Phaedra for a short time, Luca felt more of a bond and a sisterhood with her than with Naomi.

Naomi whipped her hair around, smiling and said, "Ohmygod, it feels like forever since we hung out, Luca. What, we're not friends anymore? You're forgetting about me?" It was a playful statement, but Luca saw truth in it.

"Where are we going?" Luca asked.

"I know this great place not too far from here to have lunch. Trust me, you'll love it," Naomi assured her.

She shifted the Corvette into first gear and sped off, needing to show off to the lesser people around her. Yeah, she knew how to drive stick, and soon she was going to have her own sports car.

Nonchalantly, Luca went along for the ride, becoming her old quiet and introverted self again, allowing Naomi, like always, to be the dominant one in public. But there was a raging beast that wanted to erupt from within Luca. She had felt what power and respect was like, and submerging it felt wrong. The docile side of her was gradually fading away, and while Naomi talked about herself and her fiancé as usual, Luca was seething. She could not forget that this bitch had fucked Nate and talked shit about her behind her back. What kind of friend was that?

Palmer's was an upscale waterfront restaurant with fine dining and quality service. The picturesque view of the downtown Manhattan skyline was remarkable and attracted locals and tourists alike.

The place was semi-busy with an afternoon crowd for lunch or those who did brunch. Mostly businessmen and women from the area frequented the place, along with lawyers and officers from the courthouse up the street.

Luca sat opposite Naomi at their outdoor table. She picked at her veggie burger and fries. She really wasn't hungry. Her mind was focused on business. She was moving five kis of heroin a week for Squirrel. Business was good; really good. Luca still disguised herself as the same docile woman that didn't say much. She had Naomi fooled. No one suspected that she was becoming a drug queenpin.

Naomi dug into her smoked salmon salad. She couldn't shut up about her perfect life. It was always about her and her fiancé, Abioye. Luca couldn't even pronounce his name right.

Naomi talked about her school, her cushy office job, her engagement, her future kids, and where she planned on moving to once she was married. She went on and on like a well-oiled machine.

Luca sat expressionlessly, dying of boredom. How the fuck had she remained friends so long with such a shallow bitch? Luca asked herself.

"Do you feel me, Luca?" Naomi asked.

"Yeah, I feel you," she dryly responded, not knowing the question asked.

"But anyway, enough about me," said Naomi.

It's about fucking time, Luca thought.

Naomi continued with, "I haven't seen you around in a few weeks. I was starting to think that Luca got her groove back. You feel me?" It was a teasing statement. "I mean, I wouldn't blame you if you did. It would be about time you got over Nate," she added.

"Excuse me?" Luca returned with a puzzled gaze.

"I'm just saying, Luca, maybe you need to start making better decisions in your life, because you don't want to make the same mistakes like before," Naomi preached.

"What same mistakes?" Luca asked. She couldn't believe what she was hearing.

Naomi had the audacity to speak about decisions and mistakes when she was the one who fucked Nate right before his murder.

"I'm not trying to belittle you, Luca. You're my friend and I love you. But look at the reality of your situation. You were dating a drug dealer. What did you expect? To live happily ever after with him?"

Luca was dumbfounded by her words. So dumbfounded, that she chuckled slightly.

"Luca, it's not anything to laugh about. I mean, look at my life. I was smart enough to date someone with a future, like my fiancé, who's going to be a great doctor someday. You think I'm just going to put myself out there for anyone, especially for some nigga in the streets and been around? God no. There's no telling what type of STDs these niggas are carrying.

141

"You have to leave these thugs alone, Luca. They're only going to bring you down. I had love for Nate, but he was just like the rest of these niggas around the way, going nowhere but to jail or the grave."

"You grew up with most of them thugs, Naomi," Luca said with some contempt.

"I know, and don't remind me. I'm trying to forget where I come from," she stated.

Luca tightly gripped the silver fork and stared at this bitch talking shit about Nate like they all didn't grow up together. And then had the nerve to dog out her man like he was some plague when she'd fucked him raw. Naomi was a hypocrite. Luca imagined herself leaping from her seat, jamming the silver fork into Naomi's eye, and twisting it deep until it rammed into her skull. She felt the strong urge to get violent with Naomi—to show the bitch a side of her that she wasn't expecting. It would be a hell of a way to make a statement and reveal that she was no longer was going to take her shit. Not only had her hair changed, but she had also. Luca's pussy tingled with the thought of that fork being shoved into Naomi's two-face, disfiguring and blinding the slut.

Luca gripped the fork so tightly that even Naomi saw it and had to say something.

"You okay with that fork? I mean, you're holding it kind of tight, Luca."

"Yeah, I'm okay," she lied.

"I thought you was about to stab me with it for a moment, but you're too sweet to do anyone harm."

"No, you're my best friend. And well, you've made so many great decisions in your life and I admire you so much, Naomi. You're, like, my idol."

Naomi had her head so far up her own ass that she actually thought Luca was being legit with her statement and was giving her a compliment. She smiled, reached across the table to place Luca's hands in hers, and said, "I'm always going to be there for you, Luca. And when I have my wedding, you're going to be one of my bridesmaids. I just hope your hair grows back before my wedding."

Luca locked eyes with her friend/enemy. She strongly felt that Naomi had taken everything from her the day she fucked the love of her life. Stabbing her to her death was just too simple. Luca wanted to rip away everything from Naomi and have her suffer and feel the way she always felt—torn apart.

"You know what we need to do together, Luca? Go and hit the club. Just you and me, have some fun and do us," Naomi suggested excitedly.

"I'll think about it," Luca replied halfheartedly.

"Don't think, let's just do it. How about this weekend? We can get tipsy and flirt with some cute guys."

Luca nodded. "Okay."

Naomi smiled widely. "That's my girl. I can't wait. Girls' night out."

Luca wasn't that thrilled about it, but she had a plan. It might take her a moment to pull it off, but it was going to happen. The contempt in her heart for Naomi was growing faster than a tumor.

"I gotta go," Luca said, quickly removing herself from the table.

"Go? Luca, we just got here."

"I know, but I have something important to take care of."

"Now what's more important than sitting in a nice place by the water and having lunch with your best friend?" Naomi asked.

Everything, Luca thought.

"I just have to take care of something."

"Well, I'm not ready to leave yet, Luca. This was important to me, too." Naomi made this clear by sitting firmly in her seat, always wanting to have her way.

"That's okay, I'll catch a cab."

Luca pivoted on her heels and hurried away from Naomi and the restaurant. She didn't even look back. It was hard to stomach Naomi, but until her plan came through, she was going to play nice and pretend to be the same person Naomi grew up with.

Naomi remained seated at the table looking perplexed. She wasn't chasing behind her friend. She wanted to continue to enjoy her lunch and the red Corvette on such a beautiful day.

Chapter 12

Luca and Phaedra rode in the backseat of the cab on their way to Queens. Luca looked at her friend and smiled. She was excited about this trip. She was going to learn something new. Even though she was around them, she'd never had any use for them: guns.

Phaedra carried the book bag. Inside were a few guns and some ammunition. They were heading to a remote location in Queens for target practice. Phaedra knew of a place where her uncles and cousins used to take her a few years ago to shoot at bottles, cans, trash, and everything else. It was in the cut and away from any residents and open roads.

They were coming closer to their destination where the streets became narrow and traffic became a lot sparser. Phaedra had to direct the driver to a wooded area near Far Rockaway. He came to a stop at the desolate area and was puzzled as to why two young and beautiful ladies would want to be dropped off at such a remote location.

"There's nothing out here," he said.

"We know," Phaedra replied. "Just mind ya business."

It was a costly trip. She paid him his fee, and he could only shrug. It wasn't his business to know.

The two climbed out of the cab and walked away. It was a quarter of a mile walk through the thickly wooded area to an abandoned mansion nestled in the cut with towering trees and thick shrubberies. While they wandered down the winding path, Phaedra said, "So, ya friend from the other day, she's a straight bitch. And how long have y'all been friends?"

"Too long," Luca replied.

"Well, I don't like her. She's rude, stuck-up, and she was about to get her ass fucked up," Phaedra said frankly.

"She was a friend, but not anymore. She's a hypocrite and she's gonna get hers, believe that."

"What do you have planned?"

"Something she definitely won't like," replied Luca with a wicked grin.

"I like it already. Just make sure I'm there when the fireworks go off."

Luca nodded.

The two reached a deserted area. There was nothing around but trees, land, and privacy. The mansion was dilapidated, covered with long vines and creepy looking— like it belonged in a horror film. It had been vacant for over twenty years.

Phaedra began setting up bottles and other trash that was scattered all over the area. She had seven glass bottles and other debris positioned on trash cans and rocks for target practice. She then removed four handguns from the book bag—two .45s, a .9mm Berretta, and a Glock 17. They were all locked and loaded, ready to be fired.

"This is it. You ready?" Phaedra asked Luca.

"As ready as I'm gonna be."

"So, you never fired a gun before?"

"No."

"Real talk. The business that we're in, sooner or later it's gonna get ugly, Luca, maybe real ugly. And this right here—knowing how to shoot and protect yourself—can be the difference between living or dying," Phaedra warned.

Luca nodded. "I already saw the ugly when they killed Nate right in front of me."

Phaedra gripped the .9mm, holding it down to the ground while she talked to Luca. "But are you ready to kill someone when the time comes? We're building an empire, you and me, and there will be blood."

"I think I am. I'm ready to do what I have to do," Luca replied solemnly.

Phaedra nodded. She posed in a shooting stance with her arms outstretched, pointing the gun at one of the targets lined up about one hundred meters down.

"What my cousins used to say to me was, you never pull it out unless you gonna use it. And when you do, you use it right," said Phaedra. "It's you or them out there… and believe me, I'm not tryin' to be dead anytime soon."

She fired two rounds, striking a beer bottle and making it shatter into pieces. She aimed again and fired two more rounds, destroying a detergent bottle. Luca was impressed.

"Now you try."

Phaedra handed Luca the .9mm. She still needed to get comfortable with the gun. She held it like it was some creature trying to crawl up her arm.

"Luca, you gotta get used to holding a gat. It ain't gonna bite you. It's there to help you survive."

"It's kind of heavy."

"It ain't the weight you have to worry about. It's one, when niggas shoot back, and two, the recoil. The bigger the gun, the stronger the recoil," Phaedra explained.

Luca stood with her legs spread apart and her feet planted firmly against the ground. She had both arms outstretched with the gun at the end of them. She took a deep breath and fired. She missed by a mile. The recoil of the gun was shocking to her and made her stumble backwards a bit.

She fired again; it was even a bigger miss. The third shot was out of this world. Aiming wasn't her forte.

Phaedra sighed. "No sweat. It's ya first time shooting. We gonna get you right."

"I don't know if I can do this."

"You can, Luca. Because your life and mine will depend on how well you can shoot."

Phaedra passed Luca the .45. "Maybe this one will be a little easier for you."

Luca took it, repeated the same stance as before and fired. The bullet didn't even come close to its target. She fired again—the same results. Frustrated, Luca screamed out, "Ah! I can't do this!"

"Yes you can. You just gotta know how to relax and take control. Just breathe easy and shoot. Set ya sight on what you want to hit, and don't squeeze on the trigger too hard," Phaedra explained patiently.

"How did you get so good at this?"

"I come from a rough family and rough neighborhood."

"I did too," Luca replied.

"Yeah well, ya book smart, which is cool, but this here, it was like walking for me."

They came from violent hoods, but somewhat lived in different worlds. Luca once remembered someone saying to her, "We all may live on the same planet, but we all come from different worlds."

As the day went on, Phaedra continued to train Luca in shooting. She taught her the fundamentals, from the safety of a weapon to knowing how to cock it back and load rounds into the chamber. It took time, but Luca's aim steadily improved as she became more comfortable with handling the weapon. But she was still missing her targets.

Almost two hours passed. The day was becoming exhausting, and their rounds were nearly spent. Luca was determined to get it right. Her shooting stance and grip on the weapon had improved. She stood upright with her arms outstretched and gripped the .45 tightly. Phaedra stood behind her, coaching her gently and anticipating results.

Before Luca fired the gun, Phaedra said in her ear, "Gaze intently at the target, the large glass bottle down there, and imagine it being someone you want dead. Now is ya chance. Take 'em out, Luca. Take 'em out!"

Luca fired. It was a direct hit. The bottle shattered into pieces.

"There you go!" Phaedra hollered excitedly. "Now do it again. The same as before."

Luca beamed and fired again—direct hit once more.

"Now that's my bitch! That's muthafuckin' gangsta right there," Phaedra shouted.

Luca was excited also. She had finally hit something. It was a good feeling to see results.

Phaedra was curious, so she asked, "Who or what was you thinking about?"

With a wayward smile, Luca answered, "I was thinking about Naomi."

Phaedra smiled also. "Fuck that bitch."

"Yeah, fuck that bitch!"

Both girls aimed at the remaining targets a hundred meters away and fired erratically, causing everything to explode suddenly. Watching shit being shattered and destroyed was an exhilarating feeling for Luca. She breathed heavily with the smoking gun in her hand.

"It's a good feeling, ain't it?" Phaedra asked.

"It's a great fuckin' feeling!"

Chapter 13

Stepping out of the cab in a sexy coral side-tie halter dress with a plunging cowl neckline, curve-hugging bodice, and side-tie skirt, along with a pair of YSL stilettos, Luca looked remarkable. The single-carat, princess-cut diamond stud earrings in fourteen-karat white gold and the one-third carat diamond solitaire pendant in eighteen-karat white gold were her way of indulging herself with some of the finer things in life. With her short blonde hair and her body looking outstanding, Luca immediately caught the attention of club goers who stood outside Club Rain, an upscale venue on the Lower East Side of Manhattan.

There were hordes of people standing on line waiting to get inside. She was alone and felt some trepidation. She didn't really want to be there, but there was a side of her that wanted to show off. Knowing she looked fabulous, Luca smiled and felt like a celebrity about to walk across the red carpet at a major event. It was supposed to be girls' night out, and she did need to unwind and have some fun.

She looked around for Naomi, but there wasn't any sign of her. Luca pulled out her cell phone and dialed Naomi's phone. It rang a few times, then went to her voicemail, making Luca nervous.

"I hope she didn't stand me up," Luca said to herself.

With the phone pressed to her ear, she dialed again, her eyes searching through the thick crowd outside for this bitch. It looked impossible to get inside. Security was tight and arrogant, selective about who they allowed into the place and who they made wait. Luca didn't know anyone. This was Naomi's favorite club to party at. It was popular in New York. Celebrities and athletes frequented the club, and it had been in a few movies.

Luca got her voicemail again. Her smile swiftly turned into a frown. She was ready to turn around and catch a cab back home. But, unexpectedly, she heard her name being called.

"Luca! Luca! We over here!"

She turned around, and it was Naomi down the street, waving at her. There was some slight comfort knowing Naomi didn't play her tonight. Luca strutted over to Naomi and quickly learned that she wasn't alone. Standing next to her friend was a tall, dark and very handsome male clad in a gray suit and a warm smile. It was obvious that the man was Naomi's fiancé, Abioye. Naomi was lovingly by his side with a bright smile.

"Hey," Luca greeted faintly.

"Ohmygod, I'm glad you came, Luca," Naomi joyously greeted. "You remember my fiancé, Abioye?"

"Yes. Hey."

"Hey," he greeted with a bright white smile. "I'm sorry for your loss."

"Thank you," Luca replied.

"We gonna have so much fun," Naomi hollered.

Luca stood looking confused. She thought it was only going to her and Naomi, so why was Naomi's fiancé around? Naomi nestled against her man—smiling a great deal, clad in a gold, strapless keyhole dress—and strutted toward the front entrance. Luca was behind them, finding herself the third wheel of the night. It was so uncomfortable. Once again, Naomi made it about her.

They had no problems getting in. Security outside was familiar with Naomi and her fiancé, and the velvet ropes were unhooked, allowing the trio easy access inside while everyone looked on in awe.

Like a wandering puppy, Luca followed them into the lively, forty-thousand-square-foot landmark nightclub in the heart of the city. The music was blaring, professional bartenders worked the busy crowd, and NYC's hottest DJ mixed it up.

Abioye asked for bottle service right away, and the trio was escorted into one of the many VIP areas where they had their own seated section. As they sat, Naomi stared at Luca and said, "Girl, you clean up nice. Look at you, looking your best. I love them earrings and that necklace. What are they, cubic zirconias?"

Luca smirked. Naomi was trying to play her in front of her man. She couldn't give a decent compliment without throwing acid in it. Luca knew she looked great from head to toe. The attention she received outside and while walking into the club was proof enough.

Luca commented, "No, they're the real thing, Naomi."

"Get out of here! How much? And how can you afford real diamonds? You ain't ever had a job, Luca," Naomi replied with her reckless mouth.

"Things are changing for me," Luca replied.

"Changing? Oh, are you fucking some nigga that's treating you with the best? You met another hustler, Luca?"

Luca was seething inside. It took every passive inch of her to keep her buttocks planted in the chair and to keep from jumping up and beating Naomi down. First she brought her fiancé with her into the club to show off, and now she was trying to clown Luca in front of him. It wasn't cool.

Abioye remained quiet with his arm around Naomi. He was a gentleman. He let the girls talk and stayed out of it. The only thing he was waiting for was his champagne .

"I'm still single, Naomi," Luca returned.

"Single? With diamonds like that in your ears? Girl, I gotta get a closer look at them," Naomi said.

She got up from Abioye's side and plopped down next to Luca. She attentively gazed at Luca's earrings and necklace, inspecting them like she was appraising everything.

"Shit, they do look real. Well, if you're not fucking anyone for jewelry like this, then you're boosting, right?"

Luca was ready to bark on her, but the waitress came

over to their table clutching two sparkling bottles of champagne.

Abioye smiled. "Yes, it's about time."

The champagne lady inadvertently stopped the argument that was about to ensue between Luca and Naomi. She placed the bottles that were in a bucket of ice on the table in front of them along with three long-stemmed glasses. Abioye reached for the bottle and glasses and poured everyone a drink. He stood up with his drink in his hand and said in his thick Nigerian accent, "We're out here tonight to all have fun. So let's have some fun. I have a very beautiful woman that loves me, and she has a beautiful friend, and tonight, let's leave our troubles outside."

Naomi smiled. Luca did too. They stood up with their glasses in their hands and toasted. But Luca didn't feel too cheery about anything. She only went along with the program because she had plans she wanted to set into motion.

Naomi danced with Abioye while Luca played the VIP section, sipping on champagne and glaring at Naomi. The hate for her was bubbling inside so strongly that it was making Luca almost sick to her stomach, just staring at her happiness. She watched Naomi glide across the dance floor with her fiancé while Luca sat alone.

Luca was never a good dancer, but she had a wicked body and she wasn't about to sit there alone while Naomi got all the shine with her man. The new Luca was ready to burst out. Her fierce attitude was growing every day, and she saw something she liked standing by the bar. She stood up and strutted toward the dance floor with that gleam in her eyes to finally try and outdo her counterpart. Immediately, the attention shifted to her. The dress she wore was striking. She moved by Naomi and Abioye and did the boldest thing ever: approached a handsome stranger out of the blue and asked him to dance with her. He couldn't say no to her beauty and sexiness. He smiled, and nodded. "Of course."

Naomi could only stare in awe as she watched a changed Luca take the initiative and take charge of something. John Hart's "Who Booty," blared throughout the club. Luca started to wind and grind against the man. He held her waist while her plump backside grazed against him, causing him to become aroused, a little.

"She's never done that before," uttered Naomi with disbelief.

As Luca danced with the man, she stared over at Naomi hugging up against her fiancé and winked. Tonight, it wasn't going to be just the Naomi show. Luca's alter ego decided to step up and do something. It was an eye for an eye. Her newfound company was really into her, and they moved in sync, one song after another. Luca was actually having a good time and wasn't worried about Naomi. But that dark, seething part inside of her wanted to take away something that made Naomi truly happy, that she cared about so much. And she knew exactly what to take.

The night started to wind down, and Luca's male friend didn't want to leave her side. His name was Ryan. He was an accountant in the city—an affable guy, well dressed and well groomed. He was deeply attracted to Luca and asked for her number. Naomi noticed the attention her friend was getting and it rubbed her the wrong way.

Naomi was now alone because Abioye had had to run out. He had to work in the morning, and decided to catch a cab back to his place, leaving his fiancée the car—making Naomi the third wheel in the club while Luca was really getting to know Ryan. The three sat in VIP, Luca and Ryan chatting and laughing while Naomi downed champagne and felt out of place.

"So, what is it that you do again, Ryan . . . that is your name, right?"

"I'm an accountant at one of the top firms in Manhattan," he replied.

"You know, your kind is a first for my girl. She's not used to men like you," said Naomi with a twisted grin.

Ryan chuckled slightly. "Men like me?"

Luca cut her eyes at Naomi, trying to give her a warning.

"She's from the hood."

"We're both from the same hood," Luca corrected.

"I know. And you're new to her. I mean, she's used to dating thugs and shit," Naomi added.

"It doesn't matter where she's from. I'm from the South Bronx. And I done seen it all too, crawled my way out of hell to live a better life. But it's not where you're from, but where you're going," Ryan stated nicely. "And your friend, she's sweet, beautiful, and has piqued my interest."

Luca smiled.

Naomi frowned and continued drinking. "Well, she's still getting over her last boyfriend. He was killed over a month ago," she said.

Luca jumped up, and exclaimed "Naomi, are you serious?" Enough was enough. It was clear that Naomi was hating on her.

"I'm just keeping it real," Naomi explained herself.

Luca glared at her and retorted, "That is not your business to tell!"

"Well, we're not trying to keep secrets from each other," Naomi said in her own defense.

"Ladies, it's cool, I'm not trying to start anything here."

Ryan stood up and looked at Luca. He smiled. She smiled.

"Listen, the only thing I care about is if you're single or not?" he asked politely.

"I am."

"Here's my number then, beautiful. Call me anytime and I'll take you somewhere nice. A place where we could get to know each other better."

He said his goodbyes to the ladies and walked away, leaving a lasting impression on Luca. But Naomi had something smart to say. "He might be gay. You better watch out for him, Luca."

Luca didn't reply. She was sick of Naomi and all of her hate. She glared at Naomi and said, "I'm ready to go. It's getting late."

Naomi agreed, and they both left the club after 3 a.m.

Luca decided to spend the night at Naomi's place since it was closer and Canarsie was a long distance at the late hour. It would be the continuation of their girls' night out.

When the two left the club and arrived at Naomi's apartment, Naomi threw back a few more drinks of Grey Goose and passed out in her bedroom in her club attire. Luca decided to take advantage of the moment. She wasn't tired. She was still angry. And it was time to make Naomi feel the same pain she felt.

It was 9 a.m. and Luca lingered on the couch, plotting her revenge. The morning sun was percolating through the blinds, and it was another beautiful day.

Luca stood up and checked in on Naomi in her bedroom. She was still passed out, face down on her bed with her feet dangling, one shoe on and the other off. Luca walked into the bedroom quietly and looked around for her keys. She rifled through Naomi's purse and checked the dresser. She soon found what she was looking for on the bed: Naomi's key ring, and her address book with the critical information Luca needed. She searched for one particular address, memorized it, and then snatched up the key ring and walked out of the apartment.

Knowing there was a locksmith two blocks down from Naomi's apartment, Luca took a walk to it and got a copy of all the keys on the ring. Luca knew one of the keys would work. The locksmith made a duplicate of all six keys. Luca walked back to Naomi's apartment with a grin and, once inside, placed Naomi's keys where she'd found them and went into the kitchen to make some coffee. Phase one of her plan was complete; now phase two would be the most difficult. It was going to be the ultimate sin.

Naomi woke up around noon with a serious hangover. She shed her wrinkled club dress and donned a long blue robe, smelling the coffee brewing in her kitchen.

She walked into her kitchen to find Luca seated at the table drinking coffee and reading today's paper.

"Good morning," Luca greeted with a warm smile. "I made some fresh coffee."

"Thanks," Naomi said.

"Do you remember anything about last night?"

"Did we fuck?" Naomi joked.

She had no recollection of the previous night. The only thing she remembered was Abioye leaving, and vaguely, some man Luca was with. Her drinking had gotten heavy, and with it her mouth had become more reckless.

"No!"

Naomi laughed. "Okay, at least that's off my mind."

Naomi poured herself a cup of coffee and started sipping. She leaned against the kitchen counter, looking pleased, and said to Luca, "Thanks for looking out for me last night and staying with me, Luca. I was twisted and really don't remember shit. How did we get home?"

"By a miracle," Luca said.

Naomi laughed quietly.

"You don't remember Ryan? And the things you said to him?"

"I think so. Was he tall and handsome?"

"He was fine."

"And was he trying to hit on me?"

"What?" Luca uttered in disbelief.

"You said he was tall and handsome right? And I know I was looking good in the club. Ohmygod, Luca, did I do something stupid? Did I cheat on Abioye? Did I give this nigga my number?" Naomi asked in alarm.

Luca couldn't believe it. Once again, Naomi had put on a show and now she tried to make it all about her. Luca felt disrespected from last night up till now.

"You know, Luca, I would never cheat on Abioye. He's the only man getting my cookies. Oh god, I really need to stop drinking," Naomi said.

Luca jumped up from her seat and exclaimed, "Fuck you, Naomi!"

Taken aback by Luca's harsh and unexpected outburst, Naomi uttered, "Ohmygod, Luca, why are you upset? What did I do?"

"You will never have a clue." Luca marched toward the door.

Naomi followed behind her.

"Luca!" Naomi cried out. "What did I do to you?"

Luca ignored her and rushed out of the apartment, hurrying down the hallway. Naomi found herself dumbfounded by Luca's flare-up. It was the first time it had ever happened. She tied her robe tightly and watched Luca from her doorway, disappearing into the stairway. She sighed heavily, confused about what had gone wrong, and then closed her door.

Chapter 14

Luca, Phaedra, and Little Bit stared at the towering high-rise complex in Long Island City. It was twenty-two stories tall and plush-looking with its glass exterior, like a landmark near the waters. They remained inconspicuous in the afternoon hour, dressed like schoolgirls and sucking on lollipops. No one would think that they were up to no good and were armed with pistols, ready to do the unthinkable. Their disguise was perfect. Now the setup had to be even more perfect.

Naomi had to be taught a serious lesson. She had to feel what it was like to lose something that she truly loved. She had to feel alone and scared. Luca's growing hate for Naomi was changing her into something vicious. Her alter ego, Vesta, was constantly in her mind, taking over. Subconsciously, Vesta was capable of doing something that Luca knew was wrong to do. That way, if her alter ego did it, Luca would lose the responsibility for it.

But the problem was, she was a complex individual. Some days a portion of her personality might be more dominant than the other. But it felt so good to have the courage and wittiness to do and say things that Luca was once scared to say or do. She was once unhappy with who she was socially, but with Vesta and Phaedra in her life, she started to feel more welcomed and accepted by everyone.

Today, Luca needed Vesta to take over fully—to dominate her mentally, and fortify her sanity and doubt with self-reliance. She needed to become someone hardcore and violent. She had come this far, and now wasn't the time to feel any remorse about anything or anyone. People needed to be taught a lesson, and sometimes violence was the only way to teach it. Like Phaedra had said, this was part of the ugly.

Phaedra and Little Bit followed behind Luca into the apartment building. Luca already had the keys. There wasn't a doorman around, and there were no residents. The lobby was quiet; just an ordinary day. They walked to the elevator and pushed for it. It slid open and the girls slid inside. Luca pushed for the tenth floor. They rose slowly and stopped on the tenth floor. Everyone stepped out, entering the posh and carpeted hallway. Luca searched for apartment 10G. Bingo, down the hall to their right. Luca used the duplicate key to enter.

When they walked into the apartment, an apple-cinnamon flavor immediately nourished their noses. There were two big mirrors on the side of each wall. The golden living room set sat beautifully on the tan carpet. Down the hallway to their right was an office.

"Wow, this shit is fuckin' nice," Phaedra uttered.

They all looked around the spacious apartment, each going into different rooms. The bedrooms were each tastefully furnished and decorated with a flat-screen TV and queen-size bed. Each bedroom had a full-length mirror and luxe amenities. The bathroom featured a marble tile floor, a deep, jetted tub, and a modern stainless steel sink.

Luca was impressed. The man definitely knew taste and knew how to live. Luca meticulously checked the apartment for any installed hidden cameras. She went through different steps to make sure there weren't any cameras or bugs around. She was somewhat paranoid. She listened as she walked the entire room quietly, knowing that many small, motion-sensitive cameras make an almost inaudible click or buzz when they operate.

She then turned off the lights, closed the blinds, and looked around for tiny red or green LED lights. While the lights were off in certain rooms, Luca grabbed a flashlight and carefully examined all the mirrors. She then used her cell phone to pick up an electromagnetic field. She placed a call on her cell phone and then waved the device around where she assumed there might be a camera or microphone. If she heard a clicking noise on the wall, then it meant her phone might be interfering with an electromagnetic field.

Phaedra and Little Bit walked in on Luca screening the room.

"What are you doin'?" Little Bit asked.

Little Bit was one of their workers. She was sixteen, pretty, and eager to please Luca and Phaedra by any means necessary. She also came from a broken home in Brooklyn and was poorly educated. Luca encouraged all her of young female workers to stay in school or get their GED.

"She's doin' her thang; what she knows best," Phaedra answered. "She's smart like that, making sure we don't get caught doing this shit."

The two watched on.

"What now?" Phaedra asked.

"We wait and we hide," Luca answered.

Hours passed; the diamond in the sky gradually faded into the twinkles of the night. The front door to the apartment opened and Abioye walked into his home after a long and tiresome day. Everything in his home seemed in order. It was dark and quiet. He walked into the living room and turned on the stereo system. Instantly, opera started to blare into his home: *Voi che sapete* by Wolfgang Amadeus Mozart.

He was a man of classical taste and the heart for fine arts and other finer things in life. He adored different cultures and music. He was in love with his life.

As the opera played, he loosened the buttons on his shirt and started to undress. He was in need of a long, hot shower. He tossed his clothing to the side, displaying his chiseled dark physique in his bedroom. Luca and Phaedra watched him from the bedroom closet. The clothes came off and his manhood was showing. Luca was impressed. Abioye's dick hung from him like an anaconda from a tree. It was long, black and thick.

Damn, she thought.

Abioye walked into the bathroom butt naked and ran the shower. The girls could see his silhouette from where they hid. They could hear him in the shower. He was singing something in a rich, lilting language they did not recognize. He had a nice voice—a soothing baritone tone that could easily serenade any woman. The girls loitered in the dark, organized closet, waiting for the right moment to strike. Luca breathed easily. She couldn't look weak. This was the ugly. This was payback. This was Vesta.

Twenty minutes went by. Abioye exited the bathroom with a wetness to his skin and a towel wrapped around his waist. The only thing he wanted to do was study and sleep. He removed some underwear from his drawer, dropped the towel, and got ready for bed. Luca watched, the gun in her hand. Abioye disappeared from the bedroom for a moment, the opera suddenly went off, and lights in the apartment were shut off too. Abioye came back into the bedroom with a small snack and a drink. He pulled out a book and briefly began studying some medical material. His studying didn't last long. Hearing a noise from the closet, Abioye gazed that way and then stood up to investigate.

With the shirtless man coming their way, there was no time to think, only time to react. The closet door burst open, startling Abioye. Phaedra aimed the .9mm at him. He stood frozen and wide-eyed.

"What is this?" he uttered with panic.

"It's nothing personal against you," Luca said.

Abioye at once recognized Naomi's friend. "Luca? Why this?"

"Because I can't stand your fiancée," she replied.

He stepped toward the girls. Phaedra fired a single shot, striking him in the head, and he dropped to the ground. Dead. Phaedra took a deep breath and exhaled. She gazed at Luca in awe. Earlier, the three of them, Luca, Phaedra and Little Bit, had drawn straws to see who would pull the trigger; Phaedra picked the shortest straw. It was her first murder, and Abioye's death was on her head.

"Oh shit!" Phaedra uttered. "He just came at us."

They stared down at the body. Blood started to pool underneath his head, staining the carpet with crimson. Little Bit entered the bedroom, seeing the murder scene.

"Damn!" she muttered.

It was a shock to them all. Phaedra held the smoking gun and needed to collect herself.

"It had to be done," Luca said.

Phaedra nodded.

Abioye never knew what hit him. He was dead before he hit the floor. And now wasn't the time to flip out over his death. It was their plan to kill him; now Phaedra had felt what it was like to murder someone. She stood over him, gazing at the body, feeling the power of the gun and knowing the thrill of a kill. He was a man. She started to hate men; they thought they ruled the world. Thinking about her foster father—the sexual assault and beating, and the rage she felt toward him, Phaedra scowled heavily. She pointed the gun at the body again and fired.

Bak!

Luca and Little Bit spun around quickly, startled.

"Phaedra, what the fuck? He's already dead!" Little Bit shouted.

Luca stared at Phaedra with some understanding and knew why she fired the second shot. Little Bit was clueless about the assault, but Luca knew that the pain of feeling helpless and violated by some foul-smelling man still lingered deep down inside Phaedra.

"Phaedra, he can't hurt us," Luca said softly.

Phaedra turned and looked at Luca. There were tears welling up in her eyes. She nodded. "When I see him again, Luca, I'm gonna shoot that muthafucka dead."

"And I'll help you," Luca assured her.

Little Bit was lost.

They went on with the plan. Luca placed strands of black weave hair on the pillows on the bed, and then in the bathroom sink and shower. She flooded Abioye's apartment with lipstick, heels, panties and other womanly things that Phaedra had collected from the group home from random girls. She then went extra and planted a dildo in the nightstand and transsexual porno magazines. The buffet of clues all did not lead to one particular person, which is what she wanted. And she wanted the police to be baffled.

***

Naomi was devastated when she heard the news about her fiancé. Murdered! He couldn't be dead. How? And by who? With Luca by her side, a teary-eyed and distraught Naomi hurried toward the precinct. Abioye couldn't be gone. He couldn't be out of her life. They were getting married. She was meant to be a doctor's wife and live happily ever after. This couldn't be happening. She was suddenly thrust into this nightmare. Why? She didn't know what to do. The only person she was able to turn to was Luca.

Inside the local precinct, Naomi was immediately detained and questioned by homicide detectives for a few hours. But it was clear that she wasn't a suspect. The evidence didn't point to her. She had a solid alibi.

When she received the news of the dildo found in the nightstand and the transsexual porno magazines found under his bed and in the drawers, Naomi was flabbergasted. She didn't want to believe that her man was a closet homosexual. He couldn't be. But the proof was there. Was he having an affair with another man?

A hysterical Naomi came rushing out of the precinct with her face in anguish. Luca was right there. She remained expressionless. Naomi looked at her and shouted, "Ohmygod, I can't do this! I need to get out of here!"

"Where you wanna go?" Luca asked calmly.

"I just need to be somewhere else. They want me to identify his body at the morgue," she cried out.

"The morgue it is, then."

The city morgue, used for the storage of human corpses awaiting identification or removal for autopsy, was a still and unpleasant place for anyone to be. Luca stood with

Naomi behind the large glass that looked into the cold, crude room where there was a body placed on a slab and covered with a white sheet. A knock came from behind the other side where Naomi and Luca stood. It was the indication to the mortician that the people were waiting to see the body from the other side. The mortician walked toward the slab and removed the sheet from the face, pulling it down to the chest to slowly reveal the corpse's identity. It was him. It was Abioye. Naomi suddenly collapsed and fell to her knees in grief.

"Oh god ... No! Not him! Please, nooo!!" she screamed.

Luca took her friend into her arms. Even though she was sympathetic and consoling to Naomi, inside she felt joy and fireworks going off. But seeing Naomi in that horrid state, suffering from the lost of her boyfriend, it jolted her to the night Nate was killed. Luca found herself tearing up too, while holding Naomi in her arms. Though she was the one responsible for snatching Abioye's life, it seemed traumatic still.

***

Luca remained by Naomi's side during her trying time. Naomi's apartment was dimmed and filled with sadness. Her heavy sobs continued, and her pain manifested through violent outbreaks of her breaking and throwing things around. Naomi was so tormented by the loss of her fiancé; see almost seemed suicidal.

Some hours went by. Luca and Naomi sat on the couch with everything quiet in the apartment. Naomi's face was stained with tears. Her eyes were red from the grief. She sat nestled against the couch, nursing a cup of tea that Luca had made her.

Luca stared at Naomi, who seemed distanced from everything while staring at a blank wall in her apartment. Out of the blue, Luca asked, "Did you know he was cheating on you?"

Naomi snapped out of her remoteness and sharply replied, "Abioye would never cheat on me!"

"But you heard what they found in his apartment; the dildo, the magazines. He was hiding something from you, Naomi."

"It's a fuckin' lie! He wasn't like that!"

"Are you sure, Naomi? Men are always lying to us," Luca stated.

"I know him. He was a good man! He loved me and I loved him," she vehemently cried out.

"Well, how does it feel to realize you never knew the man you were about to marry?"

Luca was being catty with Naomi. It was payback for all the hurtful things she'd ever said or did to Luca or anyone else. It was a different feeling, seeing Naomi in such a fragile and confused state of mind.

Naomi looked at Luca contemptuously and uttered, "What are you saying, Luca? You believe he was faggot?"

With a stoic stare, Luca replied, "Did you know about his secret homosexual life? I mean, did you see the signs and choose to ignore them?"

"Fuck you, Luca!" barked Naomi.

"I'm just trying to be a friend to you, Naomi. Like you always were to me," she tersely replied.

"You're not helping me with these stupid fucking questions about my fiancé. Okay?! Just shut up about him or leave!" Naomi exclaimed.

"I'm sorry." But Luca truly wasn't. "But I do think as a friend I should tell you to get tested for STDs."

Naomi erupted into hysterics. "I can't hear this shit right now, Luca!"

Naomi seemed to be at her breaking point. She couldn't stop crying. She couldn't stop thinking about Abioye and didn't understand why he was murdered. The evidence in his apartment pointed to a jealous love affair—man or woman. But Naomi was adamant that she was the only person he loved and was with. Her fiancé wasn't a faggot.

Luca gazed at Naomi, smirking behind her back, and then she started to stroke the back of Naomi's hair. Then she asked, "What are you going to do now?"

Chapter 15

Money, money, money, it was what life was all about—living big dreams and doing big things. Money, money, money, it was the cure to most of everyone's problems. Money, money, money, it could turn anyone's hell into paradise. Money, money, money, they say it's the root to all evil, but having it is almost the sweetest thing, like some good dick. Money, money, money, finally Luca had a slice of heaven—and it was the reason she was meeting with Squirrel in his Harlem place. Money—it was the reason she was risking her freedom and her life for another five kilos to cut up and distribute to her high-end clientele, from Canarsie to Wall Street. Tiffany kept reeling in the big fishes. She had a knack for marketing. So much clientele was coming Luca's way that Luca was drowning in business.

Money, money, money, it was the thing, the source that made the world go round and round—like Wu-Tang sang, "C.R.E.A.M."—cash rules everything around me.

Luca didn't mind traveling to Harlem to get her work. She substituted the train ride with a costly cab ride, paying the cabbie an extra hundred dollars more for the trip from Brooklyn to Harlem and back again.

Luca gawked at Squirrel, who was shirtless, his upper torso cut with a six-pack and a strapping chest covered with tattoos. A ten-karat, solid white-gold men's diamond tennis chain hung from around his neck. It was big and looked costly. He sported a colored diamond pinky ring. He took a pull from his cigarette, standing by the table, and seemed relaxed. Five kilos of heroin was placed on the coffee table in the living room.

"You like what you see?" Squirrel asked.

"I definitely do," Luca replied with a lecherous grin, but she wasn't talking about the kilos.

Squirrel smiled slightly. He was starting to have much respect for her. It was her fourth trip to him in over a month. But not only was she creating good business for him—earlier, Luca had done him the favor of using an RF signal detector to do a sweep of his place to make sure he wasn't being spied on with bugs, either from the city or state police, or the feds. The results were positive. Squirrel's place was bug-free. He was very appreciative. Squirrel had developed some paranoia that he was constantly being watched by someone—enemies or authorities. Luca, with her specialty in technology, inadvertently became something like his guardian angel.

"You know, you surprised me, Luca. I thought I might have to kill you, but ya savvy and adept. You're useful in more ways than you know. I like that, especially in a woman," Squirrel complimented. "My opinion—you're a better replacement than Nate."

"Thank you. I try to run my business like a brand."

"You and me both. I respect that," Squirrel replied.

It was obvious that there was a mutual attraction between the two of them. Luca had wanted Squirrel since the first day she laid eyes on him. It had been a while since she'd had any dick. Her mind was usually on business and plotting Naomi's downfall, but when she was around Squirrel, her hormones would go crazy and her pussy would start throbbing. She needed her itch to be scratched. And Squirrel seemed like the right candidate to do some serious scratching.

But there was one flaw in Luca's desire to have Squirrel—his crazy baby mama, Angel, who was the hottest bitch in Harlem and all around the five boroughs. Angel was very jealous when it came to Squirrel. They had two kids together and over ten years of history. Angel was known for slicing bitches across their face for even looking at her man wrong, and if a bitch tried to take what was hers, then Angel wasn't shy about pulling out pistols to let her position be clearly known.

But tonight, Luca wasn't worried about Angel or any other of Squirrel's wild jump-offs or other baby mamas. Her heart fluttered every time when she was around him, and her attention was always fixed on his fineness from top to bottom. Him being shirtless in the apartment didn't make things better.

Luca was constantly trying to get Squirrel to ask her out, but to no avail. Squirrel was a money-hungry businessman who wasn't easily distracted by some pussy, unlike the average nigga. Any other man would have jumped at the chance to bed down Luca and take what was clearly being thrown at him.

Luca continued to stare at Squirrel. She wanted to touch his chest, suck on his nipples, throw her hand down his jeans and squeeze, and run her manicured nails across his washboard stomach. He kept himself really fit. He was healthy, and Luca wondered if the dick between his legs was as healthy as well.

It had been almost two months of torture for Luca, yearning for something so badly that was already taken. She missed the smell and the touch of a man. Nate was a dog, but he was a good lover. Luca missed being penetrated by some long, piece of hard, natural flesh.

She began placing the five kis into the book bag. Squirrel watched her while smoking his Newport. His eyes were trained on her smooth, curvy figure in the short top she wore and tight jeans that accentuated her figure.

"How long had you been wit' Nate?" he asked out of the blue.

"Two years," she replied.

"He must have appreciated every inch of you every night."

"We had our moments." Luca smiled.

"Some really good moments by the looks of you," said Squirrel.

"Well, those moments are gone now," Luca returned nonchalantly.

"You miss them?"

"What woman wouldn't? I still have my needs," she stated. "I'm sure you do your baby mama right all the time. Just looking at you, I can see that you're all man, with a really nice body."

"I feel that a man's body is his temple. You treat it right, your body, and it will treat you right just the same," Squirrel said.

Luca nodded.

She packed all five kis of heroin into the book bag and zipped it up. She was ready to go. She slung the bag over her right shoulder and looked at Squirrel.

"My cab is waiting outside," she said.

Squirrel stubbed out his cigarette in the ashtray nearby and gazed at Luca. She was, beyond doubt, beautiful all around. He also didn't want her to leave so soon. Fuck the idling cab outside. He could wait. Something else more important was brewing in the project stash house. It was supposed to be only business between them, but somehow, sparks were igniting inside the dimmed room.

Luca slowly made her way toward the exit. Squirrel followed behind her. But, unexpectedly, before she was ten feet from the door, Squirrel grabbed her from behind, sliding a hand around her shoulders and another around her side, and he pulled her into his arms and then slammed her against the wall of the foyer. They locked lips heatedly, his tongue sliding easily between her lips. She could feel the large bulge in his pants pressing hard against her. She was ready to unzip his jeans, reach inside, and grab a fistful of dick and stroke him lovingly.

Luca found herself back in the living room, the book bag the floor; she found herself being curved over the couch with her jeans and panties sliding off of her body effortlessly. Squirrel dropped his jeans around his ankles and stepped out of them. He was completely hard and ready to fuck. Her body lit up with pleasure feeling the mushroom tip of Squirrel's eight-inch erection near her pulsating pussy. She was ready for penetration. He gripped her hips and pierced his hard, throbbing flesh inside of her wetness, and the instant his dick touched inside her kitty cat, Luca felt a great heat rush through her. She wanted to feel him travel deeper inside of her.

His thrust was powerful. She gasped and moaned, gripping the armrest of the couch tightly. He fucked her doggy style, pushing deep into her pussy, instantly finding her G-spot.

"Oh shit! Fuck me! Fuck me!" she cried out.

She could feel her juices leaking out of her and running down between her legs. Her nipples were hard as stones with the heat building up inside of her. Her pussy pulsed nonstop around Squirrel's thrusting shaft, and it felt like his dick was truly being sucked by a gulping throat—felt like it was in some kind of sexual vortex.

The apartment was empty, and they took full advantage of it. Luca took complete enjoyment from his dick. Her heat wrapped around his hard shaft as he let his own lust jerk his hips forward quickly. Luca's tight, hot walls were compressed around his bulbous head. The sensation was mind-blowing. Squirrel wanted to pull out; the suction and quivery, heated, velvet walls of her pussy were too good. He moaned with guttural abandon as he pushed his dick all the way to her cervix. He felt his balls contract and he couldn't hold the sensation in any longer. The way Luca was throwing her pussy and ass back while in the doggy-style position became extremely passionate and exhilarating and he released his seed into the woman positioned in front of him. It was the heat of the moment.

Inadvertently, he came inside her sweet pussy, leaning over her with his hand around the back of her slim neck, grunting and feeling like a balloon being deflated. He pulled out of her dripping, wet pussy and pulled up his jeans. Luca smiled, turning around to collect herself. It was nice.

"What now?" she asked softly.

"Business as usual wit' us and we keep this between you and me, that's the what now," he returned.

She nodded. Business was now mixed with pleasure.

Luca picked up the bag and went for the door a second time. Her cab had probably left already. It had been twenty-five minutes. But she had promised him an extra hundred if he stayed around until her transaction was complete.

This time she was able to walk out the door without getting fucked, figuratively.

Bad Girl Blvd

✳✳✳

Knowledge was always power. Once you acquired it, once you understood something, saw it like it was crystal-clear and knew the mechanisms of how things operated, it was something that no one could ever take away from you. And that came with an education.

Luca was learning day by day, thinking she knew the pitfalls of the drug game. She didn't want to become another statistic by either getting murdered or locked up. She was shrewd with everything in her operation; from the smallest concern to the biggest problem, it all mattered. She was the queen, and her lieutenants and pawns were all under the age of nineteen. They were still in school, a group home, or in some kind of program to better themselves, but she and her crew—her girls, they were like Dr. Jekyll and Mr. Hyde. Getting an education in life—it was everything. So when Luca, Phaedra, Little Bit, Danielle, Spirit, and Meeka passed the course and received their GEDs, it was a joyful moment. Luca passed with flying colors, almost receiving a perfect score—getting 760 out of 800. It was a wonder to so many people that she hadn't gotten her high school diploma long ago and gone on to college. It was clear to everyone that she was smart, but had probably made stupid choices in life.

Phaedra was the happiest of them all. She had finally accomplished something positive in her life. She had the approval of her probation officer and finally didn't have to worry about being stupid. With the help of Luca, the proof was in her hands.

Luca wanted a quiet celebration for herself, but for her girls, she had to do something special. They all looked up to her, they trusted her, and they were all family. In society's eyes, they were all social misfits—high-school dropouts, teenage mothers, former prostitutes, drug users, drug dealers, and more. But under one roof in a beautiful Canarsie home, they were family—sisters with a strong bond and a mutual understanding about each other. Because of Luca, they felt welcomed and accomplished, and they would all die for each other.

Phaedra was Luca's right-hand bitch, second in command. She'd been down since day one, and she was also the one to recruit the girls she knew and could trust to get money and have loyalty.

Little Bit was the wild card. She had gotten pregnant with her son at thirteen years old, and he was being raised by her grandmother. Little Bit was known for stabbing and cutting bitches and niggas.

Danielle was eighteen with a list of criminal charges, from assault with a deadly weapon to grand theft auto. Spirit was a sixteen-year-old baby mama with a compulsion for stealing.

Meeka, she was the crazy pistol-packing dyke who didn't give a fuck. She was short, cute, and had a short fuse and fierce hands, having learned how to box when she was ten years old. Luca surrounded herself with violent young women. It was her security blanket. They put up a wall around Luca, so if any hungry wolf came lurking, they had their own pack to fight back.

Luca had love for all of them, and they were her peoples—they were her friends, her muscle, and her business—without them, there was no her.

Business with Squirrel was booming, and her sneaky love affair with him was rapidly growing also. When they got the chance to see each other, despite doing business, they would fuck like rabbits. Luca was infatuated with the man; everything about him made her cream in her panties. Squirrel also loved the way she fucked. Her pussy was new pussy and the way it got super wet for him and clamped around his dick when he was inside of her blew his mind. Somehow, Luca had managed to get Squirrel open. He had his main chick, Angel, but Luca was his freak, the one who would fuck him in the backseat of his H2 Hummer while parked on the block, or let him eat her pussy out while her girls were in the other room. It was a definite thing. Neither one could leave the other alone, whether it was business or sexual. Things were good.

***

So much money was coming in from the sale of the heroin stamped "Bad Girl" spreading out—infiltrating the Brooklyn streets once again. With the strong clientele rolling in, Luca saw herself living a double life. She had a five-block radius in which to push the drug in Canarsie, Brooklyn, but a good, potent drug wasn't going to remain low-key in a quiet neighborhood forever. It was inevitable that things would expand.

She was pretending to be in school while trying to enroll herself in a good college after passing her GED test. Her scores were high, and she wanted to put in for financial aid. She needed a ruse, something to throw off the authorities if they ever came investigating her way. Luca wasn't a fool; she had to justify her means of income and way of living. She had to find some way to cover up the substantial amount of money that she was making. And with such a potent heroin, the cash was coming in by the boatload. The only means of hiding her illegal source of income was money laundering. But it took someone skilled to pull it off. Luca knew nothing about money laundering, but she was ready to learn it and apply it to her business.

But a wise hustler also knew they needed protection from the law and the IRS—maybe a mole inside the DA's office, a dirty cop to bribe, a judge to influence or blackmail, a kinky or perverted married prosecutor to sex up and take advantage of. Luca needed a strong legal and financial team to help secure her placement and freedom in the game. Her first priority was to hire an effective attorney on retainer and a strong financial advisor. She needed to go down that rabbit hole and become lost in a different world.

Power came to those who knew how to take it. Therefore, she came up with the perfect plan for herself and her girls—to make them an offer that they couldn't refuse.

Chapter 16

It was mid-August, and the heat wave in the city was unbearable. Every day for almost a week, temperatures and humidity in the city reached a scorching 100+ degrees. People walked around drenched in their own sweat, the community pools were overcrowding, and there were blackouts happening due to the intense power usage. It felt like the sun was trying to connect with the earth. People in the city were hot and miserable; every air conditioning unit was on full blast, and some hoped for rain or an early winter. But despite the heat wave in the city, business went on as usual.

Luca stepped out of the Lincoln gypsy cab on 34th Street in Manhattan clad in a white wrap dress with a flowing hemline. She sported a pair of wedge heels and a pink wig—her body and features looked more stunning than Nicki Minaj's. The different hair colors were part of her growing alter ego. It was all Vesta.

The minute Luca was out of the gypsy cab and on the bustling Manhattan sidewalk, attention shifted her way, from fleeting looks to lingering stares. It felt good to be noticed. It felt good to be wealthy and sexy at the same time.

She was looking for one particular person: Ryan. They had spoken the other night, and he had promised to take her out to lunch on the scorching summer day. Even though it had been several weeks since their meeting at the nightclub, Ryan made it clearly known that he was definitely still interested in her.

"I thought you had forgotten about me," he had said.

"It's been a really busy month for me, but I always kept your number close," Luca had replied.

"And why the pleasure of this phone call?"

"Because I've been thinking about you. Thought we could go out for lunch or dinner," she had revealed.

Luca could feel him smiling through the phone. The man couldn't hide the excitement in his voice. They talked for a moment and a date was set. Ryan couldn't wait to see her again.

Luca was attracted to him too, but there was more to her calling him than just an attraction and a smile. He was a CPA in the state of New York, and she saw some use in having him around. Luca and her girls were on a mission to solidify their hold on the top players in the city— authority, legislators, politicians and prosecutors—via sex, bribery or straight-up blackmail and extortion. Once she had them in her pocket, she would be untouchable.

The ball started rolling with help from Tiffany. Cooperate America and Wall Street were Tiffany's world.

It appeared she knew everybody important and it wasn't a secret that she was fucking her way to the top. She was using what was between her legs to get the finer things she wanted in life. The white boys were in love with Tiffany with her oozing sex appeal and sultry attitude.

When Luca came to her with another proposition, of course Tiffany wanted her cut. She was business-minded and Luca had to respect that. The scheme would benefit them both if they ever got into a jam with law enforcement or the DA. It would be their get-out-of-jail-free card.

Tiffany handed Luca a list of the most prominent men she worked with, sexed, did drugs with, or hung around. It was an exclusive list with some heavy-hitting names. Tiffany knew about these men's weaknesses, their desires, their sins, their lusts and loves—and their main loves, besides making money, were pussy and getting high.

Luca had a meeting with her young girls to talk about the scheme she had set up with Tiffany. It would be something like borderline pimping out her crew to these high-end men to insure their well-being. Phaedra was conspicuously absent for obvious reasons.

"This is y'all choice. If you don't feel comfortable doing it, then y'all don't have to," she said to her crew. "But each of y'all involved will receive a significant cut from it. And this is a higher stake."

Luca broke down the plan to them, detail by detail. She explained who they were going after and why. Those who wanted to participate would raise their hand, and if they didn't, she would understand, no hard feelings. Each girl in the room raised her hand high, each willing to whore herself out for the good of the organization, and Luca would be joining them.

With the list, the first person they went after was District Attorney Andrew Gilligan. He was a closet pervert and freak. He was Spirit's target. Tiffany made the subtle introduction between them at a charity dinner she was invited to that cost five hundred a plate. Spirit was nervous at first, but she was being coached by Tiffany. She was underage, but the sexy black John Galliano gown she wore and expertly applied makeup made her look sophisticated and five years older.

"Andrew Gilligan, this is a good friend of mine, Nancy Hogan," Tiffany introduced Spirit under a fraudulent name.

Once the towering, lanky, pale DA locked eyes with Spirit, he was hooked on her young beauty. They shook hands and Spirit took it from there. By the night's end, the man had Spirit over at his downtown suite with her gown on the floor. He was fucking her in the ass in his plush bedroom, unaware that he was having sex with a sixteen-year-old minor. Spirit was no stranger to prostituting herself. Their secret affair would continue with Andrew Gilligan unaware of the fact that his sexual rendezvous with the minor were being recorded and documented by Luca.

The second on their list was a public defender named Samuel Duncan. He'd been a functioning heroin addict and heavy drug user for more than five years and had ties to the mob. He was one of Tiffany's clients who was hooked on the Bad Girl product. Luca and Tiffany knew he had to keep a tight lid on his secret, because if it ever got out that he was a drug user, he risked being disbarred and indicted, as well as the reopening of all of his cases, and it could result in many of the prosecutor's cases being overturned.

Third on their list was a state prosecutor named James Levy, a married, overzealous and racist white man who frequented underground brothels on the down-low and had a craving for young black girls to suck him off and perform S&M on him. Little Bit would take care of him for a nice fee. While the sexual episodes went on nestled in a backroom in Brooklyn, videos and pictures were secretly being shot of the nastiness thanks to the technology set up by Luca—a pinhole-sized camera placed in the room.

The fourth was a shrewd Irish detective from a Brooklyn precinct named Henry Macdonald. His weakness and desire was pussy, young or old. He didn't give a fuck. If it got his dick hard, he loved it. Danielle had him under her thumb. He couldn't resist the starry-eyed, long-legged beauty. He was also a heavy drinker and the type of freak who liked to do lines of cocaine off her naked body. Once he was under the influence of alcohol, he was a chatterbox. Danielle had a lot of dirt on him.

The fifth was the jackpot for Luca and her girls. With the help of Tiffany, who had strong ties to the man, they were able to snatch a judge named Holland Lemansky in their loop of bribery and blackmail. He was a family man—married for ten years with five kids—but was also addicted to the heroin he acquired from Tiffany, and was a closeted homosexual. Unbeknownst to him, his life was being watched and recorded. The judge liked dick—raw dog up the ass and down his throat. And he was a repeated user of Bad Girl. The potency of the drug had him hooked.

Day after day, and week after week, Luca and her crew pimped themselves out to these affluent men of the community and the city. It was so easy to set up and trap these men in such prominent positions because of their desires—mostly strong sexual cravings. If these men wouldn't play ball if or when the time came, then Luca had enough dirt on them to destroy their careers and shame them for a lifetime. She was almost certain that none of these men would want to hit the front page of *The New York Times* like their peers—Spitzer, Barry, Weiner, Clinton, or McGreevy.

With five prominent men in useful positions in her grasp, Luca saw something profitable in getting close to these high-end figures on the city, state, and even federal level, and taking advantage of something wonderful. For her silence they would have to pay, via a favor when needed, or with hardcore cash. Their dirty, dark secrets would ruin not only their lives, but the lives of their families.

***

On the West Side, 34th Street near Hell's Kitchen, overlooking the West Side railway yard, Luca strutted toward the vintage diner where Ryan instructed her they should meet up.

Luca walked by the post office and Penn Station, which dominated the south side of the street, serving Amtrak trains. Above Penn Station sat Madison Square Garden, the world's most famous arena.

She spotted Ryan standing by the diner entrance in a sharp gray suit on the scorching day. He stood tall like an NBA player and was handsome like a print model.

Luca smiled. Her smile was contagious, causing Ryan to grin widely also.

"Hey, beautiful," Ryan greeted warmly.

"Hey, sorry I'm late. The traffic coming from Brooklyn was murder," she explained.

"No apologies. I'm just glad you could make it."

The two hugged. The pink wig stood out, and Luca noticed his eyes lingering on it.

"You don't like it?" Luca asked.

"I love it. I love a woman who's daring and different. If I wasn't in the office, I would probably change my hair pink too," he joked.

"You trying to be sarcastic?" she returned.

"I'm just trying to get to know you."

Luca blushed.

"Are you hungry?" he asked.

"I'm starving."

Ryan grabbed the door handle to the diner and pulled it open for her, escorting his afternoon date into the renowned diner that had been around since the sixties. "It isn't five stars, but that can come later," he said.

"Where there's food? I don't care. You're treating, I eat," she joked.

They both laughed and smiled.

They moved into a cushioned booth near the window, looking out onto the active city street.

Ryan fixed his eyes on Luca as she sat opposite him in the diner booth and once again proclaimed, "You are so damn beautiful. I have to thank your mother for doing a great job with you and God for making you flawless."

She grinned like a child. "Thank you. You are a very handsome man yourself."

"I try," he replied with appeal.

"You don't need to try, it's natural for you."

He grinned. "So what is it that you do besides being a supermodel?"

She chuckled. "Cute. I'm a student majoring in technology. I have a thing for computers and gadgets."

"Beautiful and smart. I think I'm falling in love with you already."

"I thought you already did at the club when we met," she joked.

He laughed. "I do believe in love at first sight, and I guess I did," he joked. "And you?"

"You guess? But I believe love at a first sight is usually corrected with a second look," she quipped.

He laughed again. "There's nothing sexier than a beautiful woman with a sense of humor. And how's my second look?"

"You okay," she said with a natural smile.

"I was handsome earlier. You were lying to me?"

"No, but the nightclub was kind of dark that night. So it was hard for me to see."

"Uh-huh, okay." He chuckled again.

The laughter and smiles were constant.

There was strong chemistry between the two of them. Ryan sat with a strong posture in his gray suit, looking like Morris Chestnut and catching fleeting looks from some of the waitresses and female patrons in the diner. His aura was golden. He seemed to be a cool guy in Luca's eyes—easygoing with a flowing conversation style. But she couldn't get too caught up in his charm and beauty. She had called him for a purpose, thinking more business than pleasure, but her approach had to be subtle.

"But all jokes aside, I'm glad that you called me. I really did think you forgot about me," he said.

Before Luca could say anything, the slim, tall waitress walked over, introducing herself with a smile, with her gaze mostly focused on Ryan.

"Hello. My name is Grace, and I'll be your server this afternoon," she said, her smile trained on Ryan. "And I have to say, you are too fine a man."

Luca found her behavior to be quite rude. Didn't the bitch see he had female company? Luca appeared to be the invisible woman sitting across from him as the waitress flirted with her afternoon date. But she kept quiet about it.

The waitress took down their orders, and said, staring at Ryan, "If you need anything, please don't hesitate to ask." Then she walked away, with Luca's eyes lingering on the ho longer than needed.

"That was rude," she uttered.

"It was," Ryan agreed.

"I mean, didn't Miss Slutty see me sitting here, smiling and staring all in your face like that?"

"Don't get jealous. I'm with you, and you have my undivided attention," Ryan said. "And besides, she don't even compare to you."

"That bitch lost her tip." Luca rolled her eyes.

The duration of their meal was spent with them getting to know each other. Ryan had been a CPA for fifteen years. He was thirty-seven with no kids, vibrant about his career and life, and ready to meet Ms. Right. He wanted a wife and kids.

"Father Time is catching up with me and I want a family…a home. I have my health, a career, savings, but no one to share it with," he told Luca.

Luca told him that she was single with no kids, the truth, but her lies to him were that she was in school and employed doing data entry at a doctor's office in Harlem. It was a job she remembered Naomi once had, a few years ago.

"I think everyone wants a family . . . happiness," Luca replied.

"And you? What do you want, Luca?" he asked.

Luca looked pensive for a moment. She'd once thought about having a family with Nate, before his murder. It was clear to see that it was only a pipe dream—especially after finding out that he had fathered several kids already. Luca stared at Ryan and replied, "I just want to be happy, too."

"It can happen. Do you want kids?"

Kids. She was twenty-three and hadn't really thought about kids since her miscarriage at sixteen. It was always a fleeting feeling for her. However, it was a miracle that she wasn't pregnant yet from fucking with Squirrel. He was making frequent deposits inside of her and she couldn't explain how she kept allowing him to fuck her raw.

Luca gazed at Ryan with some reverence. "I'm surprised a handsome man like you isn't taken already. What's the catch? You're not gay, right?"

He expressed amusement.

"No catch. And I'm not gay. I'm looking, but haven't seen anything worth taking home to my mother yet," he returned.

"Your parents are still alive?"

"My mother is. She's sixty-seven and my best friend. My father passed away when I was ten," he informed her.

"I'm so sorry."

"There's no need to be. My mother, being the strong woman that she is, was able to hold down the fort in the projects and raise me and my little brother. She always worked two or three jobs just to put us through private school in the city and then put us through college," he proclaimed with esteem in his tone.

"She sounds like a wonderful woman," said Luca.

"She is. And if we keep vibing and connecting like this, then hopefully I'll introduce you to her one day."

Luca smiled. "I might like that."

She didn't know where the comment came from. It spilled out so suddenly, like an embarrassing fart in a public area. Ryan was only an objective—part of her master scheme to strengthen her organization—and there was no time for love at first sight and romance. She had been there and done that with Nate, and she was falling in love with Squirrel.

As Luca and Ryan got more comfortable and talkative with each other, they both noticed the waitress's souring mood. It seemed that she wanted Ryan all to herself and became jealous of the chatter and laughter coming from the table. Her service became dry and her smile was transforming into a frown.

But Luca wasn't worried about her. While feasting on her turkey and cheese sandwich and fries, she subtly shifted the friendly chat toward business. Her goal was to learn something about accounting, money laundering, and more. She figured Ryan would be the key guy to explain and even help her in the near future. She needed to get him aboard either willingly or by finding some dirt on him and blackmailing the man. It was coldhearted.

"So Ryan, being an accountant for fifteen years, you must love numbers. Did you or your firm ever get involved with money laundering?"

It was a frank question, but it was time for Vesta to take over and have Luca take a backseat on their quaint afternoon date.

"Money laundering?" he replied.

"Just asking. I watched a program about it the other night, and it is amazing the things criminals will go through to wash dirty money."

"It's a vile thing to do, and me and my firm never have and never will have any part of it," he said with severity in his voice.

"I didn't mean to offend you."

"No offense. I come from morals and values, and my mother didn't work hard all of her life to give me a better future and education just for me to become a criminal," he declared.

"Oh, totally," Luca replied.

Luca saw that he was going to be a tough nut to crack. He seemed pure and humble, far from the voracious and immoral sort of man that she and her crew were used to blackmailing.

Their chatting continued. Luca felt the urge to be daring—her alter ego was becoming full-blown and she was getting tired of the side looks coming from their jealous waitress. She wanted to give her something to really be upset about. She changed her position in the booth and nestled next to Ryan. He was thrilled. Then she placed her hand under the table and landed her hand against his crotch. She squeezed; he smiled. She started to massage his private area and kissed him heavily up top, slipping her tongue into his mouth while catching some attention from other patrons and from their waitress, who turned and hurried away with a frown. Ryan had no complaints. The teasing action went on for a short moment.

Luca pulled away from him with a naughty smile displayed on her angelic face. "You can get used to that."

"I would like to," he responded.

She looked around for the waitress, whom she felt slighted by, but Luca didn't see her around. It felt good to be a bit passive-aggressive. She touched up her lip gloss and heard her cell phone ringing on the table. She looked at the caller ID—it was Phaedra calling her.

"I need to take this," she said to Ryan.

He gestured that it was cool. Luca answered the call while nestled against Ryan, and the first thing out of Phaedra's mouth was, "Luca, it's Spirit. She's hurt."

"What? What happened?" Luca hollered.

"He beat her up really bad. She might need to go to a hospital," Phaedra informed her.

"I'm on my way back to Brooklyn right now," she said.

Luca hung up and sprung up from the window booth. Her mischievous and naughty behavior quickly transformed into concern for her young worker. Ryan noticed the sudden change and asked, "Luca, what happened?"

"I have to go back to Brooklyn. My little cousin was in an accident."

"I'll take you."

"What about your job?"

"They can go without me for a few hours. This is more important."

He stood up, reached into his pocket, and pulled out a wad of bills. He dropped a fifty-dollar bill on the table, saying, "That should cover everything," and they both hurried out of the place.

Parked across the street from the diner was Ryan's silver Aston Martin. Luca didn't have time to marvel over his lavish ride. She jumped into the passenger seat and Ryan sped her to Brooklyn. The only thing Luca could think about was Spirit. What muthafucka had the audacity to harm one of her girls?

Chapter 17

The Aston Martin came to an abrupt stop in from of the Canarsie home. Luca jumped out of the car like a track star and ran inside her home like a fireman rushing into a burning building. Everyone was present inside. The atmosphere was solemn. Spirit was lying on the couch in really bad shape with her young cohorts surrounding her. Her right eye was completely swollen, black and blue and shut tight. Her lip was busted and still bleeding, and the side of her face was heavily bruised. It looked like she had gotten into the ring with Mayweather.

Once Luca laid eyes on her, she wanted to cry. What kind of monster would do such a thing to a sixteen-year-old girl? "What happened?" Luca cried out.

"That muthafucka Andrew Gilligan," Phaedra spoke up. "Somehow he found out she was underage and not who she said she was, and he attacked her. He beat her like she was a man. You wouldn't do this to a fuckin' dog!"

Luca frowned heavily. She went over to Spirit and knelt beside her. Luca took her hand in hers, gazed at

Spirit, and wished she could make everything better for her. Spirit could barely move. She could barely speak.

"Spirit, I'm here, it's Luca. Talk to me. What happened today?" Luca asked softly.

Spirit slowly turned her head in Luca's direction, her eyes trailing off. Luca gently wiped the blood from her lips and held back the tears. It wasn't the time for her to become emotional. But it was time for her to defend her girls and look toward revenge. Spirit gaped at Luca for a moment. Her lips quivered and her face was a mess. Her eyes became watery and she feebly muttered, "I'm . . . I'm sorry, Luca. I-I fucked up."

"No girl, you didn't do anything wrong. He's the one that fucked up," said Luca.

"I . . . I tried to fight him . . . but he was too strong. He . . . he found out I was sixteen and said . . . I . . . I was a lying whore. And then . . . then he attacked me. We were in his car . . . and he kept hitting me and hitting me. He pushed . . . he pushed my head into the glass and I . . . I thought he was goin' to kill me. So I jumped out and I ran."

Luca couldn't hold back the tears for her friend. She took a deep breath and said with conviction, "He's going to pay for this, Spirit. I promise you that. He'll fuckin' pay."

"She needs a hospital," Little Bit exclaimed.

"I have someone who'll drive her." Luca ran through the doorway to get Ryan, who was sitting patiently in his ride.

Everyone spun around and was in awe to the tall and handsome stranger standing in their home. Phaedra scowled at the sight of him. Ryan went over to the beaten young girl, picked her up in his masculine arms, and carried her outside. He gently placed her in the backseat of his Aston Martin. Luca and Phaedra rode to the hospital with him while the other girls stayed behind to hold down the fort.

Brookdale University Hospital on Linden and Rockaway boulevards wasn't too far away from Canarsie. They arrived there in a heartbeat, and Spirit was rushed into the emergency room to be treated while Luca and Phaedra waited outside. Ryan sat behind the wheel of his car, and Luca was highly appreciative of his help.

Phaedra puffed on her cigarette and was worried about their friend. She exhaled. "So is he a mark, or is there something more with him?"

"He's a mark, Phaedra, nothing more. I need him for something important that I want to start up. He's an accountant with an extensive history with his firm and he's good with numbers," Luca explained.

Phaedra puffed again and nodded. Her distaste for men was evident. She glared at Ryan—seated behind the wheel of his car, talking on his cell phone—and felt like taking his life. She didn't trust him.

"So, what are we gonna do 'bout this muthafucka? He needs to be got!" Phaedra growled.

"I know, but he's also the district attorney," Luca replied.

"And? I don't give a fuck what he is, he's a dead man soon!"

"Meaning if we kill him, then there's going to be a lot of heat on us, and that kind of attention is the last thing we need from anyone," Luca explained.

"So we just gonna let this muthafucka slide and have him get away wit' beating the shit outta Spirit?"

"No. He will pay, I can guarantee that. But there's more than one way to skin a cat, Phaedra. Think about it. We already have enough footage and evidence on him to ruin his entire career. And he fucked up when he put his hands on Spirit. I got this, Phaedra. I'll make this muthafucka wish he was never born when I'm through with him," Luca said with fervor.

Phaedra smiled. "I wanna be there too. I wanna see this muthafucka go down. I wanna see his bitch-ass suffer."

"You will, but not until we get what we need from him," Luca replied.

Phaedra continued smoking, anticipating news from the doctor about Spirit's condition. It was a cool night, in contrast to the heat wave from earlier. She stared at the Aston Martin and asked Luca, "How long is he supposed to stick around? I mean, do we still need him around?"

"I guess not." Luca agreed.

She walked down the stairs and went over to Ryan. She lightly tapped on the window. He buzzed the passenger window down, and she lowered herself to eye level with him. Ryan curtailed his phone conversation and hung up. "How is your cousin doing?" he asked.

"We don't know yet. The doctor still hasn't come out to say anything to us. But I'm sure she'll be fine."

"She will. She seems to be a strong girl."

"But listen, you can leave, we're good from here," Luca said politely.

"You sure? I mean, I'm all yours until everything is taken care of. I'm in no rush."

"You're sweet, but we're good, Ryan. I'm with Phaedra, and I'll call you later on. I'm sorry for any inconvenience I caused you."

"No, it was all okay. I do understand, and I had a great time with you today. I want us to do it again. I mean, except rushing your cousin to the hospital. But I really like you, Luca, and I want to continue seeing you. If that's okay."

"I'll call you."

He smiled.

"Get home safe," she said.

He nodded and looked pleased. "Well, can I get a kiss goodbye?" he asked with a slight grin.

Luca hesitated. She didn't want to show any affection while Phaedra was watching from a short distance knowing how her friend felt about men. But she had to make him believe her feelings for him were genuine. Luca opened the door and slid into the passenger seat. She leaned toward him and planted her lips against his. Their kiss was brief, but a bit passionate, with their tongues entwining.

Ryan truly enjoyed the kiss. He smiled heavily. He was always smiling—always affable—a genuinely nice kind of guy.

"I really like that. I hope to get more of that in the future," he said.

"You continue being a good boy and maybe you will," she teased.

He chuckled.

Luca climbed out of the car. Ryan started the ignition. He didn't want to let her go. He savored the taste of her on his lips. Luca stood by the curb and watched him drive off, knowing he was going to be a difficult mark—but still a mark. When she pivoted on her heels, she saw Phaedra staring at her incredulously, and then Spirit's doctor walked out into the night to give them an update on their friend's condition.

Luca hurried over to the hospital with anticipation in her stride.

There wasn't any major damage to Spirit, nothing broken or fractured. She was very lucky. She was going to be fine, as Luca expected. But her friend was going to need lots of rest and healing. Luca and Phaedra had that covered. But things were about to change in their organization. Luca couldn't risk any of her girls getting hurt.

✳✳✳

Luca held court in the living room of her Canarsie home. Phaedra, Meeka, Danielle, and Little Bit sat on the couches and chairs in the plush living room with their undivided attention on Luca, anticipating what she had to say to them all. Unfortunately, Spirit wasn't around for the meeting.

Several days had passed since Spirit's beating. The girls kept a low profile for the moment with the men they were fucking and duping. While in the hospital, Spirit was visited by a social worker and a detective who wanted to question her about the incident and her well-being. But Spirit was defiant. She wasn't snitching on anybody, not even her attacker. He would get his; Luca was going to make sure of that. Spirit had complete trust in Luca.

The social worker was ready to place her back in a group home. Spirit had run away from three so far. Luca strongly protested the decision, but to no avail. Spirit was a minor. Luca was over twenty-one, but she wasn't a parent, guardian, or sibling to Spirit; therefore, the girl had to be placed under the state's care once again. She was a minor who had been severely beaten, most likely via domestic abuse, and the incident had to be reported immediately to the authorities and a case worker.

It pained Luca that she couldn't do more for Spirit, but she and Phaedra weren't giving up on her. Their hands were tied at the moment, but Luca was going to find some way to get their girl back. And it angered them both that Andrew Gilligan was the cause of all of this. He was going to suffer some way—somehow.

Luca stood in the living room with a small, black handbag in her hand and so much concern on her mind for her young girls. They all looked to Luca with profound trust and admiration. She was their den mother—their leader. She was changing them by giving them means, along with knowledge and understanding, and they were changing her greatly—transitioning Luca into something aggressive—a cult leader. She was becoming stronger and more cunning.

Her treacherous scheme of bribery and blackmail of powerful men had to be put on hold for a while. It was lucrative, but also costly and risky. A great young girl who could have died because of it. Besides, they had their evidence—photos, videos, audio, and other documentation of these affluent figures doing unthinkable and undesirable things to her young girls, from fornication to drug use— and all it took was one phone call to a wife or boss, or the threat of taking the information public, and these nasty and cruel muthafuckas would be under her thumb for a very long time. Pictures were worth a thousand words, but videos and recordings created power.

Luca stared into the faces of all of her young girls and said to them, "I love all of y'all and love how dedicated each and every one of y'all has been to this organization in the past months. Unfortunately, Spirit couldn't be with us tonight because of some bullshit, but we will get our girl back. I promise y'all that."

The somber faces in the room displayed how much they missed the lively sixteen-year-old girl.

Luca continued with, "We all came a long way, and tonight, I just wanted to show how much I appreciate everyone, from passing y'all GED exams to helping to build this family . . . this organization. Look at us; it wasn't too long ago that we were society's misfits—the unwanted and ungodly. We were called whores, stupid, naïve, ignorant, uneducated, weak, and so much more . . . the lowest on society's pole. But tonight, we sit on a million-dollar empire. And we have fear and respect out there from the ghetto to Wall Street, because our product is superior to anything else. Bad Girl is out there. She's potent, and everyone desires her."

The girls nodded and smiled.

Phaedra stood behind Luca with a proud and accomplished look.

Luca continued talking. Her speech was encouraging and uplifting. They understood her, and she understood them. They were from the same world, having gone through almost the same tribulations in life, but they had all grown strong and wise in a short period of time.

"If we continue to stick together like this, then I can guarantee that nothing will ever break us apart," Luca proclaimed intensely.

Luca signaled for Phaedra. She walked over, and Luca handed Phaedra the black handbag. Luca nodded, giving the signal that it was time to reveal what surprise she had in the bag for her girls.

Phaedra went around the room passing out a long, square velvet gift box to each girl. The girls were excited. Luca smiled. She once again gazed into the faces of her young girls and said, "This is a little gift from me to all of you; something to display my gratitude to y'all. Go on ahead and open the boxes."

The girls opened the long, square, velvet gift boxes, and inside each one was revealed a fourteen-karat solid white gold women's diamond tennis chain, along with a fourteen-karat solid white gold women's multicolored diamond butterfly pendant. It was a costly gift to each girl.

"Wow," a few uttered in amazement at receiving such an expensive gift.

Luca shouted, imitating Oprah, "And you get diamonds! And you get diamonds! And you get diamonds!"

Everyone laughed, relishing the moment.

Luca continued smiling. "The multicolored butterfly pendant signifies our transformation from ugly caterpillars to beautiful and soaring butterflies. It's who we are— butterflies. This is our symbol. This is what we represent . . . beauty."

The girls were extremely appreciative and pleased with their gifts, but for two more girls in the room, there was more to come. Luca reached into her pants pocket and pulled out two car keys, each to a brand-new Honda Accord parked outside.

"Phaedra and Little Bit, these are for you," Luca said, handing them the car keys.

Little Bit beamed with excitement. "Are you fuckin' serious?"

Luca nodded and smiled.

Phaedra was ready to do back flips. Both girls snatched the keys from Luca's hands and rushed outside. And there they were: two spanking new Honda Accord Sedans, one in silver and the other in burgundy, parked on the quiet Brooklyn street. Luca had had them secretly delivered earlier. The car dealership in Jamaica, Queens she dealt with was known for their shady services when it came to drug dealers who wanted to buy nice cars. And with the help of her newfound attorney, Dominic Sirocco, she was making some smart investments.

"I'm taking the silver one," Phaedra hollered, snatching Little Bit's key out of her hand just in case it was to the car Phaedra wanted.

She ran to her new toy like a child running to the Christmas tree on Christmas Day. When she got in, she tossed the additional key to Little Bit, who rushed toward the burgundy one.

Luca didn't want to do the same cliché other drug dealers had done before her—walking into a lavish car lot and paying for one or several cars in cold cash. It would have definitely been a red flag to the IRS and the police. Instead, she opened up a bank account—a checking account—and wrote a check for the down payment. Then she was going to close the bank account and continue to pay the remainder of what she owed in cash.

It was subtle. It was business.

Luca had sized up the right dealer to do business with. The car dealership was known to be greedy and understanding with their seedy purchasers—looking the other way with their business transactions and dirty money in their hands, helping the buyers evade the reporting law. They weren't cops; it was their business only to sell cars.

Luca promised the car dealer she would bring a lot more business his way really soon. He could only beam with anticipation.

"Y'all wanna go for a ride?" Phaedra shouted.

She and Little Bit were the only ones with their license. Luca had her permit, but she always procrastinated on taking her road test and getting a legitimate license. Her mind was on other things, mostly business.

The girls climbed into their respective cars, Luca riding with Phaedra, and they all decided to go out to eat, Luca's treat. As they rode, Luca's phone rang. It was Ryan calling. She hadn't spoken to him in several days, and she didn't feel like talking to him now. She sent his phone call to voicemail. Moments later, Squirrel called, and Luca quickly answered.

"Hey," Luca answered in an excited tone.

Phaedra glowered. She didn't like the fact that Luca was becoming seriously involved with their drug connect—a man who could make their lives miserable if he so chose too. She despised their hidden relationship, but kept her mouth shut about it. Luca was the boss, but Phaedra's romantic feelings for her boss were growing rapidly. She was falling deeply in love with Luca, and wondered if Luca could ever look at her in the same way.

Phaedra kept quiet and listened intently to Luca talk sweetly to her main boo over the phone. It was stupid for them to get into this hush-hush relationship when Squirrel already had a crazy baby mama. Phaedra wanted to make her move on Luca—but when? And if she did, how would Luca react to her sexual advances? Luca had always helped her out and taken care of her. She did so much for her and the other girls. Phaedra placed Luca on the highest pedestal and felt she could do no wrong. She was the smartest person that Phaedra had ever met, and the two of them were unbreakable.

Unbreakable—that was who they were, and no man nor anyone else was going to destroy their bond. Phaedra would kill for Luca—and she already had.

Chapter 18

Dominic Sirocco was a genius, and Luca knew she had made the right move by securing him for smarter investments and legal advice. He was a tall, dark man with a stern, half-shaven face and short, cropped hair. He was maybe thirty-five years old—at most, an athletic forty. He was a shrewd man and at all times aggressive for his clients, in and out of the courtroom. He was one of the best defensive attorneys in the city, holding a 70 percent acquittal rate. When push came to shove, Luca was smart enough to understand that she might need this man to defend her one day. So why wait until the day when the storms came brewing to hire a lawyer?

He was expensive, but the word around town was that he was worth every penny.

Dominic Sirocco wasn't just the best criminal attorney in town; he was also selective with his services and clientele. He knew about business from top to bottom. He was a rich man who'd acquired dozens of profitable businesses and investments over the years. He'd had a law degree by the time he was twenty-four years old.

Luca had heard about him through the grapevine. She made an appointment to see him, and the two immediately had a mutual respect for each other. Dominic saw a beautiful and intelligent young woman seated in his office—but a drug dealer. He wasn't shocked about her profession. In his line of work, criminals—or better yet, clients who made a living off of ill-gotten gain—came in all shapes and sizes, even looking like supermodels.

When Luca first introduced herself to him, she was sexily clad in a sea-blue, form fitted dress. Her smooth, defined legs were nicely crossed over each other and at the end of them were a pair of pricey wedge heels.

She was impressed with his office décor. A few Picasso paintings and several degrees decorated the walls of his downtown office with floor-to-ceiling windows capturing a picturesque view of the Hudson River and the New Jersey shoreline. He sat in a high-backed leather chair behind a solid wood desk that rested on hardwood flooring. Dominic looked distinguished and impressive clad in a sharp, Gucci Grey Brera slim-fit suit.

He leaned back in his high-backed chair, gazing at Luca with his hands clasped together like he was about to say a prayer. Luca met his eyes, looking stoic in his presence.

"They say you come highly recommended," Luca had said.

"I do," he had replied with some aloofness.

"Well, I need help. Do you know what I do?"

"I'm sure you're about to tell me."

"I'm a drug dealer, Mr. Sirocco," she said matter-of-factly. "And I need help with my money, among other things."

Her direct honesty intrigued the man.

Luca didn't hide who she was from him. She stood out and was frank about it. She wanted to invest her drug money in something legal and profitable. She needed to launder lots of money coming in. She needed a front. Dominic was the right guy to employ. He was borderline shady with a few of his practices, but also fair—an oxymoron type of guy. Immediately he developed a fondness for Luca. There was something about her that would not let him refuse her his services. She was beautiful and angelic, and appeared somewhat fragile to be in the kind of business that she was in—yet she was intriguing, with some hidden transgressions about herself.

Luca had a goal—a proposal that she intended on revealing soon. It took brains and brawn to make it high in the criminal world. Dominic saw something special in her. She was well-spoken, aware, and motivated, with something rooted deep inside her that provoked her into progress.

One of her goals was to take her profits and slowly invest them so she wouldn't raise any red flags. Get a nice mutual fund started and stash some money away. She wanted to become a legit multimillionaire by the time she was thirty.

With the help of her attorney, Luca bought a $250,000 piece of property in Brooklyn. The seller accepted $100,000 of the payment in cash and agreed to list the official sale price on the closing documents at around $150,000. The transaction, though not illegal, allowed for Luca to turn the cash into equity on the place. Even if she were to sell it for exactly what she paid, she would recoup the $100,000 and have a ready explanation of how she received it for the authorities. It would be clean money.

It was smart business moves like this that kept Luca ahead of the game and the law. She was becoming Batman, and Dominic Sirocco was her Robin. Luca saw this game, this illicit drug trade, as a business to get rich off quickly and move on. She had an intoxicating and powerful product, a commodity that was constantly moving like running water.

In her mind, it took more than a gun or some muscle to make a living with a recreational drug or pharmaceutical— it was a career that touched upon any of the disciplines. One might consider the shady drug pusher or drug dealer akin to an independent distributor working for a global conglomerate, reaping billions of dollars a year. All the fundamentals of running a successful business were also part of everyday life for a dealer.

Luca had learned from Nate that if your product was really good and pure, as opposed to being cheap and generic, people were willing to pay for quality, even in a down economy.

Business is business—it didn't matter if it was legal or illegal; the same principles applied when you were trying to get rich off a product or service. It all came down to profits. What could you do to sell your goods and services at a profit?

Customer satisfaction, brand management, and advertising were all necessary to stay ahead of the competition and deter upstarts looking to snatch away the market share. If you loved it, appreciated it, then you were going to pay for it.

The way Luca saw things, there were two types of drug dealers. One was the sort who got by with scattered, urgent sales of diluted product—the get-rich-and-don't-give-a-fuck-about-quality type, selling cocaine cut with baby laxative or marijuana sprinkled with dollar-store oregano. They saw the game only as a hustle—to impress and become absorbed by violence. But the other type of drug dealer cultivated loyal customers who sought out the purity and quality of their product. They had future goals, and violence was always their last resort. These were the drug dealers who transformed themselves into businessmen and legit entrepreneurs.

Dominic Sirocco was willing to help Luca with every business transaction and the paperwork and steps necessary to launder drug money and establish legitimate income for herself and her peoples. To hide the true ownership of some properties, and to protect herself from liability, Luca set up some corporations and a few LLC's and listed properties in their names. She also acquired a few houses to convert her tainted funds into clean money.

Luca and her attorney were also using a tactic called "smurfing." This was the practice of breaking up a large cash transaction into smaller ones, in which, usually, payments were made using cashier's checks or money orders for less than $10,000. Sometimes it was tedious and daunting business covering up large transactions by using twelve checks and money orders to pay the bulk of the cost of a car or property, or using 69 money orders to make payments totaling $90,000 for a property in Queens and 159 money orders and bank checks for $75,000 in payments for another property in Brooklyn. It needed to be done subtly and right. Luca wanted to avoid the red flags. Red flags meant trouble—it meant the FBI or IRS opening up an investigation on you.

Despite the federal law that required the reporting of cash transactions involving more than $10,000, Luca had no trouble finding lawyers, merchants, and real-estate agents who would look the other way.

Dominic Sirocco also helped Luca wash her money through a series of adept laundering operations he was aware of. One was bulk cash smuggling. They would physically smuggle her cash to another jurisdiction and deposit it into an offshore bank account.

Another way they laundered her money was through a cash earning business. Luca was a silent partner with one of Dominic's associates in opening a strip club near downtown Brooklyn. This front business was involved in receiving cash, and it used its accounts to deposit both legal and drug money profits, claiming all of it was legitimate earnings.

Bad Girl Blvd

Bad Girl was meant to be a low-key drug in the quiet, middle-class neighborhood of Canarsie, and also among the high-end clientele Luca developed through Tiffany and word-of-mouth. But something as potent and demanding as Bad Girl was going to attract the wolves toward the growing nest, and—thinking Luca was a sheep—they were ready to devour her, and take what was glitzy in their eyes.

When Danielle was robbed of five thousand dollars at gunpoint by two notorious stickup kids named Ozzie and Keen, it was time for Luca to take action and use her muscle. Phaedra advised her to make a strong point—send out a lurid message to anyone who thought they were weak. The last thing they wanted to do was look weak in a vile and deadly criminal underworld.

Luca green-lighted the hit. She understood it needed to be done.

A week after Danielle was robbed, Phaedra and Meeka ambushed the two men in Brownsville. Ozzie and Keen were seated in a dark Chrysler 300, smoking weed in the back streets behind the towering projects under the glowing moon, unaware of the ominous threat looming. Little Bit was the decoy. She strutted past them in her tight shirt and short skirt, revealing her toned legs.

"Hey gal, where you walkin' to, ma?" Ozzie called out.

Little Bit turned around and grinned at his catcall. "Why you care? You gonna take me?"

"Shit, we'll take you wherever you want to go, ma. You know what I'm sayin'?"

"Yeah, I know what ya saying," Little Bit replied. "I might be goin' far, though."

"We down fo' the ride," he replied with a grin.

"Y'all are?"

"Uh-huh. You smoke, ma?" Ozzie asked.

"Of course I do," Little Bit gladly replied.

"Get in then, and let's have some fun tonight."

Little Bit hesitated to get inside the car. She was great at keeping them distracted while Phaedra and Meeka approached from behind, crouched low to the ground, creeping like bugs in the night with dark hoods over their heads and pistols in their hands.

Little Bit slowly approached the vehicle. When she was near, just a few feet from harm's way, Phaedra and Meeka sprung into action like lightening striking. Phaedra went for the driver; Meeka took out the passenger.

Bak! Bak! Bak! Bak!

Both men were instantly killed with two shots apiece to their upper torso. Their bloody bodies lay slumped in the front seat of the 300. The trio of young girls walked briskly away from the area and toward the parked Dodge down the street. It slowly pulled away from the crime scene.

"Fuck them niggas! Fuck all these niggas!" Phaedra shouted heatedly from the front seat of the moving car, breathing hard, excited about the kill.

Their adrenaline was rushing, their names ringing out strongly on the streets of Brooklyn. And Bad Girl inadvertently became Brooklyn's drug of choice.

Luca was sitting on the throne of something majestic. It was so euphoric—the sex, the money, the murder, the power. It pulled her in deeper and deeper, and made her wish she could have transformed into this person long before. The death of Nate was the birth of her, something new and exhilarating—Vesta.

Chapter 19

It was going to be a rare day together for Luca and Naomi. It had been weeks since they seen each other. Since the death of Abioye, Naomi had secluded herself somewhat from everyone, grieving in silence. But now she was back on track and ready to continue on with her aristocratic way of living. She called Luca out of the blue and decided the two should meet, talk, shop, have brunch, and catch up on lost time.

Luca agreed.

Luca stepped out of the black Mercedes cab looking spectacular, like a ray of light in a white minidress. Her pink wig flowed, her platinum and diamond earrings and necklace sparkled in the sun like fireworks, and she oozed confidence and sex appeal. She was far from the meek girl she'd been several months ago—looking like a dog running around with her tail between her legs and cowering from her own shadow. Her attitude now was fierce, her power growing. Things done changed for her.

Naomi waved energetically at Luca, spotting her exiting the cab on Fifth Avenue in the city.

"Hey, girl! Luca! Luca!" Naomi called out with a welcoming smile.

Luca was expressionless for a moment. She gazed at Naomi in a different light, and a smile appeared. However, her smile was more mocking. She wasn't going to be able to hide the coldness in her soul any longer. Soon, her harsh transformation would have to show, like a tumor growing outside of the skin.

"Ohmygod, Luca, look at you, coming outside looking like a ghetto Rihanna with that pink wig," Naomi joked.

Luca didn't find the humor funny. But she showed no reaction.

The two hugged each other halfheartedly. Naomi was definitely back to her old self with her sardonic remarks and humor.

"You look good, Naomi. How you been?" Luca asked matter-of-factly.

"I'm doing great, Luca. Really great. But I miss him so much, and it took a while for me to heal . . . But guess what, girl? He left me some money—twenty-five thousand dollars! Even after his death, my fiancé still looked out for me. So we have to go shopping."

"That's nice," Luca replied dryly. "Nice."

"But look at you . . . you look really good, Luca." Naomi leaned back and gazed at Luca in awe. "I see you must be doing really nice yourself. You have changed a lot. It's like you're a completely different person. New hair, new look, nice jewelry—what did you do, get a Maury makeover or fuck a baller?"

"Cute, but no. I just have a whole different attitude about life now."

"Girl, it's about time! I'm so glad to hear that. We both do. I graduated college, my birthday is coming up, and I look fabulous. You feel me? And right now, I'm ready to do me. Let's go shopping, because we're looking good and I have some money to spend," Naomi exclaimed vibrantly.

Luca was ready to show off her newfound wealth. She was no longer in Naomi's shadow.

Fifth Avenue would be their destination for shopping. The bustling area—lined with prestigious shops and boutiques and home to some of the most extraordinary museums, businesses, luxury apartments and parks—was a major thoroughfare in the center of the borough of Manhattan.

It was known as one of the most expensive streets in the world. Naomi and Luca felt like they were the most expensive girls in the world.

Fendi, Gucci, Tiffany's & Co., Chanel, Ralph Lauren, Donna Karan, Versace, Dolce and Gabbana, Dior, and Louis Vuitton. It was everywhere—pricey and prestigious.

Luca felt privileged to be able to walk into any store and afford it all. She carried ten thousand dollars on her. It was pocket change. And this time, there wouldn't be any window-shopping.

The ladies went into one high-end store after another, coming out with bag after bag. Then they had high tea at the Plaza and enjoyed a perfect summer day and the sprawling blue sky patched with a few clouds.

An hour later, they were having a nice lunch at Philippe Chow on the Upper East Side of the city. The ladies sat at the circular Venetian-style bar sipping on apple martinis and talking. Despite Luca's hate for Naomi, it had been a really good day. She had several shopping bags of nice and pricey clothing and shoes in the trunk of the cab they'd rented for the day. For six hundred dollars, she'd hired the cabbie to be her personal driver around town.

Naomi became curious. Where was Luca getting all of this money from? she asked herself.

"Girl, you're spending money like me. Damn, I see you definitely got it going on, Luca. You must be putting it on that nigga you fucking something really nice," Naomi said.

Luca didn't respond. She sipped her drink and remained expressionless toward the incendiary remark.

Naomi took a sip from her Martini and continued with, "But you know what they're saying about you in the neighborhood, right?"

"What are they saying about me, Naomi?" Luca asked halfheartedly.

"That you are fucking with the enemy. That you and Squirrel got something going on. From what I'm hearing from the streets, everyone is upset and is in some kind of uproar about your relationship with that nigga. You know they're saying—he killed your man, Nate, and now you fucking him, Luca. What's that about? I'm your friend. You can talk to me," Naomi proclaimed.

"I'm surprised that you even keep your ear to the streets since you always putting it down, Naomi," Luca quipped.

"I hear things."

"I bet you do."

"What are you getting at? I mean, I'm trying to be your friend here and help you out. People are talking about you, and it's not good. Nobody sees you anymore, and they're saying you are always in Harlem. You don't come around anymore. Now suddenly you have all this money to spend. Girl, I'm just going with the evidence," Naomi said in a self-righteous tone.

Luca sadly chuckled. "You are something else, Naomi. Since I've known you, you have always been a fuckin' bitch."

"Excuse me?!"

"Bitch, you heard me."

Naomi was flabbergasted by Luca's sudden choice of harsh words aimed at her. Luca had never in her life come out of her mouth like that before. Naomi crushed her hand against her chest, aghast at what she had just heard.

"Luca . . . what has gotten into you?"

"I should be asking what has gotten into you," Luca spat back. "Like Nate!"

"What?"

Luca wanted to stir up the hornets' nest and see what came out. "You know before Nate was killed, he confessed to me about you and him. Y'all fucked, right?"

"He's lying, Luca! I didn't fuck him!" Naomi vehemently denied.

Luca coolly continued with, "He said your pussy was stank anyway. And that you couldn't fuck."

Naomi nearly died. The panic and embarrassment on her face was priceless for Luca.

"Ohmygod, Luca . . . are you seriously going to believe him? I'm your friend! I've been a friend to you for so long. Do you actually think I would do that to you? I never wanted your man. You know he's not even my type. I had a fiancé. And besides, you're like a sister to me, Luca. I wouldn't dare hurt you like that. That is not me! It's not!"

It was an Emmy-award-wining performance coming from Naomi.

Luca laughed, but it was an unsettling laugh. Her cold eyes sent chills up Naomi's spine. This wasn't the same Luca she grew up with. There was something definitely different about her.

"I never believed him anyway," Luca finally responded. "Nate was always a liar."

Naomi breathed a sigh of relief. "Yes, he was."

"You would never do me like that, right, Naomi? Betray me behind my back?" asked Luca calmly.

"You know I wouldn't. We're friends, Luca. And we will always be friends. I love you."

A nearly undetectable smirk danced across Luca's face. "I love you, too."

Luca downed the rest of her apple martini and suddenly stood up. She couldn't stomach that trifling bitch anymore. She'd had enough. Luca only wanted to see if Naomi would admit the truth, but she was too much of a coward to do so. Luca had video of them fucking. It was stored away someplace safe. How would Naomi explain herself now if Luca revealed the footage?

"You're leaving?" Naomi asked weakly.

"Yes. I have other plans for this afternoon," Luca replied. She headed for the exit, but turned around to face Naomi again with an afterthought. "And one more thing, Naomi. My business is my fuckin' business. Let them all talk, because they know me. And when they get to really know me, then they're going to hate me."

With that said, Luca strutted outside to her driver, with her pink hair bouncing and behaving. Naomi stood looking listless and speechless by the bar.

***

Luca thanked Squirrel for the eighteen-carat diamond necklace by fucking him once again. It was one of many lavish gifts from Squirrel. He was spoiling her with the finest jewelry and some good dick. His dick was addictive, and Luca was always yearning for him and it. From the moment she laid eyes on Squirrel, she was drawn to his energy, his thuggish aura, and his incredible muscularity. Their masculine and feminine energies complemented one another and they just seemed to fit like a hand in a glove.

It was a shame that she had to share him, though.

But she would rather share Squirrel with Angel than not have him at all.

Her recent trip to Harlem was about pleasure this time, no business. And when Luca came by for pleasure, Squirrel made sure they were alone in the project apartment. His goons were either lingering outside or handling business elsewhere.

Luca was doggy style over the bathroom sink, her legs and ass spread from the deep penetration—her passionate facial expression reflected in the mirror. Squirrel was positioned behind her, colliding his muscular body into her, his thick penis throbbing and pulsating within the warm, wet, velvety walls of her vagina.

Luca cooed, "Fuck me, Squirrel. Ooooh, you feel so good, baby. You feel so damn good inside of me."

Her hardened nipples would ache to be pinched or squeezed, or for his mouth to devour them. His thick mushroom tip prodded the slippery folds of her pussy and rubbed against her clit, bringing about a jolt of stimulation for Luca. Squirrel's hands slid across her breasts while he thrust deeply inside of her, eliciting intense moans of pleasure from her.

"Mmmm . . . ugh! Ugh! Ugh! Damn, baby, that feels so amazing," she shrieked.

Instinctively, she pushed back, grinding the soft, full curves of her ass against him. She met each hard thrust inside of her with a passionate cry and lifted her head, her eyes meeting with his lustful expression in the bathroom mirror. She could see the concentration on Squirrel's face in the mirror and she could tell he was experiencing intense pleasure as well.

"Agh! Ya pussy is so fuckin' good, Luca. I'm takin' this pussy! I'm takin' this pussy!" he chanted.

"Take the pussy, baby. Take this pussy! It's yours, daddy! It's fuckin' yours," Luca yelped, feeling his erection engorged and rock-hard inside her.

She could feel her temperature rising, and she was on the edge of exploding. He gripped the back of her slim neck, placing his other hand on the counter beside her, and continuously pounded himself inside of her, pushing her against the countertop. Squirrel's energy was strong.

"You gonna make me cum, daddy! I wanna cum, daddy," Luca cried out.

He grunted and stayed focused on busting his nut. But then, there was that sound twittering and vibrating against the bathroom counter. It was his cell phone going off. It was loud and disrupted his mood. It stopped, but immediately it started again.

"Fuck!" Squirrel cursed.

"Don't answer it, baby . . . just keep fucking me," she whined.

He stopped anyway and snatched the cell phone into his hand. It was one of his goons calling him.

"Yo!" Squirrel answered gruffly.

"Yo, Squirrel. Angel is on her way up," his goon said.

"What?"

"I don't know why. She just barged right by us wit' this attitude and went into the building," his goon informed.

"A'ight...thanks!"

Squirrel hung up and pulled out of Luca's pussy.

"Shit! You gotta go," he uttered sharply.

"What?" Luca looked confused.

"My baby mama is on her way up, and she can be a problem," he warned Luca.

Squirrel hurried to get dressed and snatched Luca out of the bathroom and tossed her into the living room. Their sexual episode had come to an abrupt end. She was clearly upset.

"Are you kicking me out, Squirrel?"

"Luca, you don't want any part of her, believe me. That bitch is crazy. So you need to get the fuck out, now!"

Luca hesitated.

Squirrel saw her hesitation, and it angered him. He took the initiative in helping her abruptly leave his place by yanking her by the arm and pulling her toward the door. Luca slightly resisted, but she knew she wasn't in the position to protest. She was only his jump-off and he was her connect. It would be stupid to create any problems with him.

He coldly pushed her out the door with no remorse.

Dumbfounded, Luca slowly walked away with her pussy still tingling. She went into the stairway just as the elevator stopped on the floor, and Angel hurried out and marched toward Squirrel's door. Luca caught a glimpse of her from the cloudy, rectangular window embedded in the doorway. She looked upset. Luca wanted to confront her, but she didn't.

It wasn't the first time that the two had almost clashed with each other. Angel was unpredictable, coming and going when she pleased, and there were a few near-misses between them while Luca was in Harlem seeing Squirrel.

And she would have to hide or scurry off like some stray dog or a flock of pigeons being shooed away.

It was humiliating for her.

Luca didn't understand. She was becoming a major drug queenpin in the city, and Squirrel had the audacity to treat her like she was second-rate. Luca didn't want any problems, but her pride was crushed. Who the fuck was Angel? In her mind, she should have been Squirrel's main bitch. They matched perfectly. So why couldn't he let Angel go? Luca was in love with the man, but he wasn't in love with her.

Luca exited the project building and climbed into a cab. She sulked. She was still horny. Her mind was heavily on Squirrel. She was clearly frustrated and perturbed. The only thing she could think about was Angel taking her place and taking that good dick inside of her while her own pussy was still throbbing.

"Where to, Miss?" the cabbie asked.

Luca hesitated telling the driver her destination. Tonight, she wanted to be sought after and yearned for. She wanted some dick. And she knew the one person who wouldn't reject her. The one person who would love to give her what she needed.

***

Ryan opened the front door to his Harlem brownstone, and there she was, looking spectacular in the light drizzling shower outside. She glistened like a polished diamond as the rain cascaded down around her. He smiled at the sight of her and quickly invited her inside.

Luca rushed at him, throwing her arms around him and slamming her lips against his. They kissed passionately, wrapped tightly into each other. He hoisted her into his arms, and she straddled his strong, masculine body. He carried Luca into his Asian-themed bedroom like she was a feather in his arms and they dropped against the platform bed.

"Fuck me!" Luca cried out. "Fuck me so good tonight."

Ryan was ready to oblige. They shed their clothing while nestled against each other in the feng shui décor. The white wallpaper with the enormous black Japanese cherry tree sprawled across it became witness to the two's naked and heated passion. Their naked bodies intertwined with their lips locked, grunts and moans echoing throughout the bedroom.

If Squirrel didn't want her tonight, there was always someone else to take care of her needs. Luca was like a customer at Burger King; she wanted to have everything her way.

Chapter 20

A towering, dark and seasoned detective with a dark goatee and piercing dark eyes walked into the lavishly furnished Canarsie home under the setting sun. His name was Walter Charter. He was always well dressed for his job: a stylish button-down, designer tie, creased pants, black shoes, gold pinky ring. His meticulous method and adeptness at solving crimes sometimes stirred up jealousy among his coworkers. He was a smart and attractive black male with a sprinkle of superficial and self-righteous behavior.

He stood poker-faced in the home, which could potentially be a crime scene. Two uniformed cops who had been first on the scene were there in the home to meet him. A concerned neighbor had made the phone call after discovering the tragedy. She hadn't seen her neighbor in days and became concerned.

"What do we have here, fellows?" Charter asked.

"Looks like an OD to us," one of the officers replied nonchalantly.

Charter sighed. It was the second overdose in one month in the same quiet and affluent neighborhood.

The man's body was face down on the living room floor; he had been dead for three days. The officer's report listed him an immigration attorney in his mid-forties. His name was Michael White, and he was going through a bitter divorce battle with his second wife. He seemed to be a healthy male with a hidden addiction.

To Detective Charter, it appeared to be some type of foul play. There was a large life-insurance policy payable to the spouse after his death. The detective wondered if the victim's estranged wife was responsible for giving the victim a lethal dose of the dope. She definitely had motive.

But there was one thing detective Walter Charter saw near the body that canceled out his first theory: the glassine bag on the floor near the body, stamped pink with "Bad Girl." It was obvious to him—heroin.

He crouched down near the body and picked up the glassine package with a pair of tweezers from his pocket. He had seen the same thing at the other victim's home. The mark was definitely the same. Both victims had used the same type of heroin.

"Say no to drugs," joked the uniformed cop.

Charter shot a sharp and disapproving gaze at the cop.

"I'm sorry," the cop apologized.

The smell was becoming overwhelming. The body had started to deteriorate in the home when another heat wave had come over the city. The city morgue was called, and a case was brewing. Detective Charter guessed that maybe he had stumbled onto something bigger than expected. Charter's crafty eyes saw the slightest details that could easily be missed by the average mind.

"Bad Girl," he muttered to himself while staring at the package.

He stared at the body. An immigration attorney hooked on drugs. It wouldn't be the first time some big shot was hooked on narcotics, but usually their drug of choice was cocaine, pills, marijuana, or ecstasy. It was unlikely that a man of his status would do heroin, and the same went for the first victim found two weeks back: a data analyst in the city. She was found naked and dead in her bedroom with same pink Bad Girl package on her nightstand.

Detective Charter came to the conclusion that they were taking the drug nasally. He didn't find any syringes nor pipes to smoke it orally. A new and potent drug had flooded into the middle class neighborhood undetected, and people were rapidly becoming hooked on it.

Who was the mastermind behind it? Where did it originate? He thought someone of a Frank Lucas character must be responsible. The drug wasn't remaining low-key on the five-block radius it had started out on anymore. It was spreading out like a contagious virus. Two overdoses in one month—it wasn't a coincidence.

Detective Charter meticulously examined every inch of the man's home, but didn't find anything else unusual in the place. He stepped outside for some fresh air. He looked up and down the block. He felt the urge to canvass the area and see what he could turn up. He went knocking on a few doors on the block, and started to ask neighbors questions about Mr. White, and if they had seen anything unusual in the past week or so. Who was he hanging around? But no one had anything to say. It was the area where people minded their business. They went to work, came home, and stayed inside.

Detective Charter went knocking on one door right next to Luca's. An elderly couple, the Peters, were the residents there. They answered their door for the detective and were happy to help out. They were a nosy couple in their early seventies, and had been living in the same Canarsie home for over fifty years. They were sad to hear about Mr. White's death. They knew him, but barely. He seemed so nice.

"So sad. He seemed to be a decent man, Detective Charter, him and his wife, but I did hear they were having some issues. But going to drugs . . . my prayers go out to his family," Mrs. Peters expressed sadly.

"I'm just going around asking a few questions," the detective replied. "I just want to get to the bottom of things, and want to know if y'all have seen any unusual activity recently."

"Well, we haven't seen any unusual activity around here lately," Mr. Peter replied.

"George, tell them about our new neighbors," Mrs. Peters chimed in.

"New neighbors?" Detective Charter asked with a raised brow.

"Yes, Detective. They moved in several months ago,

young girls, maybe five or six of them, always coming and going," Mrs. Peters informed him. "They do seem nice, but also mysterious. I mean, I personally can't understand how such a young girl can afford such a nice place like that. I don't think she works."

"How old is she?" the detective asked.

"I would say about twenty-two, maybe twenty-three."

"And they moved in when?"

"About five or six months ago," she said.

"They're quiet people, Detective, and mostly keep to themselves. They don't have any parties or any men coming by at all, which I find kind of strange. Young girls that beautiful and no boyfriends. I asked if they were family, and the oldest one told me yes. But I don't believe her, Detective. Don't any of them look alike," Mrs. Peters stated.

The detective nodded. He saw it as a dead end. He was investigating a drug-related death, not a few young girls living next door.

"Well, thank you for your time. If y'all hear anything, please feel free to give me a call," said the detective, handing the couple his personal card.

"We will, Detective. We sure will," replied the wife.

Detective Charter walked down the stairs, lit a cigarette, and then stared at the house next door. It was a beautiful place surrounded by a wrought-iron fence and a few flowers. It was well taken care of. He didn't see any cars parked in the driveway or out front, but he did notice the security cameras on the house. It was kind of odd—

but, he thought, in these troubling times, who didn't have some type of security system to protect their home?

He gazed at every inch of the place from the street and was tempted to walk up to the door and knock. But he thought against it. It seemed that there wasn't anyone home anyway. Detective Charter took a few pulls from his cigarette and walked away. Bad Girl was on his mind, and the first thing he wanted to do was get a full autopsy done on White's body, see what came up—see what linked and how exactly the immigration attorney had died.

Deep in his gut, he knew he had stumbled onto something. He wasn't sure just yet, but you keep knocking at the wall long enough, eventually it will come crumbling down.

Chapter 21

Spirit is dead!" Phaedra cried out.

Everyone was in a state of shock. Emotions ran high in the house, and it was a hard thing to accept. Spirit was only sixteen years old. Luca couldn't believe it herself. One of her girls was dead—murdered.

"What happened?" Danielle asked with tears streaming down her face.

"They raped and killed her at this group home in Sunset Park," Phaedra informed them emotionally.

"Who?" Luca exclaimed heatedly.

"These twisted brothers . . ."

"How did some boys rape her in a girls' group home?" Luca shouted.

"They set her up. I talked to her last week and she was saying how bitches didn't like her in the place and were hating on her. I know them bitches in there set it up! I know they fuckin' did!" Phaedra screamed out.

There wasn't a dry eye in the room.

Spirit was gone.

Luca stood in front of her crew with anger and hurt clearly written across her face. She couldn't help but to blame herself for Spirit's death. She should have done more. She could have done more. Why hadn't she done more for Spirit? The beating incident by Andrew Gilligan opened the gates to Spirit's death. If that son of a bitch had never laid his hands on her, then Spirit would still be in her crew and alive.

The girls stared at Luca, waiting for her command—waiting for her instruction to exact revenge. Someone had to die, from the niggas that raped and killed Spirit to the man responsible for having her taken away from them.

The girls were ready to do something.

Luca remained quiet, looking angry and pensive at the same time. She walked away without saying a word to anyone. She disappeared into a room and slammed the door behind her, yelling out, "Damn!"

Phaedra shrugged and then decided to follow Luca into the bedroom. She was furious. She took the rape personally and was ready to kill someone. It reminded her of when she had been violated several months back. It was like a perpetual itch inside of her; like some fungus growing.

Phaedra slowly opened the door to the room where Luca had gone. Luca was seated at the foot of the bed with her back turned to Phaedra. Luca remained silent and angry and couldn't help but blame herself. A few tears trickled down her soft light brown cheeks.

"Luca, you okay?" Phaedra asked with concern, her

rage ready to spill over.

"No, I'm not okay, Phaedra. I'm far from fuckin' okay," Luca bluntly replied. "But we're going to make things okay."

"How?"

Luca slowly turned in her friend's direction and her eyes met with Phaedra's. Both of their eyes were clouded with tears. With a chilling and impassive tone, Luca didn't blink when she proclaimed, "Phaedra, I want 'em to feel pain! I want them all to feel what we're feeling!"

Phaedra proudly nodded.

***

Save the best for last—Andrew Gilligan. Luca had something special planned for him. But for now, her attention was on the two animals who had raped and killed Spirit. She had Phaedra use her connects in the streets and paid for information to track the monsters down. It took them two days. The names Thomas and Hunter frequently came up in their search. They were two lowlife brothers in Brooklyn who had a long history of violence in the streets. Word was they were dangerous men with a passion for conflict and domestic violence. They were connected and always packing heat.

Phaedra didn't care who they were connected to or how violent they were; they had to pay, and pay heavily. She and Meeka stepped out of the silver Honda Accord sedan on Eighth Avenue in Sunset Park, a culturally diverse neighborhood in the western section of Brooklyn.

The block fluttered with activity, the locals walking up and down the street and going in and out of shops that lined the avenue, vehicle traffic crowding the road, and young hoods lingering on the corners in front of common bodegas or mom-and-pop shops, selling dope or gambling.

Phaedra spotted the man she was looking for. They'd driven through the hood searching for him for hours, and there he was—in the cut, minding his business and looking aloof to the world with a cigarette in his hand, dusty, and broke. He wore a white, oversized T-shirt with sagging jeans, and his sneakers had seen better days. He was of average height, slim, with a baby face and nappy hair. He leaned against the side of the bodega with his foot propped against it, puffing his Newport with an ominous look. Phaedra knew that look of his. He was about to do something crazy.

Phaedra hurried toward him. The young boy took a few more pulls, then flicked his cigarette into the street. He pushed himself off the wall with the back of his foot, and then reached underneath his shirt and pulled a .38 from his waistband. He pivoted toward the entrance of the bodega with the gun in his hand and marched that way.

"Shit!" Phaedra uttered. He was about to rob the damn store in broad daylight. Is he fuckin' crazy? Phaedra thought to herself.

"Yo, Grape Kool-Aid! Yo! Grape Kool-Aid!" Phaedra shouted out frantically, hurrying in his direction.

He turned and glared at her coming his way. He squinted to see who was rushing toward him. If it was a foe, he wasn't going to hesitate and open fire on them. Nigga or bitch, he didn't give a fuck; anyone was capable of catching a bullet.

"It's me, Phaedra," she quickly made herself known.

"Phaedra, what the fuck?"

Phaedra finally approached him and slammed her hands against his small chest, pushing him away from the bodega exit. She scowled at him. "Nigga, what the fuck is you doin'?"

"What the fuck you think I'm doin'? I'm 'bout to jux this place and get this money!"

"In broad daylight wit' everybody watching!" she hollered.

"I don't give a fuck, Phaedra! I need to get this paper up. I'm thirsty right now—starving and shit! Look at me!" he exclaimed.

"Grape Kool-Aid, put that shit away. It's me, and we need to talk."

"'Bout what?"

"Qwap."

"Yeah, I'm listening, start talkin'," he replied dryly.

"Not here. In the car."

"Word, you driving now, Phaedra? What ya pushing?"

"You'll see."

He nodded and smiled somewhat. He decided to hear Phaedra out. He stuffed the .38 back into his waistband and followed her to the parked Accord down the block.

He climbed into the backseat. He was introduced to Meeka and then was ready to hear about some business. He was anxious to get paid somehow and had turned to committing petty crimes throughout Brooklyn just to eat and survive. Grape Kool-Aid—he was Phaedra's murdered boyfriend's cousin. She had always had respect for him. He was one of few men she actually had respect for.

"Damn, I see you comin' up and shit, Phaedra. Nice ride. My cousin Demetrious would definitely be proud of you," he mentioned.

Hearing Demetrious's name bought back some fond memories to her. But now wasn't the time to reminisce. It was time for action and business.

"But what's good, though, Phaedra? I ain't seen you around since my cousin's murder. What you been up to?"

"I'm doin' big things now, Grape Kool-Aid."

"Grape Kool-Aid?" Meeka mouthed to Phaedra with a questioning stare and smile.

"Funny story," she said to her friend.

"What's a funny story?" Grape Kool-Aid asked.

"She was wondering about ya name," Phaedra mentioned.

"Yeah, that's my fuckin' name . . . that's what they call me everywhere. I grew up liking grape Kool-Aid a lot. It's what I always used to drink, you know what I'm sayin'? But don't get it twisted—ain't no fuckin' sugar or anything sweet running through these veins, ya know what I'm saying? I gets it fuckin' in out here. I don't get fucked wit', you know what I'm sayin'..." he hollered.

"And that's why we need to talk," Phaedra said.

"I'm listening, Phaedra. Talk."

"I know you tired of being broke out here on these streets, and we need you for sumthin'. You know everybody out here in Brooklyn."

"Yeah, you know I get around, do my thang, fuck wit' real niggas and ain't got no time for lame niggas, you know what I'm sayin'. But you my peoples, Phaedra. Whatever you need, I got you."

"Do you know the names Thomas and Hunter?"

"Vaguely. Why?"

"We need to find them."

"A'ight. What they do?"

"Disrespected the crew I'm wit' big time, and they need to get got," Phaedra explained.

"You payin' fo' this, right?" asked Grape Kool-Aid with a firm stare.

Phaedra tossed a wad of cash into the backseat at him. He stumbled to catch it and his eyes widened at the hundred-dollar bills stacked together and bound with two colorful rubber bands. "Oh shit!"

"That's five stacks for you, and there's plenty more where that came from, Grape Kool-Aid. You know I don't fuck wit' everybody, but you my peoples too, and I hate to see you starve out here. I got somebody I want you to meet, and believe me, you fuck wit' us, and we'll definitely take care of you," Phaedra said with conviction.

Grape Kool-Aid leafed through the stack and smiled. "Damn, y'all banking like this?"

The girls nodded.

"When do I start?"

"By helping us kill these two muthafuckas that raped and killed a good friend of ours, and we'll put so much money in ya damn hands that you'll be bleeding green till the day you die," Phaedra returned.

"Yeah, I definitely like the sound of that. I'll find them for you, no doubt. I got you, Phaedra, best believe that, you know what I'm sayin'," he replied, nodding his head and counting his money.

***

Luca wanted to argue with him, slap the shit out of him, or curse him out about the other day when she had to leave his place so abruptly for the next bitch, even though the next bitch was his main bitch and baby mama. But she didn't do any of the above. She couldn't. Once again she found herself trapped in his web of seduction and lust. And like some twenty-dollar backstreet whore turning tricks in the front seat of his truck, her face was in Squirrel's lap, her sweet, full lips wrapped around his fat, hard dick, going up and down, up and down. Squirrel looked down at the mass of purple hair that was planted in his lap and moaned heavily.

He loved her interchangeable looks. The purple wig was different; fashion forward.

"Ooooh, you feel so good, baby. Ooooh, I missed you," he moaned.

If he missed her, then why push her off every time? Why make her an option when she should be his priority? And why was she doing this? Sucking his dick? Why did she continue to subject herself to the same degrading acts, becoming some second-rate whore, sucking dick in the dark area of the West Side in Harlem and in the front seat of his Escalade—going extra hard to please a man who didn't love her like she loved him? She was a growing queenpin with wealth, status, and class, but tonight, she was his personal whore.

Each stroke of her tongue against him brought about a pleasing quiver and sensational moan inside the vehicle. Each time Luca's lips would wrap completely around the base of his dick and slide up to the tip, Squirrel went crazy.

"Damn girl, what ya doin' to me?" he cried out with enjoyment.

Luca released his penis from her mouth, jerking him off satisfactorily, and looked up at Squirrel with her eyes hungry for his dick and his attention. He breathed deeply. He wanted her to finish.

"I love you, Squirrel," she said out of the blue.

"I got love for you, too, Luca. Don't stop, keep doing what you was doing to me," he uttered excitedly.

Luca lowered her lips back to his dick and wrapped them around his erection. Her suction and salivating mouth continued to bring him closer to an orgasm. She cupped his balls, her manicured nails tickling the back of his scrotum. Her other hand gripped the base of his cock and became like a vise. She sucked him harder and faster.

She moaned while giving him head, and the vibrations flowed along his shaft, past her fingernails, and into his balls. Squirrel squirmed and moaned. His flood was rushing out. Squirrel felt her strong suction pulling his cum out of him. She worked his dick until he was ready to release like a fountain. He poured his fluids into her mouth, his sperm mixing with her saliva. He moaned and hummed like an animal. And then he rested back in his seat looking spent.

"You feel good, baby?" she asked with a smile.

"I'm good, baby. I needed that tonight."

"I'm glad I was able to help you out."

"You definitely did," Squirrel said.

The minute he said that, his cell phone rang. It was Angel. When Squirrel answered, Luca frowned. This was her moment with Squirrel; why did that bitch have to call and interrupt a good thing? She wanted him to ignore the call, but he refused. Once again, she was his priority.

"You be quiet, a'ight?"

The nerve of him!

Luca scowled like she had just sucked on a rotten lemon. He had the audacity to hush her after she sucked his dick and let him bust into her mouth and swallowed his babies.

"Hey, baby, what's up?" Squirrel answered like he was Mr. Brady.

"Where you at?" Angel exclaimed. Luca could overhear the conversation because the bitch was so loud through the phone.

"Taking care of business on the streets. Why, what's up?"

"I'm calling you and calling you, and why you ain't pickin' up ya fuckin' phone, nigga?!" Angel shouted out.

"'Cuz I'm fuckin' busy," Squirrel snapped back.

"Busy doing what, nigga?"

"He's busy doing me!" Luca abruptly shouted.

Squirrel shot a murderous look at her.

Hearing Angel's ghetto voice on the other end triggered something inside of her, and the comment just came out. Luca felt that she was ten times better than Angel. She was educated—not in degrees, but she was smart and she was running an empire that she had started from the ground up, and it was rising like dough being baked. She was meeting with important people and lawyers, acquiring property throughout New York like she was Donald Trump. So why did she have to take a backseat to some loud, ghetto-ass bitch?

"Squirrel, who the fuck was that?" Angel shouted angrily. "Is it that same fuckin' bitch that I been hearin' about you creeping with in Harlem? I'm gonna fuck you and that stank bitch up!"

"Fuck her, Squirrel. You with me, right, baby?"

Squirrel glared at her like he was ready to tear her apart. But he focused his attention on Angel for the moment, screaming into the phone, "Angel, you need to chill the fuck out! It ain't that serious!"

"It ain't that serious! No! You a dumb-ass nigga, Squirrel! I swear, I'm tired of ya cheating, fuckin' ass! I hate you, nigga! I fuckin' hate you! I'ma fuck you up! You fuckin' wit' the wrong bitch, nigga! And that bitch, I'ma see that bitch!"

"See me then, fuckin' bitch!" Luca snapped back.

What came over her? She didn't know. But she did know. It was jealousy. Squirrel was hers and she didn't want to lose him, and she damn sure didn't want to share him with Angel, despite the fact that Angel had had him first and had given him kids.

"Angel, it ain't nuthin', and you need to stop trippin' the fuck out. Matter of fact, I'll call you back," he said quickly, and hung up.

Now his heated attention was mainly on Luca.

"What the fuck is ya problem, Luca! Are you fuckin' stupid?"

Luca looked dumbfounded for a moment. She was far from stupid. Squirrel palmed the side of her face, pushing her head against the window of his truck so hard, she spiderwebbed the glass.

Luca was in awe.

"You don't fuck wit' me, Luca! That's like my wife you causing tension wit'!" he shouted. "You play ya fuckin' position like the side bitch you are!"

Luca sat soundless. Anger and hurt were displayed on her face. She held back her tears. Blood trickled down the side of her face from a small wound, but the hurt was greater on the inside.

"Now I gotta fix this fuckin' shit!" Squirrel yelled.

"I'm sorry."

"Yeah, you fuckin' are!" he spat back. "I swear, you pull that fuckin' shit again, and we're fuckin' done! You don't fuck wit' me! Do you fuckin' understand me?"

She meekly nodded. She wanted to know what he meant by done—business or pleasure. She was afraid to ask.

The drive back to the projects on the East Side was an unpleasant one for Luca. She had pissed Squirrel off so much that she was afraid for her life. She knew he had a gun under his seat and that he was a murderer. That side of him that made her uneasy, bringing chills down to her bones.

They arrived back to the Wagner Houses where the area was flooded with Flow Boyz and 20 Blocc gang members. With summer coming to an end in just a few weeks, everyone was taking advantage of the warm weather and bright sun. Squirrel parked his truck in the middle of the block and harshly said to Luca, "Get the fuck out my truck."

"What about my product?" she asked.

Squirrel gazed out his window and nodded to one of his goons holding the block down. He nodded back and went trotting off. He came back several minutes later with a black book bag and handed it to Luca through the passenger window. She took the bag, but hesitated to get out of the truck.

"Squirrel—"

"Don't say shit to me, bitch. Just get the fuck out and leave. You got six kis in that bag, and I'm keeping my composure at the moment, so don't say shit to me. You got what you came for, so fuckin' step," he replied through clenched teeth.

Luca took a deep breath and sadly stepped out of the Escalade. She had fucked up. She had let her emotions get the best of her. She'd allowed her personal feelings for him get in the way of her business. Now she couldn't help but wonder where she stood.

Chapter 22

Luca remained in her bedroom with tears pouring out over Squirrel, thinking she'd lost him and her drug connect permanently. She couldn't help who she fell in love with. It just happened. He was the man she always thought about and was excited to be around. While Ryan was pursuing her, she'd only wanted Squirrel in her life. She was reclusive from her crew for a while, thinking heavily about her next move. Loving a man who didn't love her back the same was tearing her apart.

But Luca was starting to feel that love was some parasite, a growing fungus, a disease that attached itself to you and spread, plaguing the human body with disaster and deformity. First there was Dennis, who'd gotten her pregnant at sixteen and given her an STD. He'd left her, thrown her out like trash. Then there was Nate, who was a womanizer and had broken her heart plenty of times. He was dead. Now there was Squirrel, the epitome of the bad boy that she yearned for. He only wanted her for the pleasures she serviced him with and their business, but besides that, she was only his jump-off, the side piece. Maybe it was wrong, mixing business with pleasure, but it was too late now.

But even with these ambivalent and painful feelings, she couldn't stop thinking about Squirrel.

The knocking at her bedroom door interrupted her thinking.

"Who?" Luca called out.

"It's me, Phaedra. Can I come in?"

"Yeah, come in."

Phaedra walked inside the bedroom and instantly knew that her friend was hurting over that Harlem nigga. Luca sat in the dark, gazing out the window on a beautiful September night. "He's not worth it, especially if he keeps hurting you and got you trippin' like this."

"I'm fine, Phaedra!" Luca snapped.

Phaedra walked deeper into the bedroom. "I know you're not. You're not fine. And I'm your friend, Luca, and what I'm saying to you is don't let this ignorant muthafucka distract you. We have business to take care of. Money to make. There are better things out there—someone who will treat you better than him. We don't need him. And yeah, I know he's our connect, but we can always go around him and—"

"No!" Luca suddenly shouted out. "We do need him; his product. It's the best on the streets right now, and there's no way we drop down to some inferior brand. I won't hear anything of it, Phaedra."

Phaedra scowled. "I understand. But on a lighter note,

Grape Kool-Aid is on his A game out there, and he's hunting for Spirit's killers night and day."

Luca laughed quietly to herself. "Grape Kool-Aid . . . what kind of name is that for a thug, or a supposed killer at that?"

"Don't underestimate him, Luca. He's a very serious muthafucka, despite what his name is. I grew up wit' him in Bed-Stuy, and he has heart and he is loyal. He's fearless, Luca, best believe that, and we gonna need a nigga like that on our team."

"Well, I'll call him Kool-Aid for short."

"It ain't 'bout the name, it's 'bout the reputation out there."

"Well, you make sure Kool-Aid earns his keep around here. Put his fierce reputation on the streets and make us look good," said Luca.

"Oh, he will, I can definitely vouch for that. He will. Whoever I recruit, I can vouch tooth and nail for."

"That's good, Phaedra. I'm glad to hear that. Now leave me and let me be in peace for a moment. I have a lot to think about," Luca said impassively with a stoic look at her friend, like she was a different person.

"Cool. I'm always here for you, Luca. Remember that."

"I know."

***

Manny, the local crackhead, briskly walked toward the dark green Yukon parked on the narrow Brooklyn street in the heat of the night. Clad in tattered clothing and showing a toothless smile, he was eager to get to the truck and reveal the information he had obtained. He desperately approached the driver's side with his smile. Cigarette smoke came from a opened window on the driver's side. The block was quiet, the neighborhood violent and rough. But the four occupants of the Yukon were more violent and rough.

Crackhead Manny leaned into the driver window like a common panhandler, and this angered the driver.

"What the fuck you doin' nigga? Get the fuck back! I don't want ya nasty hands all over this fuckin' ride," the driver heatedly shouted.

"I'm . . . I'm . . . so sorry. I'm sorry," Manny meekly apologized with his stuttering. "No . . . no harm."

"What you mean no fuckin' harm? I just waxed this shit this morning, and I don't need your dirty fuckin' hands staining my ride."

Manny nodded submissively. "I'm . . . I'm sorry."

"Yo, Benny, chill," said Kool-Aid from the backseat.

Benny sighed angrily, glared at Manny, and followed orders. Manny, frightened by the bunch of hoods, stood back a few feet until Kool-Aid waved him back over to the truck. Kool-Aid and Phaedra were seated in the backseat with two of their notorious henchmen, Benny and Dallas, taking up the front. They were ready for some action.

"What you got fo' us, Manny?" Kool-Aid asked.

"There's . . . there's f-five of them . . . up there, serv . . . serving us, through . . . through a wide slot," Manny informed them.

"And you sure Thomas and Hunter are in that apartment?" Phaedra chimed.

"I've . . . I've seen them in . . . in and out myself. They are baaad…muthafuckas. They al-almost beat a g-good . . . friend of mines t-to death the other day . . . and for only . . . only . . . four dollars missing."

Phaedra laughed at his handicap. He was used to being laughed at.

Kool-Aid didn't care for the particulars of his sad story, only the details of the place on the sixth floor. Kool-Aid took a pull from his cigarette and thought about things. He was itching to get things started. He loved it—the danger, revenge, and plotting against niggas and getting ready to kick in someone's door, shoot up the place and cause havoc. This was his world; this was what he felt he was bred to do.

He was with a crew now, and was grateful to have a real roof over his head, some money in his pockets and that he belonged to a family like Luca's and Phaedra's. He was willing to do almost anything for them. The money was good, but the excitement was a hard-on for him.

"You copped yet?" Kool-Aid asked Manny.

Manny shook his head. "No, not yet."

"A'ight, this is what you do, we all go up there together. You knock on that door and cop what you need to get. But you come up short; say you ain't got it. They won't serve you, but you don't leave that door, you make a scene, you get loud, you want ya hit and ain't leaving until you get served. You do whatever you got to do to get that door opened for them to confront you. You understand?" Kool-Aid asked.

Manny nodded.

"Don't fuck this up, Manny, 'cuz if you do, I'ma fuck you up," Kool-Aid threatened.

"I . . . I . . . I got you, Grape Kool-Aid. I . . . I ain't gon' fuck it up," Manny stammered.

The four doors to the Yukon opened simultaneously and everyone stepped out onto the concrete. They had guns, but Kool-Aid thought of a more sinister way to do things. He tucked the .9mm into his waistband and opened the latch of the truck. He removed three aluminum baseball bats and handed one to Benny and one to Dallas.

"Let's make this a lot more interesting," he said.

They nodded.

Inside the building, everyone masked up.

The narrow, bricked hallway on the sixth floor was covered with gang graffiti and smelled of something cooking or something burning. The group took the stairs up, and was ready to move in like predators lurking for their kill. Manny did what he was told; he knocked aggressively on the apartment door, indicating he was ready to pay for some crack.

The rectangular slot embedded into the thick, brown door slid to the side and a pair of eyes appeared. "Manny, what you lookin' for?"

"I . . . I . . . need two," Manny said. He pushed fifteen dollars into the slot and waited for his purchase.

"Nigga, you short five."

"I'll . . . I'll pay it back . . . promise."

"Nah, nigga, this ain't no charity. Come back when you right," the man said sternly.

The slot closed. Manny knocked again, this time harder. The slot slid back like a chamber to a gun. "What the fuck, Manny?"

"I . . . I . . . I need two! You know . . . know me. I . . . I need two," Manny repeated.

"Yo Manny, you pissing me the fuck off! Get the fuck away from this door and come back when you got all of it," he warned.

The slot slid closed again.

Kool-Aid and his goons stood out of view from the door and waited for the mistake to be made. Once they did, they were going to be all over them like flavor on candy.

Manny knocked aggressively again. And then shouted, "I . . . I need . . . two. I . . . I'm good for it!"

He was creating a scene like he'd been told to. It was coming—the breaking point, and Kool-Aid knew it. Fiends were exceptional at pissing off dealers most times, from their begging to their ignorance.

"I . . . I need this! Please!" Manny begged, giving a stellar performance.

As predicted, the brown door flew open with the man behind it charging out to confront Manny. He had a pistol in his hand and was ready to cause some serious bodily harm. But before he could put his hands on Manny, Kool-Aid swung the bat and smashed him in the face with tremendous force, breaking his nose and spewing lots of blood. He hollered and dropped down, while the others rushed inside to perform a hostile takeover.

Before he rushed inside behind his cohorts, Kool-Aid stared down at the man lying defenseless on his stomach, his blood pooling on the floor. He was badly hurt and crawling toward the elevator. Kool-Aid stood over him, smiled awkwardly, and before smashing the back of his head in with the bat, he gruffly said, "Where the fuck you goin'?"

Kool-Aid raised the bat over his head and swung downwards repeatedly. The back of the man's head exploded like a piñata. The brutal murder made Kool-Aid hyped; he was ready for some more.

Kool-Aid joined his cohorts in the deadly assault on the apartment. They stormed into the apartment and Dallas stabbed one man in the neck while he was seated on the couch, caught off guard. Within minutes, Kool-Aid and his crew had bludgeoned four victims to death and tortured and killed two more men and a red-nosed pit-bull—the dog was beaten multiple times and stomped to death.

Thomas and Hunter were two of the victims. Kool-Aid and Phaedra made sure to torture them, stripping them butt-naked. Phaedra went to work on their testicles with the aluminum baseball bat, then cut their dicks off before stabbing them multiple times in the throat, stomach, and chest.

Phaedra was completely satisfied with her work, as she

stared down at their bloody bodies. Now she felt Spirit could finally rest in peace, since her murderers lay dead. The group rushed out of the apartment, leaving behind a gruesome and probably one of the most horrific and bloodiest mass-murder scenes that the city had seen in decades.

Kool-Aid felt he was just getting started.

***

Luca walked into the Starbucks in Midtown Manhattan, wearing a bright red wig this time. She was on the spot of attention from the majority of the customers in the bustling Starbucks. But Luca only wanted one man's attention, and she saw him seated at a corner table near the window, sipping on a latte and reading the day's paper.

The flat-screen television perched over the patrons in the establishment caught Luca's quick attention when the anchorwoman announced, "A bloody and gruesome massacre in Brooklyn, New York, where six victims were found bludgeoned and stabbed to death, has residents living in fear. According to local authorities, the brutal killings may have been drug- or gang-related. The names and ages of the victims have not been released. Residents are horrified by the murders, so close to home . . ."

The breaking news had a few of the patrons' attention.

Luca listened and knew it wasn't drug-related. It was personal revenge, and the other victims who were murdered were unfortunately at the wrong place at the wrong time. But the message had been strongly sent out:

"Don't fuck with her or her crew." And now Luca had to take care of another personal vendetta. Luca turned away from the TV and went toward the counter to give her order, the same latte her target was drinking. She received her cup and walked toward the man with a keen eye on him. She needed his attention and she was going to get it.

When she approached him, planning to take a seat near him, she stumbled purposely near him and spilled some of her latte on him and his paper. He quickly jumped up, cursing, "Got-damn-it!"

"I'm so sorry, I'm so sorry," Luca apologized repeatedly.

"Damn, can't you see—" he started to be rude and obnoxious, but with one look at Luca's beauty in her flowing red wig and eye-catching dress, he paused and uttered, "Oh, wow!"

"I'm so sorry. It's these shoes, they hard to walk in sometimes," Luca explained.

"No, no, it's okay. Accidents do happen, right? No need to call 911," he joked.

Luca laughed.

She attempted to clean him up, taking a napkin and wiping away the latte from his suit. He was tall and handsome for a pale white boy and was dressed nicely. Andrew Gilligan locked eyes with Luca and smiled. His predilection for young, beautiful black girls was evident on his face. Luca knew it. It was the advantage she had.

Andrew sized her up from head to toe and smiled as if he liked what he saw.

"Please, have a seat with me," he offered.

"I don't know. I should go. I damaged your suit, and I'm so clumsy," she replied ruefully. "I'm so embarrassed."

"No, you're not. Things happen, and I would love for you to sit with me and let me get you another latte."

Luca smiled. "You sure?"

"I'm very sure."

"Okay."

Luca sat opposite him and now had his undivided attention. Andrew Gilligan was in awe over her loveliness and her bold red wig. He couldn't keep his eyes off of her.

"You are so beautiful," he complimented.

"Thank you."

"And may I have the pleasure of knowing your name?"

"Denise."

"Denise, I'm Andrew Gilligan," he introduced courteously with a handshake across the table.

"So, what is it that you do, Mr. Gilligan?"

"Please, call me Andrew."

Luca smiled. "Okay, Andrew."

"I'm a district attorney."

"That is a very prominent position to have."

"It is. I enjoy my job," he said with conceit. "And what do you do, Denise? If you don't mind me asking you."

"I'm a model. And I was on my way to a shoot. I only passed through to get my usual latte."

"I never have seen you in this store before."

"It's because I'm always in Harlem or Queens."

"Well, you are gorgeous, and I know I'll see you on billboards and TV soon," Andrew said.

"I hope so."

The two continued talking. Luca kept her composure even though she wanted to slash his neck open and rip his heart out for what he did to Spirit. But she had to stick to the program. She smiled and flirted with the prominent district attorney in the active Starbucks. She laughed at his corny jokes and touched him lightly here and there, feigning interest. As predicted, he was falling into her trap.

"You are such an intriguing woman. I really like you," Andrew stated.

"Thank you. And you are interesting yourself."

"I am?"

"It's not every day that a woman like me meets a handsome DA. Maybe if I ever get into trouble, I can call on you for advice or support."

"I always love to assist a beautiful young woman like you in any time of need." Andrew reached into his suit pocket and pulled out his card. He passed it to Luca, and she took it with ease.

"We should go out sometime," he suggested.

"I would like that."

She gave him her number too, and the connection was made. With the end of their conversation and meeting ensuing, the district attorney was pleased with everything and stood up hurriedly. "Please, call me and I'll take you out to the finest places this city has to offer."

"I will. And I'm looking forward to it."

Andrew took Luca's hand in his and kissed the back of it, like a mannered gentleman. He walked away, and once he was out of sight, Luca frowned and crushed his card into her hand. She yearned to see him suffer.

***

"You are truly beautiful, Denise," Andrew Gilligan complimented with a pleased smile aimed at his date for the evening.

He couldn't take his eyes off of her. Andrew wrapped his arms around Luca tightly and gave her a passionate hug. The look in his eyes said he wanted to slide his hand up her dress and fondle her goodies.

They went out to eat at Jean Georges on Central Park West, a refined bistro where jackets were required for entry. The plates started at a hundred and twenty-one dollars. Afterwards, they went for a horse-and-carriage ride through Central Park, then toured the city in his lavish black Cadillac STS. After midnight, Andrew Gilligan couldn't keep his hands off Luca. During the carriage ride, he tried to fondle under her dress and kiss on her. Riding in the Cadillac, he hinted that she should give him a blow job, but she refused. He was jerk; a nasty, pale-looking sleazeball who used his money and power to influence young girls, especially black girls, and Luca was ready to put a stop to it.

Luca flirted; she teased him reluctantly by finally giving into his sexual advances and allowing his hand to move up her dress and feel on her shaved pussy. He got excited. She hinted that she was ready to please him somewhere more secluded. He was ready to go anywhere she asked.

Andrew parked his Cadillac uptown on the West Side near the Hudson River and George Washington Bridge. It was a dark enough place for them to get their freak on. Once the ignition turned off, Andrew unzipped his pants, pulled out his long, pink sausage and his mouth formed into a lecherous smile. It was bigger than she thought it was, but looked raw and odd.

"I know you have some nice, sweet lips, Denise. Suck me off," Andrew said.

Luca smiled and suddenly exited the vehicle, stunning Andrew.

"Hey, where you going?" he called out.

She didn't answer him. She positioned herself in the front of the hood and lifted her skirt over her hips, showing her luscious curves and pink thong. She turned, smiled glibly and said, "Let's do it outside the car. It's more exciting like that, don't you think?"

Andrew Gilligan was more than willing to oblige. He jumped out of the car and met up with Luca. But before he could place his grimy hands all over her, a force from behind attacked with lightning speed, throwing Andrew into a submissive chokehold and thrusting a syringe into his neck. The drug, M99, also known as etorphine, quickly took effect, seeping into the district attorney's bloodstream and causing him to pass out within seconds.

"Bitch-ass nigga," Kool-Aid uttered with contempt for the white man.

Luca smiled. "Job well done, Kool-Aid. He'll be out for hours."

"I can't stand white people," Kool-Aid declared with venom.

"C'mon, let's put him in the trunk," Luca instructed.

***

Andrew Gilligan woke up several hours later in a strange, barren and cold room. He tried to move, but found his movement completely restricted by being strapped down tightly to a large table. He was also naked. Panic set in his voice as he cried out, "What is this? Where am I?"

"This is judgment day for you, Andrew Gilligan," Luca exclaimed.

She came into his view and the man was stunned. "Denise?"

"No, I'm not Denise. My identity is of no concern to you. You should be worried about other troubling things coming your way," Luca replied in a chilling tone.

"Why are you doing this to me?" he cried out.

"Why? I'll tell you why, muthafucka!" Luca shouted as she placed her face mere inches from his and then shoved a picture of Spirit in his face.

"Do you fuckin' remember her?" Luca screamed out.

Andrew stared at the picture. It seemed he had no remembrance of the girl. "Who is she?"

The question angered Luca even more. It angered everyone in the room: Phaedra, Meeka, Little Bit, Kool-Aid, and the two goons.

"Look again! Her name is Spirit, but you probably remember her by the name Nancy Hogan. You used to fuck her, found out she was sixteen, and beat her damn near into a coma," Luca proclaimed strongly.

"Nancy? Listen, it was a mistake. I didn't mean to. I just lost my temper and I thought she was going to blackmail me. I'm not that kind of guy," Andrew exclaimed loudly.

"Not that kind of guy! You are that kind of guy!" Luca screamed out, knowing he was lying through his teeth.

She showed him photos of his previous works, other young girls, mostly black and Hispanic, badly beaten up and used by him. There were over a dozen photos, and some of the girls were as young as fourteen, but because he was a district attorney in the city and the girls were young and ethnic, he was never prosecuted and had gotten away with the crimes.

"You're a sick and fuckin' twisted pervert!" Luca exclaimed.

"You know who the fuck I am! So this would be stupid of you! I'm the district attorney, and I have very powerful friends—influences that you can't even comprehend, you little bitch. It would be stupid of you to kill me!"

"We have you dead to rights. And yes, it would be stupid to kill you, when I could find you very useful alive," Luca replied coldly.

Andrew looked at Luca befuddled. She continued to show him photos of his private life and then showed him videos of his lifestyle. She had everything recorded and had enough footage and evidence to bury him with criminal indictments and end his career. He was shocked.

"Where did you get this?" he screamed out.

"I have my resources, too, Andrew Gilligan. You are so stupid. Now, shall we begin?"

Andrew squirmed in his restraints, knowing something bad was about to happen to him.

Everyone was ready to kill him, but Luca had something more calculated up her sleeve. She looked at Phaedra and nodded. Phaedra knew the routine. She disappeared into a different room and came back out with a tall male stranger wearing blue scrubs, a scrub cap, latex gloves, and a surgical mask, and carrying a nylon medical bag.

Luca looked at him and handed him an envelope filled with cash. "That's twenty-five thousand, as we agreed."

The man nodded. He moved closer to his victim and focused on the district attorney's earlobe. Andrew Gilligan had fear written all over his face. The surgeon opened his medical bag and methodically started to set up his sharp tools and bizarre instruments on the table near the man.

"What the fuck is this?" Andrew screamed out.

Luca fed on his fear and panic. She smiled devilishly. "We're not going to kill you, but only maim you so each time you look in to the mirror and see your missing ear you will see the monster that you truly are. Each time you go to shake someone's hand and see your missing ring finger it will represent how less of a man you are and a constant reminder of what you did to not only Spirit but also countless women."

"No! Don't do this to me! No! Please, oh god, please don't do this to me! Please, stop, I beg of you, don't do this!" Andrew screamed hysterically as he squirmed and writhed violently in his restraints, but to no avail.

Everyone in the room was unaffected by his desperate pleas for mercy.

Luca nodded. The tall surgeon started the procedure; he was going to do the operation while Andrew felt every bit of the pain.

"This is for Spirit, muthafucka!" Phaedra shouted before spitting into the man's face.

The surgeon took his time with his victim tied down to the table. He sterilized Andrew's ear with pepper water. They still needed Andrew alive, not bleeding to death. His agonized screaming echoed throughout the isolated concrete room. It almost sounded inhuman—unnatural. Everyone watched with aloofness as the sharp knife and metal blade cut into his ear cartilage and in due time, both his ear and ring finger were removed. There was blood and flesh displayed everywhere on the table. The callous act had everyone in the room feeling queasy.

Luca remained cold. A year ago, she would never have thought to be a part of something so barbaric and cruel. But a year ago, she was nobody—now, she was someone people didn't want to fuck with.

Luca went up to the barely conscious district attorney and whispered in his remaining ear, "I know you want to die, but you won't. You do anything stupid, and we'll not only ruin you and your career—we'll go after your family, your kids, and your elderly mother. Yes, we've been watching you, Andrew Gilligan, and this isn't pain—

this is the appetizer compared to what we have planned. Now, when you heal, which you will in due time, you will continue your work like this incident never happened. But I warn you, when I call on you for a favor, you will grant me that favor and many more, Andrew Gilligan. Why? Because now, I own your ass. And if these pictures or videos ever get out, you and your legacy will be ruined."

The man whimpered and wished he were dead. Luca smiled a little. She then turned to grab her crew's attention and with a tense stare and much conviction in her tone, she exclaimed, "Nobody fucks with me. Nobody fucks with this crew. Nobody!"

Phaedra smiled and nodded proudly.

Kool-Aid smiled too and felt right at home.

Chapter 23

With all that was going on in her life—building an empire, murder, and business—Luca was still a young and beautiful woman who wanted to have some fun. Why have money when she couldn't enjoy it? With her new attitude about life, why not show the world what she was now about? The perfect place for her to show off would be at Naomi's birthday/graduation party that she was having in the Hamptons. It was going to be a big event, knowing Naomi, and in spite of her dislike for the woman, Luca wanted to be a part of it.

Luca's invite had a plus one, and she was bringing Phaedra along to join in on the fun. Naomi didn't like Phaedra, and seeing the girl at her party in the Hamptons would definitely get under her skin. It was going to be a fun thing to watch for Luca.

She rented an onyx Maybach for the day, and she and Phaedra drove to the Hamptons in style, sipping Cristal and listening to loud rap music like teenagers. It was the girls' first time in the Hamptons, and they couldn't help but be excited. It was an escape into a different world for them.

A few days earlier, Phaedra and Kool-Aid caught another body in the streets. The mark was a young dealer encroaching on their territory and was viciously gunned down in cold blood in front of a nightclub. It was another bloody message for the wolves that came sniffing around.

Phaedra and Kool-Aid were becoming two notorious enforcers on the streets. The Luca Empire was becoming a permanent threat in the criminal underworld. Bad Girl was spreading like wildfire, and Luca's name was right behind it.

But drug dealers and killers needed leisure activities too.

The Long Island Hamptons region had long been the summer playground of the rich and famous. It consisted of a string of chic seaside communities where the most well-known celebrities owned summer homes. The spectacular beaches, fine restaurants, first-rate shopping, and historic sites made it a popular destination. The area was replete with enchanting bed-and-breakfasts, local inns, and hotels, which made it the ideal spot for a getaway at any time of the year.

The sun was fading, and Phaedra and Luca took in the wonders that the Hamptons had to offer; street after street, the scenery became greater. They were close to the beachfront property that was hosting Naomi's party.

"Why she just having her graduation party now?" Phaedra asked. "You think she's tryin' to compete with you now that you done came up?"

"Compete with me?" Luca smirked. "My money's too long for that."

"But she been graduated. Why not have it in the summer?"

"Why do you care so much?" Luca rolled her eyes, unable to admit that she felt pangs of jealousy. She should be the one graduating from college. "There are so many reasons why she probably didn't have it earlier. Maybe she didn't have the money. Maybe it's cheaper to rent in the Hamptons off-season. Maybe the fact the we fucking murdered her fiancé put a damper on things."

"Chill out, Luca. I was only asking a question."

Luca didn't realize her voice had elevated. "And I was only answering it."

The onyx Maybach pulled up to the sprawling beachfront property on Notre Dame Road in Sag Harbor Village, New York. The beautiful Sag Harbor Village waterfront home overlooked the Sag Harbor Cove. The .040-acre and 2200-square-foot property with its state-of-the-art, inside/outside sound system was teeming with revelers enjoying the lavish birthday/graduation celebration of Naomi Waters. They all enjoyed the 42-foot waterfront infinity pool, the private boat dock, bulkhead, and being reserved from any outsiders at the luxuriant residence privately nestled in a quiet cul-de-sac in the Redwood section.

Luca's mouth dropped open. How could Naomi afford such extravagance? Even if it was only a rental property, it was truly impressive by anyone's standards. She must have used Abioye's insurance settlement, Luca thought. What a dummy.

Luca and Phaedra stepped out of the Maybach looking like two lovely queens in their finest wardrobe. Luca looked stunning in a white, one-shoulder Stella McCartney dress with a zipper-front and sexy, high split. Her red wig and red Fendi heels were explosive.

Phaedra matched Luca in beauty, substituting the boyish image—the baggy jeans and oversized T-shirts— for a black Gucci dress that highlighted her young and alluring figure. It was the first time she had ever worn a dress in her life. But she wanted to impress Luca.

The ladies strutted toward the opulent residence, something that was far beyond Luca's expectation. The outer décor of the place resembled a fairy tale. The white coordination and glamour was remarkable. And Naomi had more security detail around than the First Lady. But the shock came when Luca and Phaedra tried to enter the event and was stopped at the entrance by two beefy men in black, not allowing them inside.

"I'm on the list," Luca declared.

He checked, and she wasn't.

"I don't see your name on the list," he said frankly.

"It's Luca Linn. Check again," she demanded.

Both men gave her blank stares and looked at her like she was invisible. She and Phaedra were pushed off to the side by the security team, discarded like day-old trash. Luca had never been so embarrassed in her life. She felt played at the party. She and Phaedra traveled so far only to be turned away because Naomi didn't put her name on the list and her gut said it was done intentionally. She was Naomi's best friend for many years, and despite their problems or differences, it was a childish thing to do.

For a brief second her paranoia kicked in and she wondered if Naomi had an inkling that Luca was responsible for her fiancé's murder. As quickly as the thought rushed in, she pushed it back out.

"Y'all need to fuckin' check that list again!" Phaedra exclaimed. "You know who this is?!"

"No, and we don't care. If her name isn't on the list, then she's not getting in and she needs to leave the property," the bouncer replied rudely.

Phaedra scowled and wished she had her gun on her so she could shoot them down. Luca pulled out her cell phone and dialed Naomi a handful of times, only to keep getting her voicemail. And even when other known faces from the neighborhood vouched for her and explained it might have been an oversight, the security team wasn't budging.

For a quick moment, Luca felt like her old self again, being treated like she was second-rate and overlooked. She felt vulnerable for a moment and wanted to cry, but her alter ego wouldn't allow it—not in front of Phaedra and not in front of strangers.

Luca kept her composure, suppressing her frustration and embarrassment, and decided to keep things classy and leave. Naomi had made the mistake, and she didn't know how grave a mistake she'd made.

"Let's go, Phaedra."

"What?" Phaedra replied looking confused. Phaedra wanted to stay and make a scene—how dare they be turned away?

"It's okay. It's only a misunderstanding. We'll be okay," Luca said calmly.

The two climbed back into the Maybach and headed toward Brooklyn. When they were almost back into the borough, Luca's cell phone rang. It was Naomi calling. She had the audacity to call back after they were a hundred miles away and almost back home. Luca decided not to answer the phone call; she had endured enough of the charades from her former friend. She sent Naomi's call to voicemail. Naomi didn't realize that by pulling that stunt at the Hamptons, she'd just upped the date of her death.

***

Luca walked into her attorney's office with a suitcase containing 1.2 million dollars. She dropped it on his desk and took a seat opposite of him. Dominic Sirocco looked at her and asked, "What is this?"

"That's one million and two hundred thousand dollars I need to hide for a rainy day. I want this to be put in a safe-deposit box in a bank you trust. And I'm ready to go global."

Dominic stared at her and replied, "You bring this to me. Why? What are your intentions, Luca?"

"I trust you, Dominic. I ventured out into other things—something major. I'm going to have a lot more money coming in, and I need your help making it clean."

"How much cash are we talking a month?"

"Five to ten million."

Dominic leaned back in his high-backed leather chair, locked eyes with his female client and said, "Luca, it's already becoming difficult with the cash I'm washing for you now, and your investments are paying off, but aren't profitable enough to make legal this large amount. I know you're smart, and we talked about this—so far you've been very careful because you listen and you do your homework. You're shrewder than any of my other clients. You have the hedge fund we started, the businesses, and the proprietorship of a few estates, and your strong investment in property developments. Within a few years, you could become completely legit, Luca, and walk away. But I tell you this: Keep a low profile, keep on building up your financial portfolio, and continue crawling until you're able to get up and walk, then run. The last thing you need to do is stir up any red flags with the IRS or the feds."

Luca nodded, but unbeknownst to her attorney, her empire was growing and growing fast, and because of that, a few more bodies started to pile up. And she was becoming a little gaudy with her spending. The jealousy on the streets was stirring up like grits in a boiling pot. Luca kept her cool when she needed to, knowing violence and murder always brought unwanted attention from the police and the feds. However, the wolves were out there snarling and showing their teeth, ready to attack. But with Phaedra and Kool-Aid ready to kill anything that moved, it made them think twice about trying anything.

Luca had held a meeting with her crew and expanded her business throughout the boroughs of Brooklyn and Queens, and as far out as New Jersey, Long Island, and Albany. Bad Girl was starting to show up everywhere. She began sending her young drug dealers large loads of heroin from her connect at fair prices. She expanded this way, and within weeks, she was making money hand over fist. Harlem and the Bronx belonged to Squirrel, so she kept from encroaching in his territory.

Luca's organization had started to handle multimillion-dollar loads of heroin in several states. She controlled the cutting, packaging, and sale of heroin in several East Coast cities, from Philly to Portsmouth. She was showing the world how smart she was by outdoing her late boyfriend and other rival dealers from all over by operating two massive drug mills in Brooklyn that were heavily fortified and secured, with walls reinforced with steel and concrete and protected by armed men with machine guns and state-of-the-art surveillance equipment. Besides controlling the retail sale of heroin, her organization supplied other major dealers throughout the East Coast with multi-kilo shipments for up to twenty-five thousand dollars per kilogram.

She was becoming the female Scarface of the city.

With earlier advice from her attorney, Dominic Sirocco, and the CPA she was fucking, Ryan Miller, Luca took key steps in generating some sizable income and kept from being audited and investigated or drawing unwanted attention by showing the IRS and the feds that she knew the rules, too. She planned on filing her tax return on time, continuing to invest and launder her funds guardedly, and employing the necessary precautions that would help limit her risk of any investigation and arrest.

She decided to buy her first car—a CLS customized pearl-white Benz with custom pink interior and white rims. It was her baby, and Phaedra and Kool-Aid acted as her chauffeurs and bodyguards. Luca rode in the backseat of her expensive vehicle with a MacBook, iPad and iPhone, thinking she was Mark Zuckerberg. She started looking into stocks and bonds and reading the Robb Report. Luca had a knack for business and investments. If she wasn't a drug dealer, maybe in a different lifetime she could have run a Fortune 500 company; she was ready to Lean In.

Switching up cars—from Phaedra to Little Bit's, she would take impulsive and frequent trips into Harlem, having Phaedra drive her. Unbeknownst to Squirrel, he was constantly being observed or stalked by Luca. She would sit parked outside his building, sometimes for hours, and watch Squirrel's comings and goings. She even planted a GPS tracking device under two of his vehicles to track his every movement around town. She was obsessed with the man. And on a few occasions she was tempted to confront him and Angel when she spotted them exiting the project building smiling and hugging each other lovingly. It made Luca's blood boil to see the affection he gave Angel, something that she yearned to have herself.

Phaedra hated it. She hated that Luca was in love with a man like Squirrel and not in love with her. Luca was Phaedra's heart, and she was willing to do anything for her boss. Luca had saved her life, made her rich beyond her dreams, and taught her so many things over the months. Because of Luca, she was becoming educated and becoming somebody important. However, Phaedra would hide her true feelings for Luca deep inside, keeping it a friendship and only business between them. But her love—her genuine confession—was dying to come out at times. Phaedra wanted to become impulsive and shout out, "I love you," to her.

Everyone was in shock to find out about Luca's newfound wealth. There were so many questions. Where did Luca get the Benz from? How did she get the money? Did it belong to Nate? Did she steal from him after he was dead? Did Squirrel buy it? Was she fucking another big-time dealer? The information traveled through Brooklyn very quickly, like telephone wire. And soon the gossip of Luca's immaculate wealth reached the ears of Gloria and Tanya via Naomi. While Luca loosely explained that she'd acquired her money through luck in playing the Lotto scratch-off, a plot was developing to cause her demise.

She wasn't low-key on the streets anymore.

Naomi didn't help with the gossip. During their rendezvous in the city a few weeks back, she'd noticed the jewelry, the heavy spending in Manhattan's cream-of-the-crop stores, and the Rolex watch on Luca's wrist. It was the same watch that Nate bought her, but Luca had lied and said it was stolen. It made Naomi suspicious. There was something fishy going on and Naomi was ready to get to the bottom of it.

What Luca didn't know was that Naomi had rejected Luca from attending her Hamptons celebration once she saw her with Phaedra from afar. Naomi didn't want that hood bitch at her party and told her security not to allow them in at all, even with Luca's name on the list. And since the day Luca cursed her out in the city, Naomi felt slighted by the disrespect. She was Luca's friend and felt jealous and threatened by Phaedra.

Chapter 24

I'm gonna fuck that bitch up, Mama!" Tanya shouted heatedly. "She stole from us and she's a fuckin' liar. I swear, when I see Luca, I'ma tear her fuckin' face off. That's Nate's shit she's getting rich off of. That's our shit, Mama!"

"I know. I know. Don't worry, Tanya, we gonna see that bitch," Gloria replied.

Gloria and Tanya were furious. From what they heard, Luca came off with over a million dollars of Nate's drugs and money—which was highly exaggerated, but Gloria and Tanya wanted to believe the worst because they wanted to get paid. They were still living in the projects and struggling. Without Nate around to sell drugs and help take care of them, things were bad. Neither of them had a job or an education. Tanya wasn't cute enough to snatch up her own baller, and they were reaching hardship.

Gloria wanted to live the good life and retire wealthy. She and Tanya weren't getting any younger and were desperate for a huge payoff. They hadn't seen Luca in months; she was still a sheep in their eyes, ready to be lured to the slaughter by Nate's family. Whatever she had on her, jewelry, cash—it was all getting taken, and with Naomi's help, the setup was made.

"Naomi, you better not fuck us, 'cuz I fuckin' don't like you already," Tanya said.

"I'm not. I want my cut of what y'all take from her, too. I need the money," Naomi replied.

"You need the money." Tanya laughed. "Miss Princess here, too good for the ghetto with her doctor boyfriend. Bitch, you's a joke, too."

Naomi took the abuse from Tanya. Her funds were dwindling fast. With both of her lifelines gone, Nate and Abioye, the gravy train was derailed and about to head off a cliff. The party she threw herself in the Hamptons put her finances in the red, but she had to keep up with the Joneses. Shit, she thought she was the Joneses. Naomi needed some income from somewhere, and fast, to continue her lavish lifestyle, and it seemed easier to set up a friend who now had everything.

Mother and daughter glared at Naomi with little trust. They came together for a common goal—money. Naomi was a snake bitch, but for now she was their gateway into what would probably be one of their biggest payoffs ever.

Luca wasn't coming around anymore, and not a soul, not even Naomi, knew where she lived now. Her life was secluded from her former world, and she kept herself away from the old world.

But there was one thing that could bring Luca back to the projects.

"Her grandmother is really sick," Naomi told Gloria and Tanya. "Luca loves her grandmother and she'll definitely come back to see her."

"She better," Tanya warned. "'Cuz Mama and me wants what is rightfully ours."

"I'll talk to her and find out exactly when she'll be around to see her grandmother," Naomi said.

The trap was set and now it only took for the mouse to try and snatch the cheese to trigger the release.

***

Luca traveled into the Brooklyn projects in style in the backseat of her high-end Benz, conducting business via laptop. The news of her grandmother being sick had saddened her. She loved her grandmother deeply and rushed to go see her, with Phaedra and Little Bit.

The CLS Benz came to a stop in front of the towering project building in the early evening. There were a few residents lingering outside and admiring the sleek Benz. When Luca stepped out of the car, everyone around was in awe.

"Luca?" they uttered in disbelief.

The purple wig, platinum jewelry, and short skirt had mouths wide open. She had left the projects a broken pawn and come back a queen, dominating the chessboard. The dramatic change had everyone amazed.

"Hey, Luca," someone greeted.

"You look really great, Luca," another resident said.

"We missed you, Luca."

They were all fake.

With a cold expression, Luca didn't bother to say a word to anyone. She marched into the lobby with her grandmother her only concern. She didn't miss any of it; the piss in the elevator, the stink in the hallway, the graffiti on the walls, the residents gossiping about everybody's business, the abuse from so many people. Once you've seen a piece of heaven, then why go back to hell?

Luca knocked on her grandmother's door a few times until a caregiver answered in her colorful scrubs. She was Latino, short, and seemed sweet.

"Hello," the woman greeted in a thick Spanish accent.

"My grandmother," Luca said.

"Oh, you must be Luca, I'm Maria."

Luca didn't care about the formalities. She pushed by the caregiver and went into the apartment to find her grandmother seated at her usual spot at the kitchen table, gazing out the window and being her nosy self.

Her grandmother smiled at seeing Luca. "Hey, baby. I'm glad you finally could make it and see an old woman. I thought the next time you'd see me would be in my coffin."

Luca smiled and went to hug her grandmother. "Grandma, don't say such a thing. I'm here now."

She wrapped her arms around the woman so tightly it felt like an eternity before she let her go. Her grandmother was more frail than usual. Her long, gray hair was thinning out and there were still remnants of her having just come out of the hospital with the tag around her wrist.

"Luca, what did you do to your hair? It's purple." Grandma took the purple hair into her hands and gawked at it like it was something from out of space.

"You like it, Grandma?"

"It's definitely different. Your mother is going to raise a fit when she sees it."

"It's the new me, Grandma. I've changed and I'm doing big things."

"Big things. I know about the big things you're doing out there, Luca. I have ears and the streets are always talking," her grandmother replied with a change of tone. "I'm hearing about you. Have a seat."

Luca obeyed and sat opposite her grandmother. Maria, the caregiver, brought them two cups of tea and left the kitchen to give them some privacy to talk. Luca took a sip of tea and stared out the barred window for a moment. Autumn had landed in the ghetto; the leaves in the trees were progressively changing colors, decorating the hood with a Crayola scheme.

Luca was snapped out of her daydream by hearing her grandmother say, "So you decided to take over your dead boyfriend's business."

"Grandma—"

"No Luca, there aren't any explanations, I'm no fool. I've been around for over seventy years and seen a lot. And you always been such a smart woman, but I guess you don't need no man to bring you down; you're bringing your own self down," her grandmother proclaimed with unhappiness in her voice.

"Grandma, I'm somebody now," Luca protested.

"Somebody? Luca, you always been somebody to me and to yourself. What you are becoming is poison to this community."

"Poison? You always told me to stand up for myself and be outspoken, and right now, I feel very outspoken and important. I have come a long way, Grandma. Why can't you respect that I became my own woman?"

"Your own woman? Luca, you haven't gone anywhere. You are even more lost and naïve than you was before . . . and if you keep going down this road of self-destruction, then you'll end up just like your father, and your mother had to learn the hard way."

"They haven't accomplished even half what I have in a few months. I've made millions for myself, Grandma, and acquired property and earned my respect out there. I can do for you, Grandma. You don't have to ever worry about medical bills or this place ever again. Finally, I can get you and my mother out of here," she stated proudly.

"And then when it all comes crumbling down and it's all gone—because it will come crumbling down sooner or later—then what, Luca? Then where will we go? No, I'm not giving up this place. Your grandfather and I worked very hard for the little that we had, but it's ours and nobody can come and take it away from us."

The tears started to trickle from Luca's eyes as her grandmother scolded her. She felt terrible that her grandmother was upset with her. She wanted to please the old woman and make her proud.

"Luca, it's never too late. You're so smart and you can always go back to school and get your degree. You can become anything you want in life, girl, especially now that you got your GED."

Luca hadn't thought her grandmother knew.

"Yes, I know you passed the course, Luca. I'm your grandmother. I hear about everything, especially when it concerns my granddaughter."

Suddenly, her grandmother went into a violent cough. She hunched over in her chair, clutching her chest and trying to breathe.

Luca jumped out of her chair to aid her. "Grandma, are you okay?"

After a moment, the aggressive cough subsided, bringing the caregiver into the room to tend to elderly woman's condition. The grandmother took a few deep breaths and uttered, "I'm okay. I'm fine."

"Grandma, you sure?" Luca asked.

She nodded.

Luca continued to be concerned. She brought her grandmother some water and, with the aid of the caregiver, began tending to her to make sure she was doing well. Luca stared at her and asked, "Grandma, do you need to go to the hospital?"

She shook her head, no. No more hospitals. If she was going to die, then she was going to die in her own home. Lucinda looked at her granddaughter with sad eyes and decided to reveal the truth. "Luca, I have breast cancer."

It was tragic news to Luca.

"What? Why didn't you tell me this before?"

"Because I'm an old woman and you do not need to be concerned with me. I lived my life and I lived it well. I have no regrets. Now I want you to live your life well and live it right, Luca," said her grandmother. "I am dying, but I want you to be on the right track before I'm put into the ground."

"Grandma, don't say that."

"It's the truth, Luca. We are only temporary on this earth, and after my death, there is someplace better for me; someplace with everlasting love and eternity, and I—"

Before her grandmother could finish her statement, she coughed aggressively again and almost keeled over from the pain in her chest. The caregiver immediately went into action, injected the needed medication into her grandmother's arm, and had her take a few pills.

"Grandma! Grandma, you'll be fine," said Luca with a weak smile.

Lucinda smiled back. "I know I will. But will you be fine? Get out that life, Luca. It's not worth it, no matter how much money you make. It will always end the same no matter who you are."

Luca continued to cry. Her grandmother was her world, but she didn't understand that Luca was in too deep to get out now. She had invested in so much and had people looking up to her. But her heart sank like it was in quicksand, knowing her grandmother was sick and one of her final wishes was for Luca to live a legit lifestyle and give up the glamour and riches.

"Luca, promise me that you'll get out of that wicked life. It's not for my granddaughter. It took away your father, your boyfriend, and almost your mother. I don't need it to take away my granddaughter, too," she said despondently. "Promise me that."

She took Luca's hands into hers and held them firmly. For an older, sickly woman, she had a strong grip.

Luca sighed and reluctantly lied, "I promise, Grandma."

A smile appeared on the elderly woman's face. "When I'm gone, God is going to watch out for you. He'll always be around."

Luca smiled. God? She didn't believe in him. But her grandmother strongly did.

Luca continued spending some quality time with her grandmother. They talked and reminisced for over an hour. They had more tea and some cookies. It took Luca back to a time when she was young and innocent, before the world labeled her weak and naïve—before she had ever known what pain or shame was, and before she was corrupted by men and their lies, and friends who smiled in your face and stabbed you in the back. Being with her grandmother made Luca feel sheltered and loved.

She hugged and kissed her grandmother and left the apartment with a nostalgic feeling swooping over her. She loitered outside the apartment door for a moment. She'd made her grandma a promise that she didn't intend to keep, and it was a sick feeling in her stomach. Going back to who she once was—it was impossible for her. How could she go back to shit when sugar was in her blood?

Luca exited the building and climbed back into her CLS white Benz where Phaedra and Little Bit were waiting patiently in the front seat.

"Everything okay?" Phaedra asked.

"I'm fine," Luca replied tersely.

Luca sat back in her cushioned leather seat with her grandmother heavily on her mind. She was in her own world and didn't see the threat coming. Phaedra started up the car, but before she could put it into drive, from out of the blue the back door was snatched opened and Luca found herself being forcefully dragged out of the backseat.

"Get the fuck out the car, bitch!" Tanya yelled heatedly. "Where the fuck is my brother's money!"

Gloria and Tanya were ready to beat Luca down, not knowing things done changed. Luca was thrown to the pavement and bruised her elbow. She cried out. Phaedra and Little Bit swiftly sprung from the front seats of the car to protect their boss and fight the threat. Before the mother and daughter could get a kick or punch in, or snatch Luca's jewelry off of her, Luca's two ferocious girls were on them like white on rice.

Gloria didn't see it coming. She was violently punched in the face by Phaedra while Little Bit jumped on Tanya in a vicious assault. A brutal fight ensued, drawing many residents out to watch. Luca watched from the ground as Phaedra pulled out a sharp razor and slashed Gloria in her face repeatedly. Blood spewed, and Gloria fell to the ground grasping her wounded face and screaming out in pain. When Tanya went to aid her mother, Little Bit hit her with a rock and she collapsed. The situation went from violent to extremely ugly.

Luca had to defuse the situation. Too many eyes were watching, and too many witnesses were around. Phaedra and Little Bit were heartless and unemotional about the brutality they created. Their only purpose was to protect their boss, especially Phaedra, who was secretly in love with Luca. Gloria and Tanya had met their match and were severely beaten in front of the entire neighborhood.

Luca pulled out a wad of hundred-dollar bills and started to pass money around to buy everyone's silence and loyalty. There were hands everywhere grabbing for the money. The hood vowed not to say a word to the police. She had their respect, and the area was sick and tired of Gloria and Tanya's bullying ways.

"Let that bitch bleed out," one coldhearted neighbor replied.

Luca passed out over a thousand dollars to those around. She told them to always have her back and she would have theirs. Police sirens could be heard blaring in the distance; it was time to make her exit.

However, before Luca could get into her Benz, she gazed up and noticed her grandmother observing everything from the kitchen window. Luca's heart sunk deep into her stomach. It wasn't the image that she wanted her grandmother to see, and it pained Luca.

She climbed into the Benz and sighed heavily.

"Fuck," she uttered.

Chapter 25

Luca's true enemy had already revealed herself for the snake that she was. With Brownsville treating Luca like she was the first lady, Naomi could only watch and feel jealous of her friend's sudden rise in popularity and notoriety. The tides had changed and the wind started to blow in a different direction. Naomi couldn't walk two blocks without someone asking her about Luca. After Gloria and Tanya's vicious beatdown, with Gloria receiving fifteen stitches on her face, it was clear that Luca had true power in the hood.

Little old meek Luca. The bitch done came up—and came up so fast and suddenly. She took over where Nate left off. How did it happen? No one could believe it. She was feared and respected like a diva. And Naomi was envious of it all, especially seeing that Luca now had a new best friend in Phaedra.

Naomi unexpectedly found her life spiraling into a different direction. She was now the outsider with a college degree but few funds. Months ago she was happy with a fiancé, selling weed on her school campus making a substantial profit, and on her way to living a super life.

Naomi chose to remain on the chessboard and become the queen that she was meant to be. One day she ran into Lucia, Luca's mother, on the streets and started up a casual conversation with the woman. It happened again, a week later, Naomi running into Luca's mother, and they started to talk again. Naomi would ask about Luca and then reminisce about old times.

After a month going by, Naomi and Lucia started to hang out while Naomi started to call Luca incessantly. Subtly, Naomi was trying to work her way back into Luca's life via her mother. She refused to be an outsider and have some hood bitch named Phaedra take her place Luca's best friend. She was Luca's best friend, since day one, and she felt she should reap the benefits of Luca's rise. Naomi was determined to live the good life by any means achievable.

Seeing the level of respect Luca was getting, how she was running her empire, and how the once weak and dumb bitch was making moves somewhat frightened Naomi. Since the day they met, it was the first time Luca was actually outshining her.

Luca and Naomi would causally talk here and there, and Naomi would become the sweetest and nicest person. Luca to some extent let the bitch back into her world, but she wasn't a fool; she knew what Naomi was trying to get in her good graces. It was all an act, and Naomi was transparent.

Luca wanted to squash her former friend's ego and pride by showing her who the boss was. Yes, Luca was running things. She was expanding her operation every day and was picking up clientele from Connecticut, Pennsylvania, New Jersey, and Massachusetts. Luca wanted to rub it in her friend's face and shout out, "How you like me now, bitch?"

Chapter 26

Detective Walter Charter sat in the parked gray Chevrolet Impala across the street from the young girls' residence in Canarsie and kept a keen eye out for any unusual activity. The unmarked car was inconspicuous with its dark tints and unassuming appearance. He had his binoculars, camera and his wit. It was early evening, and for the past two hours, things had been quiet on the street. At first he was nonchalant about the information he was receiving from the elderly couple next door; maybe they were delusional and lonely. They would always call him up and gladly give him information of the young girls, sometimes filling him in on Luca's or the others' whereabouts—their comings and goings.

At first he didn't think anything of it, but his gut kept telling him to further pursue the lead. He had gotten the results back from the medical examiner who had performed autopsies on both overdose victims. The final results were similar—both victims had died from respiratory failure due to the toxic dose of heroin into their system, which caused their breathing to slow and eventually stop. It was a powerful drug—too potent—and people were starting to die from it.

But when Bad Girl took the life of a third victim in the well-off area, the community caught on fire, and now it was catching some outside attention. In the projects or the ghetto, a third victim overdosing on heroin wouldn't have been an issue—it wouldn't have been a blip on the radar. But now the people dropping dead were prominent figures in the community.

Councilmen looking to be reelected, or anyone who was involved in politics, saw this as an opportunity for attention and votes and began using the threat as a campaign mission. With it being election year and the mayor wanting the drugs and drug dealers flushed out of many areas, the heat was on.

Bad Girl wasn't just a local or elusive drug anymore; it was catching citywide exposure. Fiends and drug users from all over, especially Brooklyn, realized that the distinctive heroin Blow Torch was back in town, but it was now called "Bad Girl," and they ached for it with a sickness.

Now it left many people wondering, who brought the Harlem heroin back into Brooklyn? Who was the mastermind behind it all?

Detective Charter was in charge of the investigation, but it was a complicated one. He knew he could probably be able to get his superiors to issue a search warrant for the house, but then he needed probable cause for the search. The detective felt like he was the smartest man in the room and he had to play this hand carefully.

Detective Charter observed the neighborhood for almost three hours—and then something came to life. He watched the beautiful young woman exit the place with fiery red hair, dressed to the nines in a Fendi dress and red heels. She was always stunning and looked expensive since his first observation of her several days back. For some reason, he was becoming infatuated by the ever-changing woman with her costly outfits and variable hair color. Next he observed the young girl that was always by her. She looked to be no older than seventeen, maybe eighteen. And last, a slim male of average height with baby-faced features.

Detective Charter quickly snapped pictures of the trio as he watched them climb into a silver Honda sedan. He got what he came for: pictures of his suspects. But it was going to be difficult to link the drug known as "Bad Girl" to them, if it was even linked to them. They all looked like kids. And they didn't actually stand out like the average kingpins.

He watched the sedan pull off with the young girl driving, the lady in red in the backseat. When it was about to pass him, he slouched down in the driver's seat a little and remained hidden. They didn't even notice him.

When they were gone, he rose back up in his seat and thought about doing something unethical, breaking into her home and gathering whatever evidence he could for maybe a search warrant or connection. He had been watching the place for a while, and there wasn't anything suspicious on the outside. But there was something intriguing about the woman with the fiery red hair. He wanted to learn more about her, and thought against involving his coworkers with his case. He didn't know why, but he wanted to really get close to this unique looking woman and feel her out.

But first, he planned on disconnecting her alarm system and breaking into her residence.

***

Luca made her way uptown to see Squirrel for her regular pickup. Each time, her pickups were growing and growing, and business was booming from state to state. This time, she had Phaedra and Kool-Aid with her, and she was dressed with style, scantily clad in a short dress and blazer. She knew she had fucked up with Squirrel and wanted to regain his trust and his love again. But it wasn't going to come back so easily. She'd missed him since the day of their conflict and wanted to keep apologizing to him. She forgave him. She couldn't lose Squirrel and refused to.

As they crossed over the Robert Kennedy Bridge going into Harlem, Luca's cell phone rang with an unknown number. She answered, and on the other end of the line, one of Squirrel's goons immediately informed her that plans had changed. She was told to meet up outside of Harlem, somewhere in the Bronx. He gave her an address and when she asked why, the caller quickly hung up. This made Luca nervous, but she still went along with the program.

Luca had been in the Bronx only a handful of times when she was with Nate, and even being with him she was never comfortable being in the South Bronx. But business continued no matter what borough she was in. Kool-Aid and Phaedra were fearless and ready to make their presences known in the BX, and she always felt safe around them.

The address was a warehouse in an industrial area of the Bronx. Phaedra's Honda pulled up and into the warehouse garage on the still and dark block. The trio stepped out and were greeted by Speedy, one of Squirrel's trusted lieutenants. Squirrel didn't want any direct contact with her and sent one of his men to drop off the work for him. With the drama with his baby mama, Squirrel didn't want Luca anywhere near his buildings in Harlem.

Luca took offense to it. "He couldn't come see me himself?" she asked.

"This is business, Luca. Squirrel ain't coming, and I ain't got anything to do wit' ya personal business," Speedy replied.

Kool-Aid frowned at Speedy's frank comment. He didn't like the nigga or how he talked to Luca. He was ready to protect his boss by any means necessary.

Speedy continued. "We got thirty kis for you. I'm told to make this transaction and leave. From now on this is how things will be with him."

Luca was upset and Phaedra knew it. However, now wasn't the time to be a shoulder to lean on. Luca had her heart set on seeing Squirrel, but she moved on with the transaction with a frown and watched her peoples load thirty kis of the purest heroin in the city into the false bottom of the trunk of the Honda sedan.

As this was taking place, the alert on Luca's smart phone caught her attention and she saw it was her home security system alerting her to a home invasion in Canarsie. Luca hit the button and observed some strange man snooping around in her house, unaware that he was being watched. She kept her cool, not telling Phaedra or Kool-Aid. They were busy with the drugs.

Who the fuck is he? Luca silently asked herself.

Danielle and Meeka were out of town, and Little Bit was taking care of some business for the organization in New Jersey.

Luca watched the stranger go from room to room, looking for something. Was he a rival? A killer? Then she saw the badge. He was a fucking cop. Why was he in her home? What was he looking for? Did he even have a warrant? But she wasn't too concerned. If he was looking for drugs, cash or guns, he wasn't going to find them. She had a secret panic room built into her home. It was disguised behind a well-built bookshelf and had an intricate code that Luca had designed herself. Only she had access.

As she gazed at the video, she started to recognize the man. It was the man she'd seen a few times at her elderly neighbors' door. She kept her cool outside, but she was furious inside. It appeared that she was hot and a cop was investigating her for some reason.

No matter the reason, Luca understood it was time to make some changes. When a cop came snooping around, it was never a pretty thing. The first change was to stash the thirty kis of heroin in a different location. The next was to move out of the Canarsie home. From her nosy neighbors to a snooping cop, it was time to call her attorney and to get out of Dodge. And it was also time to clean house.

Once the transaction was done, both parties went their separate ways. Luca climbed into the backseat of the sedan and made a phone call to her lawyer, leaving a message on his answering machine.

On their way back to Brooklyn, Luca was quiet and pensive. She had a lot of things going through her mind, from love, business and murder. Kool-Aid noticed something was bothering her and asked, "Something wrong, boss?"

"I'm fine," she replied.

"Then what's next for us?" he asked.

Luca gazed coldly at Kool-Aid. "More murder."

Chapter 28

It was time for her to ball her fingers into one fist and finally punch back. She had the power, and now it was the perfect time to abuse it. Luca tried to fight the paranoia of being arrested and indicted. She felt somewhat threatened by the cop snooping through her place unannounced. It didn't take a rocket scientist to understand that cops were like ants; once you saw one, then chances were there were many more coming your way. And when that happened, it was time to pack up the picnic and move it somewhere else. But before she took her picnic elsewhere, it was time to clean house. And with the heat looking like it was coming down on her from some unknown direction, there were a couple of things that needed to get done.

If her reign was coming to an end, and if an arrest was imminent, then she wouldn't be able to face the embarrassment with Naomi, Gloria, and Tanya still being alive. If she was going down, then everyone else was going down—down into the ground.

She got her killers together—Phaedra, Kool-Aid, and Meeka—and gave them names of the people she wanted murdered, saving the best for last. She didn't give a fuck. She was sexually frustrated from not having Squirrel around and she wasn't going to look stupid or embarrassed. Being the boss was just too much fun. It was really time to get her hands dirty.

***

Gloria and Tanya—there wasn't a time when the two of them weren't together like Siamese twins. They were an item, the Bert and Ernie, Mutt and Jeff, Albert and Costello of the ghetto. For many years, they'd been two greedy and ruthless bitches causing havoc in the hood. They always took what they wanted and intimidated everyone in their paths. And when Nate was alive, they always believed they were untouchable because of him. Nate was the foundation of the fear of them in the projects; now with him gone, the two only had their fading reputation to utilize. But that was taken away from them the day Phaedra and Little Bit severely beat them down and Phaedra cut up Gloria's face. She had healed tremendously since then, but the scars stilled showed.

They were starting to be mocked and heckled everywhere they went, thanks to Luca. Luca was public enemy number one on their list, and they were plotting their revenge. They did the unthinkable: went to the police to snitch. Their reputation on the streets was becoming a mockery. The mother-and-daughter team was being pushed to the side.

They frequented the beauty shop on Rockaway Avenue in Brownsville. It was a place where they always felt comfortable to get their hair done and gossip. They knew the owner and were close. Tanya sat in the stylist's chair getting a relaxer done to her hair, while Gloria was seated near her daughter with her mouth talking reckless about everyone who was going against her.

"Just because my son ain't here anymore, muthafuckas think they can shit on us. They don't know who the fuck we still are. We still a fuckin' threat out there," Gloria exclaimed.

"Tell 'em, Mama, that's right," Tanya concurred.

"And Luca, she gonna get hers, I bet you that! Bitch think she hard now, she don't know who she's dealing wit'," Gloria continued. "What her friend did to my face, this shit ain't over, it ain't. I'm the head bitch in charge in these streets. I run this shit!"

"You do, Mama. You do," Tanya agreed.

The other customers remained silent, and so did the stylists, allowing Gloria to blow off some steam with her foul language and idle threats. The word was out—they were done. Nobody wanted to fuck with them anymore. They were washed up. Since Nate's murder several months back, the two were hanging on to their respect, and everything else, by a string.

Gloria continued to run her mouth about Luca and her crew, and she used every curse word imaginable and slandered Luca's name so much, it was starting to become redundant to everyone else.

"I'ma fuck that bitch up…fuck that bitch, that bitch is a fuckin' cunt, and she's gonna get fucking killed for fuckin' wit' the wrong fuckin' bitch, cuz I don't give a fuck…she has my fuckin' face cut up and think she fuckin' gangsta…"

"Gloria, ohmygod, we do have customers in here," one of the stylists in the shop said, finally speaking up.

"I don't give a fuck!" Gloria snapped back.

Tanya smirked.

"Well I do," the woman returned sternly.

"So you tryin' to be fuckin' against me too?"

"I think she is, Mama," Tanya interjected.

"If my son was still alive, bitch, you wouldn't be able to say shit, 'cuz you know what would happen," Gloria shouted.

"Well, he's not. He's been dead for months now. Get over it!" the stylist hollered back.

Gloria stood up and was ready to confront the young, slender stylist for talking shit about her son. She had enough people thinking she was soft. At that moment, she was ready to make an example out of that bitch. But before that could happen, the doors to shop burst open and two masked gunmen came charging in. Panic ensued as the gunmen trained their attention on Gloria and Tanya. Without hesitation, they rushed toward the pair and opened fire in front of everyone. Gloria was instantly shot in the head and fell to the floor. They shot her repeatedly. Tanya was also shot multiple times while seated in the stylist's chair. Screaming echoed all over the place with the masked gunmen fleeing the crime scene.

Gloria and Tanya were dead. A terrifying message sent out.

A day later, a drug dealer named Snipes was gunned down in front of a Brownsville bodega. He was accusing Luca of murdering Nate, of probably having him set up, and he was steadily talking shit about her in the streets. The following night, Snipes' right-hand man, Loony, was shot in the head while walking outside his building.

Four murders within a twenty-four hour time period. Brooklyn was on fire; people were whispering and scared, and the cops wanted arrests. But no one was talking— everyone knew who the new power was on the streets, and to speak her name in a vile way meant serious problems.

***

The black Benz came to a stop in front of the isolated and dilapidated building in a remote location in Staten Island. It was a brisk October evening with heavy rain predicted in the forecast. Two scowling men clad in black leather jackets stepped out of the car and walked around to the trunk. They looked around briefly, checking that everything was clear, and opened the trunk. Inside was a bound, blindfolded woman. She squirmed and tried to fight off her captors, but to no avail. They roughly pulled her out of the trunk and dragged her inside the building.

Once inside, she was stripped naked, tied up, beaten,

and severely tortured. Naomi felt her body being violated in so many ways. She cried out profoundly while her captors sodomized and fondled her. When Luca walked in, Naomi was a bloody mess. When the blindfold was taken off, Naomi was shocked to see Luca in the room.

"Luca, what the fuck is this? What is going on?" Naomi cried out.

Luca walked toward Naomi with a cold stare. She looked at her and plainly said, "I'm just tired of your shit, Naomi. And enough is enough."

"Why are you doing this? I'm your friend, Luca! Pleaseeeee!"

"My friend." Luca laughed. "Since the day we met on that playground, you always treated me second-rate, and always looked at me like I was some charity to you. You are nothing but a snake, a manipulative fuckin' bitch, and hypocrite, and you can't talk or fuck your way out of this."

"Luca, I never done anything to you," Naomi cried out.

The statement angered Luca greatly. She slapped Naomi and shouted, "You haven't done anything to me, bitch? You done plenty to me. First, you fuck my man and talk shit behind my back."

"What…?"

"Bitch, don't fuckin' play me like I'm stupid! I know you fucked Nate and talked shit about me behind my back. I have it all on video," Luca screamed out.

Naomi looked stunned. "Luca, I'm sorry . . . I never meant to hurt you. It just happened. Nate, he came on to me." It was a dirty lie that angered Luca more.

"I always thought you were my friend. Since the day you came into my world, I wanted to trust you and believe in you. But you are a selfish bitch, Naomi. You hurt me, and for a while now, I wanted to hurt you back. It's the reason I had Abioye killed," she confessed dryly.

Luca's confession brought heavy tears and hurt into Naomi. "What?" she murmured. "Why . . ."

Luca locked eyes with Naomi. "I had your fiancé murdered, and it was fun to watch his life being taken and to see you suffer the way I used to suffer."

"You fuckin' bitch!" Naomi screamed.

"That's right, I'm a fuckin' bitch. And you know what? It feels so good to be one. Finally, I'm getting the respect I deserve and not being stepped on like some insect, and I have you to thank for it, Naomi. You created me," Luca proclaimed.

Naomi was in full-blown tears, but she managed to shout out, "Go fuck yourself, Luca!"

Luca smiled and chuckled. She looked at Phaedra and was handed a .357. Luca gripped the gun. She wanted to do the deed. It would be her first kill. She gazed at her former friend, placed the tip of the .357 against Naomi's forehead, and took a deep breath. "This is the end of the road for you, Naomi. I have to close this chapter in my life, and to be honest, you fuckin' deserved this a long time ago. Do you feel like pleading for your life?"

Both girls looked at each other hardheartedly, and instead of pleading for her life, Naomi unexpectedly exclaimed, "Fuck—"

Bang!

Luca didn't even give her a chance to finish her sentence before she pulled the trigger. She blew her friend's brains out the back of her head. Naomi's body lay lifeless in the room, her blood spilling onto the floor. Luca frostily gazed at the body and remained stoic in front of everyone. She walked out of the room to be alone for a minute. Even though Naomi became a foe, her death was still an emotional thing for Luca. The transition she was going through was heavy. There seemed to be nobody else around to defy her. Her reign was rising faster than floodwater.

Luca took a deep breath and then exhaled, remembering the Shakespeare quote: "Uneasy lies the head that wears a crown."

Chapter 29

She had to see him again. Her mind was always on the man she loved and not having Squirrel in her life was driving her crazy. Why did she love him so much? She had no idea. But it was the type of love that ached so badly it made her sick with his perpetual absence. He was trying to separate himself from her and make it only about business. Although Luca was generating a lot of cash for him, he would ignore her phone calls, and eventually he changed his number. It made Luca furious. Luca couldn't take no for an answer. They were still in business together, but she wanted to continue her personal and passionate relationship with Squirrel.

From the backseat of her Benz with Phaedra behind the wheel, Luca watched Squirrel step out of the large H2 Hummer and walk into a towering glass complex in Midtown Manhattan. The GPS tracking systems on both his vehicles were coming in handy.

"Luca, why are we here?" Phaedra asked.

"Because I want my man back," Luca replied.

"Your man? He wasn't yours in the first place," Phaedra corrected.

"Phaedra, why don't you find some business, and stay the fuck out of mines?" she barked.

Phaedra frowned and remained quiet. It was the first time Luca had snapped at her. Love wasn't making her think straight. Phaedra continued to hide her feelings and follow orders. She sucked her teeth and slouched behind the wheel. If she had the chance, she would cut out the middleman, Squirrel, by locating his pure heroin connect and killing Squirrel.

She strongly felt that she and Luca could truly take over the entire fucking city and control it all—heroin, coke, weed, and ecstasy. It was sickening to depend on Squirrel when it was obvious he didn't want anything to do with Luca on the relationship tip.

Phaedra and Luca could become lovers and gods at the same time.

"I'll be right back," Luca said.

Phaedra nodded.

Luca stepped out of the car and covertly followed Squirrel into the complex. She assumed it was where he rested his head. The area was posh, the lobby pristine with its marble flooring and round pillars. It was mid-October, the orange sky above spreading throughout the city and the cool fall air bringing the cold winter behind it soon.

Clad in a black blazer and snug riding pants, Luca took a deep breath, and before Squirrel could step into the elevator, she called out to him. "Hey, baby."

Squirrel turned around, shocked to see Luca in his building. No one knew where he lived, not even his drug lieutenants. But, hand it to Luca, she was conniving and shrewd.

"What the fuck you doin' here, Luca?" he shouted.

"I missed you, Squirrel," she replied with a sad face.

Squirrel marched toward her and wrapped his hand around her neck, threw her against the wall of the lobby, and squeezed. Luca locked eyes with him, not flinching, not gasping, but ready to die for her love.

"I'd rather die than live without you, Squirrel," she managed to say with his hands around her neck. "Go ahead, kill me, I don't give a fuck!"

He puffed and his red eyes burned into her. He could have killed her for following him, but he didn't. She was too valuable to his organization. And, though he did not let it be known publicly, he did have some love for her.

He released his grip and growled, "How did you fuckin' find me?"

"I placed a GPS tracking system on both your vehicles."

He chuckled. "You fuckin' bitch."

"I told you, always sweep and check your car or place for any bugs. But you look good, baby."

It had been almost two months since they had physically been together. And though she was casually fucking Ryan, her choirboy and square-cut accountant, he couldn't bring the intensity and excitement in the bedroom that Squirrel brought to her. She needed her fix. She needed that big dick to plug her filling.

Squirrel stared at her with great intensity, and no matter how much he wanted to strike her and tell her to get the fuck out, there was just something about her that made him horny and passionate. She looked great in her black gear and high heels. He felt the urge to take her in his arms and devour her from head to toe.

"I missed you, baby. And I know I fucked up, and I promise you, take me back and I'll behave. I'll be your side bitch as long as I get to have you," Luca proclaimed. "I just need you in my life."

Squirrel stood silent, pondering and glaring at Luca while taking in her plea. He pressed his body close to hers, his lips a mere inch from hers. He smelled the freshness of her breath and slowly slid his hand up her tight pants and fondled where he found her treasure. She clamped her legs around his touch and moaned from his touch.

"I want you, baby. I want you to fuck me right now," she cried out.

Squirrel didn't say a word. He pushed her into the elevator, and before the doors could slide shut he had her pinned against the wall, pulling up her blouse and groping her ass and hips. He wanted to welcome Luca back with a good nut.

An hour later, Luca came strutting out the building with a huge smile on her face. Phaedra scowled, knowing her boss just got fucked and had her waiting for over an hour in the car.

It was a great day for Luca. Her enemies were dead, she had Squirrel back in her life, and she continued to get richer and richer. As she climbed into the backseat of the Benz, she was unaware that parked across the street was Detective Walter Charter keeping a keen eye on her. He was following her and had snapped some random photos of her from a distance and couldn't keep his eyes off of her. Little by little, he was coming into her life, learning more about the intriguing young woman, and now he knew about Squirrel, too. He planned on vetting the young dealer and figuring some way to get even closer to his mark.

Detective Walter Charter was on his job, but he wasn't sure anymore if he was investigating Luca for an arrest and indictments, or if he was doing it for his own personal reasons.

Chapter 30

She didn't recognize him. It took a while, but Luca was shocked that the detective actually staged a fake run-in with her at a nightclub in the city. He looked different from the phone footage of him breaking into her Canarsie home, the one she'd moved out of several weeks back. She admitted to herself that he was very attractive; the man was tall and handsome with his dark eyes, trimmed goatee, and smooth black skin that wrapped around him like Saran wrap.

He had volunteered to buy her a drink, and she accepted.

"You're so beautiful," he had told her.

"Thank you," she had replied.

Luca smiled.

"I've been watching you," he had admitted.

Luca was somewhat taken aback by his honesty. "Watching me," she had responded with a raised eyebrow.

"Yes, since I've seen you in the club."

"Oh," she chuckled.

"And what's your name, Ms. Beautiful?" he had asked.

"Luca," she said, knowing since he was a cop, he had probably vetted her already.

"Luca, nice name. I'm Walter," he said.

The introduction was formally made, and both parties came up with extravagant lies. She wondered what his motive was. Why pretend he didn't know who she was? Luca didn't let on that she knew he really was a cop. The man lied about his occupation and said to her that he did security. They sat in VIP and talked for a while. Unbeknownst to Luca, Detective Charter had become obsessed with her after weeks of following her around and surveilling her.

For a cop, he had swag, was well dressed, and was smooth with his words. He was extremely intelligent and charismatic.

Several days after their meeting, things between them became sexual. He was good, but he wasn't Squirrel. He tried to fuck her better than any man she'd been with, pounding his dick into Luca the way she liked it—rough. However, he could never be Squirrel, and the detective knew this.

Luca captivated the detective's mind on so many levels. She was honest to him about her past, and confessed about the trials and tribulations she'd been through while growing up and living in the projects. She told him about Nate and his demise. She had dreams like everyone else and seemed to be a really nice and caring woman with a troubled past. But was she the one responsible behind the drug Bad Girl? Was she a female kingpin? It was his case and he was getting in too deep.

Detective Charter was intrigued by this woman, from her intelligence, and style, to her alluring sex appeal. Was he falling in love?

Three weeks after their meeting, with continuous sexual and explosive rendezvous between the two of them, the detective was becoming extremely jealous of Luca's constant involvement with the big-time drug dealer. He knew Luca was still fucking him. It was as clear that Luca's heart was with Squirrel. Some days, she wasbe cold toward him—aloof. The drug dealer could buy her anything expensive, and though Charter was a well-paid detective, it was a cop's salary, and Luca was an expensive woman to be with. Squirrel was his main competition vying for her love, and he needed to do something about it.

He had a badge, a gun, and authority. Despite Harlem being out of his jurisdiction, he traveled to Harlem to confront Squirrel anyway—hoping he could bust the notorious drug dealer for guns or drugs in order to keep him away from Luca.

On a late November night, and while alone in his car, Detective Charter hit the lights and pulled over Squirrel and a friend on Third Avenue. The luxurious SUV pulled to the side. Charter cautiously got out, pretending it was a routine stop.

Squirrel was the passenger and kept his cool. When the detective approached the driver's side, Squirrel immediately asked, "What's the problem, Officer?"

"I need your license and registration, and for the both of you to step out of the car," Detective Charter said.

"And for what? Did we do something wrong, Officer?" Squirrel asked coolly.

With a hard, intent look aimed at Squirrel, Charter kept things professional, firmly repeating his command for both men to slowly exit the truck with his hand placed on his holstered weapon.

"You fuckin' wit' us, right?" said Squirrel.

"Do I look like I'm trying to be on Def Comedy Jam?"

There was silence for a moment; the driver looked at Squirrel waiting for instructions. Squirrel nodded, gesturing to do what the cop said. They slowly exited the truck and put their hands on the trunk of the vehicle.

Detective Charter started going through the SUV, searching for any guns or contraband.

"You alone out here, Officer? Why no backup?" Squirrel asked.

The detective glanced at Squirrel. "I don't need backup."

"You sure you a cop?" Squirrel spat out.

"Come and try me then, and give me a reason to use deadly force," Charter dared through his clenched teeth.

Squirrel was tempted, but he wasn't any fool—going against cops was always bad for business and across the street were three heavily armed goons watching their boss's back. The SUV was clean and he and his goons were clean. He ran Harlem like a don. His reputation preceded him, and some lone detective who seemed to have a sudden hard-on for him wasn't going to get him upset.

For ten minutes, detective Charter meticulously went through the SUV but found nothing to arrest the drug dealer on.

With a smug stare, Squirrel asked, "Satisfied, Officer? Because I got someplace important to be."

The detective frowned heavily and didn't say a word. He glared at Squirrel and despised everything about him. The thought of this nasty, perverted dealer sticking his dick into the woman he was falling in love with made him sick to his stomach.

Charter walked over to him and sternly warned, "This isn't over . . . and stay away from her."

"Her?"

"Don't play stupid with me."

The two men glared at each other with so much tension, it could be cut with a knife. The detective turned to walk away, but Squirrel had to have the last word. "Where you from, Officer? Brooklyn? Yeah, I hear it in your voice. Is Harlem even your jurisdiction, Officer?" he exclaimed smugly.

Charter kept on walking back to his car, but before the detective could climb into it, Squirrel chuckled, knowing who he was probably talking about. "And officer, you should be asking that bitch why she can't stay away from me. I fuck her real good, that's why."

The comment rubbed the detective the wrong way. He spun around and charged toward Squirrel. His goons quickly jumped out of the vehicle ready to protect their boss and use force against the cop. The detective wasn't intimidated. He forcefully grabbed Squirrel by his shirt and slammed him against the SUV and shouted, "Don't fuck with me, you piece of shit! She's a nice girl and she doesn't need your type in her life."

Squirrel laughed. "Nice girl?"

Squirrel kept his cool and gestured for his goons to stay back. It was obvious the candid remark had hit a nerve with the detective. After the laughter stopped, Squirrel's expression became serious. "Go ahead, keep fuckin' wit' a Harlem don and lose your badge. You know who the fuck I am."

"I don't give a fuck. You stay away from her." He released his grip from Squirrel and walked away.

"Luca's fuckin' a cop?" the driver asked his boss. "This could be a problem, Squirrel."

Squirrel didn't respond to his goon. He fixed his attention on the detective climbing into his car and leaving. What was Luca thinking, messing around with a cop like him?

"Bitch-ass muthafucka," Squirrel uttered.

Chapter 31

The dick sliding in and out of Luca felt so good—so magnetic—and everything between Luca and the detective felt so explosive in the bedroom. Luca savagely rode his dick like a jockey with her hands pressed against his masculine chest. She leaned forward, her soft, full, sensual lips kissing him, tasting him.

"You feel so good, baby," he muttered.

He was deep inside her core. Her long, toned legs straddling him. His thick, hard dick up in her. Her pussy coaxing him to the verge of an orgasm. He moaned softly and inhaled deeply her feminine scent.

He was about to hit a collision course with a mind-blowing, earth shattering orgasm, and there was no stopping it. The cop needed his sexual release. The way Luca's pussy massaged and pulled at his dick made him reach the point of no return. He was betraying all that he was and represented with his sexual partner in crime.

It had been a stressful week. Being with Luca was his escape from being a detective and away from his superiors. The 69th Precinct had been heavily on him to find out who the distributors of Bad Girl were. They demanded arrests. The potent heroin made the media. It was famous—on the A-list and becoming America's most wanted. There were a few more overdoses. The drug was spreading everywhere.

He threw a few more upward thrusts inside of her, gripping her curvy, sweet hips, and it was that level of vulnerability, that release of inhibitions inside of Luca, that moment of complete emotional honesty that made the detective explode into some pillow talk.

He couldn't hold back any longer. His secret of being a cop had to be revealed. Nestled against Luca after such an exhilarating moment, he started to talk to Luca about the cases he was working on, informing her about drug dealers who were about to get busted. He discussed the murders going on in Brooklyn. One particular murder caught her interest.

"Mother and daughter, a month back, were gunned down in cold blood in a beauty salon. And last week, a fourteen-year-old kid, shot six times in the chest and head. It's really ugly out there, baby. These animals are killing each other like it's the apocalypse out there." He sighed heavily. "These people are like zombies and savages out there for this new heroin, baby. They stamped it Bad Girl and it's everywhere. My superiors are cracking down to find the ones responsible behind it. People are being brutally murdered behind some new power taking over in Brooklyn, and yet, we don't have a name or even a clue."

Luca listened intently. She appeared to be amazed and wide-eyed by his story and his cases. He was like the old man telling ghost stories behind a campfire.

"You have a dangerous job," she said.

"Fuckin' Iraq out there," he agreed.

She laughed.

Charter started to look pensive about something. Luca massaged his chest, comforting him in her bed. He looked at Luca and admitted, "You know at one time, I thought you were a suspect behind Bad Girl. It was brief, though."

"Me?" Luca was in awe. "Do I look like the type to be behind some master criminal organization? I mean, look at me."

He chuckled lightly. "Yeah, I know. But when I was observing you, the house, the cars and the teenage girls I saw you around. I couldn't explain it. You seemed so innocent, yet, so mysterious at the same time."

She smiled. Luca was so intelligent, that the detective believed her lies about where the money was coming from, her technique when it came to gambling and card counting, lying about her deceased grandmother leaving her some money, and even winning the lottery scratch off. Luca made sure to have hardcore evidence to support her income—financial paperwork, a forged last will and testament from her grandmother, lottery winnings she paid the actual winners for. Some things were fabricated and some were authentic. But Walter Charter believed her. He believed she was in college, that she was a civilian instead of a criminal. He was blinded by love.

They continued talking throughout the night, and then he hit her with a bombshell. "I know you're still fucking with Squirrel."

The cat had Luca's tongue. Where did that come from? She was stunned. She had promised him that Squirrel was out of her life, but it was a lie. He was part of her, like her own anatomy. But there was more.

Charter gazed at Luca and disclosed, "He don't want you, Luca. I want you. I'm in love with you. And anyway, the streets are talking: The man is getting married to his baby mama."

The news was crushing for Luca. She felt her heart in her stomach. It couldn't be true. She didn't want to believe it. She tried to remain unemotional after hearing this, but on the inside, it felt like she was about to implode with heartbreak and grief. She squarely looked detective Charter in his eyes and replied, "I don't care. I'm done with him."

But it was a boldfaced lie.

***

It was inevitable that the two girls would meet, since they were vying for the attention and affection of the same man—but the outcome became more severe than anyone expected. Luca and Phaedra finally ran into Angel and they went ham on her when they spotted her in a city night club with some friends. Instantly, the devil and Vesta got into Luca.

The nightclub was live like electricity flowing through the dance floor, with Miguel's "How Many Drinks" blaring through the venue. Luca, Phaedra, and her crew sat in VIP across from Angel and her peoples in a similar VIP section.

Luca couldn't take her eyes of Squirrel's baby mama and bride-to-be. Hate and anger surged through her blood while watching Angel have a good time with a bottle of Moët clutched in her hand as she danced to the song and mingled with her peers.

"I already know what ya thinkin'," Phaedra said. "It would be stupid, Luca. Not here."

Luca didn't respond to her friend. She sat frozen against the red lounge chair with her eyes fixed on Angel like she had personally offended her entire family. They didn't personally know each other, but indirectly, a feud was brewing between them.

It was supposed to be a fun night. It was Phaedra's eighteenth birthday, and they were all in an extravagant VIP area, partying like rock stars and spending money like it was water. Expensive bottles of champagne were everywhere; the place was packed with beautiful people, and Phaedra was looking stunning in a sexy black mini dress. She was starting to look like a lady, but it was Luca who convinced her to dress grown and sexy for her birthday party. In fact, each girl in VIP looked classy. They had a lot to celebrate; not only was it a friend's birthday, but they were making so much money they didn't know what to do with it.

Luca hadn't expected to see Angel in the club. She felt it was some kind of sign. Phaedra read her friend's expression. She focused on Luca intently while everyone else was absorbed in the music and alcohol.

"That bitch think she's fuckin' cute; like she got it like that," Luca said through her gritted teeth. "What the fuck does he see in her?"

Phaedra didn't respond. She stared over at Angel, who wasn't paying them any attention. She was in her own world—as Luca and Phaedra should have been, too. But love had a way of contorting one's emotions and making things crazy.

As the night went on, Luca continued to watch Angel like a hawk, and she finally saw her opportunity when Angel strutted off to use the bathroom down the hallway. Luca jumped up and followed Squirrel's baby mama with Phaedra right behind her. The two walked into the women's bathroom where Angel was already occupying one of the stalls. There was only one other girl in the rest room; she was finishing up her hair and makeup in the wide mirror. When she walked out, the girls had their chance in private. The toilet flushed, and when Angel walked out of the stall, she was abruptly attacked from behind by a swinging fist to the back of her head by Phaedra. She stumbled, but by the time she caught her footing, she was hit again. Luca and Phaedra jumped on her viciously.

"Fuckin' bitch!" Luca shouted.

Angel tried to protect herself, but with the liquor in her system, she was defenseless, and it felt like there were a dozen bitches beating her down. The punches came from everywhere. Luca wasn't much of a fighter, but with Phaedra's help, she became Mike Tyson in the bathroom. She punched Angel twice in the face and busted her lip. When Angel went down, the assault continued with her being kicked in the side by high heels and dragged across the bathroom floor like a mop. Then, out of the blue, two ladies entered the bathroom and briefly caught a glimpse of the assault. It made Luca and Phaedra stop beating on Angel and they hurried out, pushing by the two stunned females.

"Get the fuck out our way," Luca shouted.

There was blood on the floor. Angel lay still, breathing slowly, her dress torn and her face heavily bruised. Once Luca and Phaedra made it back to their VIP section, Luca informed her crew that it was time to leave. There wasn't any argument; everyone stood up and hurried out of the club while security went rushing toward the ladies' bathroom.

***

Squirrel was completely enraged when he heard about the attack on his baby mama and fiancée in the nightclub. Whoever dared come at his family was dead. Angel had been rushed to the hospital and later found out she was pregnant—she was going to be okay, but the disrespect toward him had to be handled with deadly force.

When word got out that Luca was the one behind the attack, Squirrel didn't waste any time racing toward

Brooklyn with a few of his goons. They were heavily armed. His affair with Luca had gotten out of control, and once again she had stepped out of her lane.

Squirrel arrived in the posh Brooklyn neighborhood and violently kicked in Luca's door like a police raid was happening. Luca was alone and completely caught off guard. How had he found her? Squirrel came rushing into the nicely furnished apartment, smashing things, and he punched Luca in the face so hard she went flying back and crashing to the floor.

"I warned you, bitch!" he screamed.

"Baby, let me explain!" Luca cried out.

She couldn't explain herself this time. Squirrel hit her again, a harder punch than the first, and it felt like her cheekbone exploded.

"Baby—"

"Don't fuckin' 'baby' me," he shouted and kicked her insides in.

She screamed and folded over from the pain, clutching her side. He roughly dragged her off the floor, punched her repeatedly, and then threw her across the room like she was a Barbie doll. His goons stood around and watched. Luca was becoming too much of a risk factor. There was the cop she was dealing with and her uncontrollable jealousy toward Angel.

How could he allow her to live?

He pulled out his chrome .9mm and pointed it at Luca. She didn't even flinch. Her pride was bruised. Her heart was crushed.

Squirrel glared at her and exclaimed through clenched teeth, "Tell me why I shouldn't take your life right now."

Bloody and bruised, hugging the floor in pain, she lifted her head, locked eyes with him, and said, "I'm pregnant with your baby."

The news took Squirrel for a ride. "What?"

"The doctor says I'm six weeks," she cried.

Squirrel didn't want to believe her. But suddenly he couldn't pull the trigger. Even though he was a hardcore killer, he had morals for himself and he didn't kill children, alive or even unborn.

He shook his head.

"Ya fuckin' done, bitch," he uttered with contempt in his voice. "No more work from me. Our business is done. You can keep your life, but you stay the fuck away from me and mines."

Squirrel pivoted and walked away leaving Luca behind in full-blown tears.

"No, don't leave me! I love you, baby. Please don't do this to me. Squirrel! I love you!" she frantically screamed.

He ignored her feverish cries and walked out of her apartment and out of her life, leaving Luca glued to the floor in widespread anguish. When the door shut, her heart felt like it was about to stop beating.

***

When Charter saw Luca's bruised face, he was devastated and furious. He went running to her to console and comfort her. He had dozens of questions. Who had done this to her, and why? Luca couldn't tell him the truth. Her explanation was that she was jumped by some project chicks in her old neighborhood while visiting her mother—an old rivalry coming back to haunt her. She was living a double life, having to conceal who she truly was from the detective and Ryan. But with Squirrel, he already knew her dirty little secret, and she didn't have to hide anything from him. It was one of the reasons why she loved him so much.

Several days had passed since the incident and she was slowly recovering from her attack. She made sure her story was consistent when repeating it to the detective. She wanted to forget about it, but Charter wasn't the type of man—or cop—to brush things under the rug and forget it like it never happened, especially when it came to someone he loved. He was investigating it and had his snitches in the streets coming to him with any information.

Luca wanted to forget about Squirrel, but he was on her mind every single day. Even when she was wrapped in Charter's arms on cold winter nights, she would think about him with her belly growing. Charter was excited about the pregnancy, believing the baby was his, when the truth was, Luca didn't know whose baby it was.

She had whored herself out to three different men.

***

It was a week before Christmas and all through the house, everything seemed perfect, even Luca's troubling life. She was still a queenpin in the mean Brooklyn streets, and her crew was more murderous than ever, crowning themselves the new Murder Inc. Luca held onto her lucrative drug reign while pregnant with either a crime lord's or a cop's growing seed, and feigning that she was just innocent. It was the season to be jolly, but in Brooklyn, bodies were still dropping, and Phaedra's love for Luca was still concrete and solid. But the shock would come to all, when the detective asked Luca to marry him, presenting her with a modest-looking diamond ring, and Luca, with a slight smile, happily accepted. It made everyone say, "What the fuck?" Things were becoming more twisted than ever.

Epilogue

Surprisingly, with Squirrel out of her personal life, life, love, and business were still good for Luca. Miraculously, Squirrel gave in and began supplying her with product again under the strict condition that Luca stay the fuck out of Harlem and away from his family. Phaedra was the only one allowed to communicate with Squirrel or his goons.

Luca was apprehensive about reconnecting with him, especially after how things had gone down. She thought that Phaedra would be assassinated when she went to do the transaction. But Phaedra was a soldier and didn't show any fear. Although things had gone smoothly, Luca always kept one eye open when it pertained to Squirrel. She just had a strange feeling that one day he would exact revenge on her.

She had grown closer and warmer toward Detective Charter. He was treating her like a queen. She had a life in the suburbs, with her cooking and cleaning, investing, and trying to run a few legit businesses—but on the side, she was also still ordering murders, flooding the streets with Bad Girl, and laundering tons of drug money.

But her past suddenly came back to haunt her. Her cousin World had just come home after doing almost a bullet in Riker's Island. It was a shock to her. She didn't expect World to get out anytime soon, but he was home and already stirring up trouble for Luca.

He came around for his payday.

Unbeknownst to everyone, Luca spontaneously hired him to kill Nate right before he got locked up. She sent her cousin the Harlem address and he followed her and Nate on that fateful night. She hadn't expected World to have help with him when he gunned down Nate and Cheez.

Now World heard the rumors about his cousin being with Squirrel and figured she came off lovely with Nate's money, and he wanted a nice piece of the pie.

World wanted a Bentley Phantom, because he wanted to ride through the streets like Batman. He also wanted more money. Why couldn't they have kept him locked up? Luca knew her cousin was going to be a problem. When she hired him to kill Nate, she had been in a bad state of mind after watching the real-time footage of the man she loved fucking her best friend. That pushed her over the edge, and she'd reached out to World prematurely, knowing he would do anything for his cousin when he wasn't locked up.

World had mental issues, and since he was seventeen years old, he had been in and out of the Kings County

Hospital's G building. He had been diagnosed with paranoid schizophrenia and needed to take his medicine daily. When he didn't, it was easy to spot with all his strange behavior.

Now it seemed he was ready to extort her. With her crazy cousin back on the streets knowing her dark secret, Luca realized World was going to be a problem.

***

It had been a lovely night of intense and heated, passionate lovemaking for Luca and Charter. Their love seemed like it was two worlds away from everything else going on in their lives. The two planned on spending New Year's Day together. He had taken the night shift, and his job had been overwhelming lately, between the murders being carried out in Brooklyn by a notorious crew who called themselves Murder Inc. and Bad Girl becoming well-known and Enemy Number One for the authorities.

Charter lay nestled against Luca in the king-size bed of her rented beach home in Rockaway Park, New York. It was twenty miles away from Brooklyn and even farther away from the city. While Brooklyn was on fire with murder and drugs, the mastermind behind the chaos was living in comfort and paradise away from it all, engaged to the head detective in charge of the investigation.

Charter woke up butt naked with his lovely fiancée. It was late in the night when he heard his cell phone going off. He answered the call; it was his partner informing him about a new case in the projects. A violent shooting. Another homicide was nothing new in his life.

He removed himself from the arms of Luca, donned a long robe, and went into the kitchen to make himself a cup of coffee before heading out to the crime scene in Brooklyn. While in the kitchen, Charter noticed something strange: a minor light spilling out from somewhere behind the wall of the bookshelf in the hallway. It appeared that the strange light behind the wall had been unintentionally left on.

Charter walked closer to the reddish light and the bookshelf. He started to thoroughly inspect the surrounding area. He ran his hand across some fixtures and inspected every single thing. He knew there had to be something to trigger open an entryway—a secret passage that led to somewhere secluded. It was an old house, so there was no telling what trickery came with it. As he examined the bookshelf meticulously, he inadvertently triggered something that made the bookshelf slide open like a doorway, and behind it was a narrow, bricked passageway that led to a lower level inside the house.

"What the fuck?" he uttered silently.

The light was coming from the security system left inactivated. Slowly, he made his way down the oval corridor that was five feet wide and dimmed. It took him to a room that was a treasure trove of evidence, revealed. Charter stood aghast at what he was seeing. Bad Girl was everywhere. The kilos of heroin were lined up and packed neatly in the room. There had to be over fifty kilos of the stuff, along with several machine guns, assault rifles, and handguns. There were also triple-beam scales and stacks and stacks of money—maybe in the millions. It looked like the secret vault of Tony Montana.

Detective Charter was speechless. How could he have been so stupid? It was all right under his nose.

Luca, who was she?

She had lied to him.

He loved her, but he felt himself at a crossroads.

What the fuck was he going to do now?

There's More Where That Came From

All the Bad Girl You Can Handle

HOUSE RULES

NOW AVAILABLE

KNOCK, KNOCK.

The Highly Anticipated
Part 2 Coming Early 2016

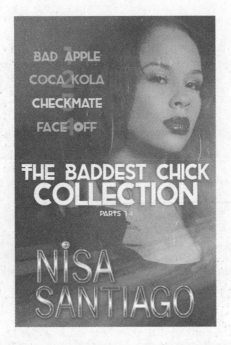